I0660149

A Wedding for

Felicity

A Wedding for Felicity

Willow Wood Brides Book 4

by

Teresa Slack

Copyright © 2020 by Teresa Slack

Published by: Grace Arbor Press
ISBN: 978-1-732786240

All rights reserved. Except for use in any review, the reproduction or utilization of this work in whole or in part in any form by any electronic, mechanical, or other means, now known or hereafter invented, including photocopying or recording, or in any information storage or retrieval system is forbidden without written permission of the editorial staff at Glory Road Press.

This book is a work of fiction. The names, characters, incidents, and places are products of the author's imagination, and are not to be construed as real. While the author was inspired in part by actual events, none of the characters in the work is based on an actual person. Any resemblance to persons living or dead is entirely coincidental and unintentional.

Other Titles

Nine Brides for Cowboy Creek

Rennie
Eliza
Carrie
Bridget
Katie
Marianne
Scarlett
Rachael
Amelia
Candace

Four Sisters Ranch

The Christmas Quilt
Priscilla's Promise

Willow Wood Brides Series

A Promise for Josie: Willow Wood Prequel
(Available to Newsletter Subscribers)
A Lawman for Lisette
A Love Letter for Jessa
A Dream for Harper
A Wedding for Felicity
A Hero for Ellie
A Cowboy for Meggan

Jenna's Creek Series

Streams of Mercy

Redemption's Song
Evidence of Grace
A Jenna's Creek Wedding: *A Christmas Novella*
Legacy of Faith

Tender Blessings Series

Love Begins
A Little Goodbye

Sterling Family Tree
(Family Life Contemporary Short Stories)

Cheater, Cheater
The Money Tree
Carla Comes Around

Stand Alone Novels

The Ultimate Guide to Darcy Carter
Runaway Heart
Joy Redefined

What Readers are Saying

"**From stagecoaches and sheriffs to outlaws and saloons,** your cowboy loving heart will be satisfied. Add a new lady doctor in town (when lady docs weren't exactly the norm --that's an understatement) and a romance, and you've got a great cozy read to hunker down with." –Linore Rose Burkard, award winning romance author, *Forever Lately*

"**Teresa Slack is a one click author for me!!**"

"**Great romance & suspense read.** ...will keep you turning the pages and won't let you put the book down. Highly recommended, though of course, I recommend the entire series as well."

"**Meet another Willow Wood lady** who learns about love, unrequited at times. All this and more in a Christian inspirational novel. Teresa Slack hits one out of the ballpark again." –Leone Bihl, Editor, Greenfield Times

"**I was pulling for Jessa from the start!** Truth and honesty won out in the end. This is a story of a faithful friend who puts her own happiness aside and always tries to see the best in her friend! Looking forward to more stories in this series!!" –Dottie Koehler, Library Editor

"**Outstanding series had me binge reading!**"

"**Wonderful story with a huge twist.** Author Teresa Slack does a great job of weaving everything together in the end. ...An element of faith intertwined in the lives of the characters that was nice as well. If you enjoy a good clean western type mystery, this is a good one for you!"

"**Mystery, a twist I didn't see coming,** and lots of suspense. ...A story of forgiveness, new relationships, new love, and accepting yourself and moving on."

"**...Loved this book by Teresa Slack.** I couldn't put it down."

"**...Suspense, intense action, and tender moments** to warm your heart. Well written...and the ending wrapped everything up nicely. I highly recommend reading it."

"**Once I started reading I had such a hard time putting it down!** It's one of those books that makes you feel good while you're reading it, and after you're through! BUT I really didn't want it to end!! I'm so ready for the next one in this series!"

"**A good balance of action,** life in the West, danger and romance. The characters were well developed, and the settings described so well that the reader feels right there."

"**Another wonderful read**... These kinds of stories keep you intrigued, wondering how the love story will pan out."

"**Rating this book a 5!** ...Teresa's work never fails to keep me on my toes from beginning to end. I am never disappointed with any of her work." –Reader review

Dedication

For one of the kindest, most generous people I
know; my friend & neighbor,
Bonnie Cooper.

Chapter One

October, 1891

The crash accompanied by cries of pain and surprise, jerked Felicity Trego away from the mirror where she had finished preparing for her day.

She ran into the hallway, slipping and sliding across the smoothly polished floor. Regaining her balance as she ran toward the sound, her heart thudded in her chest. At the bottom of the stairs, she saw a heap of gray skirt and faded white petticoats.

"Belinda!"

Imagining the worst, she rushed down the stairs as quickly as her trembling legs would allow.

Her older sister was always in a hurry. It was a wonder she hadn't fallen down the staircase years ago. At thirty-four, Belinda was as stubborn as the day was long. She never paid heed to how a lady of grace and refinement should walk and comport herself. Such matters never gave her a moment's pause.

"Belinda?" she repeated, this time a fearful question. Dread weighed heavy in her chest when she got no response from the crumpled mass.

Oh, Lord, let her be all right, she prayed.

"Sister, can you hear me?"

The gray skirt shifted as Belinda struggled to sit up. Her disheveled blond head appeared. One hand went to the side of her head.

Relief flooded through Felicity as she knelt beside her sister. If Belinda had the wherewithal to complain yet again about the injustices and confining nature of women's garments compared to the freedom of men's clothing, she would surely survive her injuries.

Running footsteps sounded from the rear of the house. "Oh, dear. Oh, dear. Oh, dear," the housekeeper Johanna Casey cried as she ran into the hallway. She arrived more breathless and red-faced than Belinda.

"Miss Belinda. Whatever happened? Are you all right? Can you move?"

Belinda scooted toward the wall to prop herself up. Felicity put her hand on Belinda's shoulder to keep her from moving further. "Lay back. Don't try to get up. Johanna, we must summon the doctor."

"Oh, dear. Oh, dear. It's that rug on the stairs. It must've come loose again. Miss Belinda, have you gravely injured anything?"

"Stop fussing," Belinda snapped. "I'll be fine as soon as I catch my breath. It's only a bump on my head. And my ankle." She pulled her skirt to her knee to assess her injury. She grimaced at the sight of it. Felicity and the housekeeper gasped aloud. The bruised flesh showed dark through her stocking and was already swelling over the top of her boot.

Not typically a delicate person, Belinda's face turned ashen. She fell back against the wall. "Oh, dear, it does hurt."

The housekeeper wrung her hands. "How awful. I'll get the scissors. We must get rid of that boot before it cuts off your circulation."

"No," Felicity exclaimed. "Yell for Shane to go for the doctor. Tell him to hurry. And then make some ice packs. We can slow down the swelling while we wait."

"Oh, dear," Johanna repeated.

"Go!" Felicity shouted.

Her uncharacteristic bark spurred the older woman to action. Still fretting, she turned about on her squat frame and hurried toward the kitchen from where she had come, calling for her son Shane as she ran.

Belinda groaned again. "Please don't bother the doctor, Felicity. Shane can help me upstairs. The swelling will go down as soon as I prop up my foot."

Felicity was secretly alarmed by Belinda's complexion. Her usually pink cheeks were devoid of color, and dark circles Felicity attributed to the pain had already appeared beneath her eyes. "You can't put any weight on that foot. If you were to go upstairs, it would be with Shane carrying you."

That sparked color in Belinda's cheeks as Felicity knew it would. "No one will carry me anywhere. I'm perfectly capable—"

Felicity cut off the rant before Belinda could get wound up. "Dr. Dutton will be here in a few minutes. You'll go upstairs after she has had a chance to examine you and diagnose the damage."

Belinda scowled, clearly furious with the situation and not a little irritated that Felicity was telling her what to do. No one told Belinda Trego what to do, especially her kid sister.

Felicity bit back a smile. Belinda was eleven years older than her, and had been the one in charge of the household, even before Papa died when Felicity was fourteen.

"Dr. Dutton can't come," Belinda said around a wince of pain. "She just had a baby."

"That was two months ago. She makes house calls in town when she's available, as long as she doesn't have to lift or be on her feet too long."

Belinda snorted. Felicity knew she admired Lisette Pelletier—now Dr. Dutton—the lady doctor who had come to town a year and a half ago and forever changed Willow Wood's views on women in positions of authority. But today, when she was the one in need of a doctor's services, she expressed only annoyance.

Felicity ran into the sitting room and grabbed some cushions off the davenport. She gingerly propped Belinda's foot on two pillows and placed another behind her head.

"I can't believe I did something so stupid," Belinda groused. "I don't have time for this today. I'm expected at the factory in..." She glanced at the watch pinned to her jacket lapel. She gasped. "Ten minutes." She moved to sit up. "I must get moving."

The family's factory Trego Leatherworks had started out as a small leather tooling shop in a shed behind Mama and Papa's house when Belinda was a baby. Now it was a booming plant that took up an entire block and employed thirty percent of Willow Wood's workforce. Since Papa's death, the two sisters had taken over the running of it and it continued to expand.

Felicity put her hand on Belinda's shoulder and pushed her back to the floor. "Just relax.

You're not going anywhere. You can get that notion out of your head this instant."

Belinda glared at her again. Felicity enjoyed the momentary rush of power over her strong-willed sister before taking a handkerchief from her sleeve and dabbing perspiration off Belinda's forehead.

"When Shane gets back with the doctor, I'll send him to the factory to tell them you aren't coming today."

Belinda jerked upright. "You'll do no such thing. I'm not laying around this house all day. It's a twisted ankle, for pity's sake."

She reached for her ankle. "My goodness, it is tender. Help me unlash this boot. Don't let them cut it off. I can't bear to waste good shoe leather."

Felicity brushed her hands away. "It's not happening, Sister. We're not taking off that boot and you're not leaving this house. Your ankle could be broken and your boot is acting as a splint."

"This is..."

Felicity glowered, a completely new expression for her. "I don't want to hear another word on the matter. I know you have things to do, but you're not doing them today. As soon as the doctor determines the severity of your injury, I'll go to the factory and take care of whatever matters can't wait until tomorrow."

Belinda gasped. "You? You don't know anything about the factory."

"I guess I'll have to learn."

The sisters glared at each other. Belinda was right. Felicity knew next to nothing about running the plant. She had an office there and showed up nearly every day. She worked mostly with the advertising department where she sometimes contributed input into the sales catalogs mailed around the country. The all-male department patiently listened to her ideas before politely dismissing each one and continuing on with whatever they planned in the first place. Everyone at the plant—and in Willow Wood for that matter—tolerated Felicity, but no one took seriously. She was Belinda's beautiful little sister, and little else.

She didn't have Belinda's grit, that was for sure. After the men in the advertising department explained why her ideas weren't prudent or feasible, as if discussing the matter with a small child, she acquiesced. They were the professionals, after all. All she had were her own experiences as a shopper and ideas about how a product's description in a catalog might appeal to a customer. The rest of the department had combined decades of experience and financial proof the catalogs brought revenue to the company.

Felicity was only in charge of a few small sales accounts that didn't amount to much, which the rest of the staff hoped she wouldn't sabotage. During board meetings, she sat, silent and invisible, in an inferior chair with the rest of the staff. Belinda occupied Papa's former seat at the head of the table while Mr. Hughes, the factory manager, sat at the other end. All decisions were made by Belinda and Mr. Hughes, with little influence from the board members. Felicity left the monthly meetings confused, overwhelmed, and annoyed by her lack of understanding. But she had never done anything about it.

She knew better than anyone that if her name wasn't Trego, she wouldn't be allowed within a country mile of the conference room.

Starting today, that would have to change.

Twenty minutes later, Dr. Dutton arrived in a flurry of green serge skirts. "Shouldn't you be home tending that baby?" Belinda said in greeting.

Felicity scowled at her before turning to the doctor. "How is your little one? I haven't had a chance to love on her yet. At church, she's always surrounded by the older ladies. I can't see a thing beyond a few red curls."

Lisette beamed with maternal pride, even as she crossed the foyer to where Belinda still sat against the wall. "I seldom get a chance to see her myself when we go out. Little Jo is certainly the center of attention. I'm afraid she'll grow up thinking the whole world revolves around her."

Belinda snorted. "Jo? Why did you give her a boy's name?"

The doctor's hands started their examination at the top of Belinda's head and moved down the length of her body. "Her name is Josephine, after Grayson's mother. Josie married Owen when he was on his way down here from Montana to take possession of his ranch."

The housekeeper clasped her hands to her breast. "Theirs was such a romantic story. Willow Wood wasn't much more than a crossroads settlement in those days, but they did a lot for our community. Josie was a right fine lady, and we all miss her to this day."

Lisette smiled appreciatively as she carefully manipulated Belinda's ankle. "Thank you for saying that. I wish I could've met her myself. We'll have to wait till our homecoming in heaven for her to meet me and her little namesake."

She set her medical bag aside and got to her feet. "Good news, Belinda. It appears your injury is confined to your foot and ankle."

"You call that good news."

"Yes, you could've broken your neck. Felicity and I will help you to the davenport in the parlor where I can examine you fully."

It took longer for the two women to practically carry Belinda to the next room and get her settled than for the examination.

"You have a nasty break, Belinda," the doctor announced, "in two places. Possibly three."

Johanna covered her mouth with her hands. Even Belinda paled a few more shades. She quickly recovered. "What does that mean? I won't be able to go to the office for the rest of the week?"

Lisette nearly rolled her eyes. "No, Belinda. Unless you plan to move the factory into this room, you won't see the inside of it for at least two months."

Felicity braced herself, and just in time.

"Two months?" Belinda bellowed. "That's unacceptable. I can't spend two months on this couch like a loaf of bread waiting for my yeast to rise."

Lisette was nonplussed. "I'm afraid your injury has taken the matter out of your hands. You have Mr. Hughes, and Felicity here," she added as almost an afterthought.

"Felicity? Mr. Hughes? Why, I..." Belinda sputtered. She looked apologetically at her sister and took a breath to rein in her frustration. "I'm sure you mean well, Doctor, but this simply won't do. I'll stay home the rest of the week, but then I truly must go back to work. The company depends on me. This town depends on me."

Lisette began putting her instruments into her medical bag. "I certainly can't lash you to this davenport. So I'll wish you the best as a cripple for the rest of your life."

Belinda's face darkened. "A cripple? What's that supposed to mean?"

"It means exactly what you think it means. If you don't give your foot and ankle the proper time to heal, you will do irreparable harm from which they will never recover. You may never walk again. And if you do, it will be with a painful and debilitating limp."

"Oh, Belinda," Felicity said.

Johanna couldn't speak at all.

Reality began to register in Belinda's midnight blue eyes. "Are you... Isn't there anything..."

Felicity had never seen her sister at such a loss.

"It's up to you, Belinda," the doctor repeated. "I realize how difficult this is for you. You surely have no choice. You can lie here and give your body time to heal for a few months, maybe longer. Or you can spend the rest of your life in a wheelchair in unimaginable pain." She glanced around the lavishly appointed room. "You're fortunate. At least you can afford a live-in nurse to tend you around the clock. Most people couldn't. I can help you locate one if you're interested."

She must've known the effect her dismal proclamation would have on Belinda.

"I most certainly am not interested!" Belinda exclaimed.

Her eyes narrowed as she realized the doctor had meant to shock her. Her gaze sought out Felicity. "Sister."

Felicity circled the doctor and sank to her knees beside Belinda. "Everything will be fine, Belinda. There are some matters at the factory you can take care of from right here. We'll set up a desk in this room so you can work while staying off your feet. Is that satisfactory, Dr. Dutton?"

"Of course. In a few days, though. I'll give her pain medication to take the rest of this week. After that, there's no reason she can't see to paperwork or whatever else can be done without moving around. But Belinda, you must not get off this couch. I'll have Shane bring some crutches from my office, but those can only be used to go to the necessary."

Tears of frustration filled Belinda's eyes. Felicity felt like crying herself. For the first time in her life, Belinda needed her. She prayed she was up to the challenge. She leaned forward and kissed her cheek. "Please don't worry, love. You'll see. You'll be fine and the factory will be fine."

As she walked Lisette to the door, she silently prayed, *Please, Lord, let Belinda handle her recovery with the same dogged determination she does everything else. And help Mr. Hughes, Johanna, and me survive it."*

Chapter Two

The sign over the door read: *Simonton and Yates, Esq.* Felicity had passed under it nearly every day of her life. Papa used to carry her past the law office on his shoulders. He would dip his shoulders, and she would duck her head, laughing, as he sang out, "Watch your noggin, Lissie Girl."

Mr. Simonton, Papa's attorney, always met them at the door when they had business inside, one hand outstretched to shake Papa's while the other secreted a candy to Felicity, though they both knew Papa didn't mind. Papa didn't mind anything when it came to his daughters.

Felicity barely remembered Mr. Yates, Mr. Simonton's partner. He was considerably older than the other attorney, with a white ring of thin hair surrounding his head right above his ears and a large, round middle straining at the vest he always wore, regardless of the temperature outside. By the time Felicity reached her third or fourth year of school, Mr. Yates had disappeared from the office. She almost forgot he existed until Papa came home one day and announced the attorney had passed away surrounded by loved ones in Denver or Dallas or wherever he was from.

The lettering on the sign over the door never changed. Every year, someone freshened the paint. Despite the blistering sun and relentless wind that faded paint and chipped siding off buildings on Main Street, Mr. Simonton's office front always looked brand new.

She turned the shiny doorknob and stepped inside. The familiar office with its high back brocade chairs and heavy oak desk in the lobby were also the same. The rug on the floor looked the same as she remembered, somehow not dirty or faded or worn in spots. Mr. Simonton paid as much attention to detail inside his office as he did the outside.

Catherine Murphy, the woman at the desk facing the door, looked up in surprise. "Felicity. What a pleasure. I haven't seen you in here in ages. Where's Belinda?"

A case of nerves closed Felicity's throat. Shane had gone to the factory ahead of her to tell Mr. Hughes and the office staff Belinda was indisposed and that Felicity would take her place today and for the foreseeable future. Catherine was the first person she would tell she was now in charge. Not the capable Belinda, but the pretty, unproven, younger sister no one took seriously. The secretary always treated Felicity with respect, but like everyone else in town, she knew Belinda oversaw the success of Trego Leatherworks while Felicity was mostly window dressing.

"Belinda fell and broke her ankle this morning."

"Oh, the poor thing. I'll pray for her. I'll pray for you, too." She arched graying eyebrows. "You might need it more."

Felicity didn't need to ask what she meant. Belinda was stern enough on two legs. No one thought she'd make a good patient.

"I appreciate that, Catherine. I stopped to pick up some papers Mr. Simonton has ready for Mr. Hughes."

"Oh, honey, you didn't need to do that. We would've sent them over later today."

Felicity suppressed a sigh. She had tried to tell Belinda the same thing, but she wouldn't hear of entrusting an errand of such importance to a delivery boy. "Belinda wanted to make sure Mr. Hughes had it first thing. I'm on my way to the office. I had to pass this way anyway."

Catherine gave her a knowing look before moving to the filing cabinet behind her. She shuffled through one drawer and then another. She turned back to Felicity. "I don't see them. Mr. Simonton is out for the next few weeks. He and Lois are visiting her family in Meridian, and I can't find a thing he files on his own. I'll see if Mr. Yates knows which ones you need."

"Mr. Yates?"

"Yes, I don't think you've—"

As if on cue, the door to the back offices opened. A tall man in a dark gray suit stepped out. His nearly black hair was combed straight back from his face revealing clean-shaven angular features and the most penetrating green eyes Felicity had ever seen. They reminded her of a stormy sea crashing against a distant cliff. She immediately wanted to step forward and gaze into them.

"Mrs. Murphy..." He noticed Felicity and looked momentarily startled. His gaze swept past her mass of sunshine-blond curls, down her slender neck and shoulders, glided over the pale gray form-fitting dress with narrow indigo stripes she'd ordered from the dressmaker's last month, to the black pointed toes of her boots and back again. The inspection took barely the blink of an eye. Felicity hardly noticed. She'd been receiving admiring glances from men for as long as she could remember.

"Mr. Yates," Catherine said, "let me introduce you to Felicity Trego. She's Belinda's sister."

"Ah, yes." The man stepped forward and extended his hand. "Norbert Yates." He smiled a disarming smile that caught her momentarily off guard. "Everyone calls me Ned."

Thank goodness, Felicity thought. She smiled in return. "And everyone calls me Felicity." She winced at the flippant remark, especially in front of Catherine. Little wonder no one at work took her seriously.

Mr. Yates smiled charitably. "Are you here for the government contract your sister had us write last week?"

She hoped her lack of knowledge about a government contract remained safely concealed behind her sapphire blue eyes. She vaguely remembered Belinda telling the board about competing for a lucrative contract with another company in Virginia at last month's meeting. Apparently, Trego Leatherworks won the bid; another coup for Belinda while Felicity barely understood what a government contract meant for the company.

"Belinda is looking forward to going over it tonight." Felicity swallowed. If she had time, she would look it over before handing it off to Mr. Hughes. In case he or Belinda asked for her impression, she wanted to contribute something more than what they'd get from a delivery boy.

"I just finished it this morning." Ned stepped aside and motioned to the inner offices. "In here, please, Miss Trego."

Felicity preceded him through the open door. He closed it behind them. She hadn't been back here since she came with Papa while Belinda was busy learning the ropes at the factory.

"I didn't realize Mr. Simonton had taken on a partner," she said.

"I'm not a partner yet." He moved around the desk as he indicated the opposite chair for her. "Soon, I hope."

His fingers rifled through the papers on his desk. Felicity couldn't help but watch his hands and hope he wouldn't find the contract right away so she could talk to him longer.

"How long have you been in Willow Wood?"

"Almost a year."

A year? Why hadn't Belinda mentioned him? A new attorney in the office was an important development considering how often Trego Leatherworks required their services. She probably didn't tell Felicity about him because she hadn't noticed. Unless Mr. Yates was robbing the company blind, Belinda would not give him a moment's thought. Felicity wished she could be as dismissive. She had more important things to occupy her mind than those direct green eyes and the tiny tuft of unruly black hair sticking out from one eyebrow.

But again, it was her fault for not staying abreast of changes that affected the company. She hadn't given Belinda a reason to think she cared about anything pertaining to her family's holdings.

"Are you the former Mr. Yates' son?"

Ned's fingers closed around a sheaf of documents. "Nephew." He turned the contract to face her and slid it across the desk. "I can answer any questions you have."

She pulled the contract closer and looked down at it as if she knew what she was reading. She needn't bother to impress Mr. Yates. Her life had no place for men. Papa had seen to that. But she couldn't deny an attraction to him even if it wouldn't lead anywhere.

"Are you also from Denver?"

He looked confused for a moment before his expression cleared. "Omaha."

"Oh, that's right. How could I have forgotten?"

He smiled, revealing straight white teeth and little crinkles at the corners of his mouth. "You couldn't have been more than a child when Uncle Daniel returned home after his health began to decline."

She nodded. "My only recollection of him is that he was very round."

Ned laughed. "You remember correctly."

"I'm sorry. That was terribly rude of me."

"Not at all. Aunt Dorena was a wonderful cook, and Uncle Daniel loved showing his appreciation."

"Your uncle meant a lot to my family."

Ned dipped his head in reverence. "He held Willow Wood in high regard, as did Aunt Dorena. They were both sorry to leave. They spoke highly of your father. I'm sorry I never met him."

"Thank you." Felicity fixed her eyes on the contract. After nine years, it was still hard to believe Papa was gone, and so many people in Willow Wood now depended on her and Belinda to fill his shoes.

Ned misread her concentration for interest in the document. "After you and your sister go over the contract together, you will each sign here...and here. Mr. Hughes will sign here."

Felicity nodded as if she'd done this a hundred times before. The few times her signature was required on a document, she signed wherever Belinda pointed without reading a word.

She noted the places Ned pointed, though she doubted it was necessary. Belinda would know where to sign.

She wouldn't be distracted, the way Felicity was now by the hint of his pine soap in her nose, the deep timbre of his voice in her ear, and the way his long fingers brushed hers when he pointed out the signature lines.

Oh, why hadn't Belinda told her Ned had joined the firm? If she'd had a bit of warning, she wouldn't be sitting here like a ninny, barely able to remember why she walked through the door.

But she already knew the answer to that one. There was no reason for Belinda to mention a new man in town. Men were irrelevant to the Trego sisters. They had the factory. They had each other. They had the church, and Felicity had the children at the foundlings' home. A relationship with a man was something that would never complicate their well-ordered lives.

She slid the contract into her satchel and prepared to rise. "Thank you for your time, Mr. Yates. It was nice meeting you."

Ned beat her to his feet. "Ned," he reminded. "It was nice meeting you, too, Felicity. I'll be happy to come to the factory in the morning to collect the signed documents. Belinda can ask any questions then."

"Belinda won't be in the office for a few weeks. She broke her foot this morning and will do what work she can from home for the foreseeable future."

A spark lit and then died in the attorney's eyes. Was it her imagination, or was Ned happy he'd be dealing with her the next few weeks? For the first time since her sister's accident, she found a bright spot in spending more time at the factory.

"I can come to the house and discuss the contract with you and Belinda if it's more suitable."

"That really isn't necessary. Belinda is supposed to take it easy this week. I'll have someone from the office return the documents in a day or so after she's had time to go over them."

She clutched her satchel in front of her and left the office. She hoped Catherine wouldn't notice the color in her cheeks. She had too much to do today, too many responsibilities thrust upon her, to entertain romantic notions about a man who would never be more to her than the family's legal representative.

•••

Ned counted to ten in his head to give Miss Trego plenty of time to exit the building before he circled his desk and stepped into the hallway. He counted to ten again to make sure his expression wouldn't betray the effect the woman had on him.

He had seen beautiful women before, but Felicity Trego was stunning. Literally. It had taken all his concentration to form an intelligible sentence with her sitting across the desk making polite conversation.

"Idiot," Ned hissed at himself. Why had he offered to pick up the signed documents himself? Felicity must've recognized the offer as an excuse to see her again. She was surely used to attention from men. Used to them falling all over themselves to open a door for her or carry her package or make an observation just to see those sapphire eyes light up in approval at their wit. She probably hoped for more from the attorney who handled their business dealings. He'd just gone and proven all men were the same.

"Idiot," he repeated before going to the lobby.

"Catherine, if someone from the factory doesn't return those signed documents by the end of the week, can you remind me to pick them up myself?"

She looked up, her eyes alight with amusement. He didn't need to tell her about collecting documents from clients who sometimes dawdled in returning them. What he really wanted was details about Felicity Trego, and he could see she saw right through his ruse.

She picked up a stack of papers and tapped them against the desk to straighten them. "I've always been surprised that neither of the Trego sisters ever married."

Ned gratefully accepted the nugget of information but managed to keep his face neutral. He wasn't surprised to hear it about Belinda. It would take a strong man of courage—perhaps with a death wish—to tangle with her.

He had never met a more determined, single-minded woman in his life. She seemed disinterested in anything but business. But Felicity; that was a different matter. How could she have possibly remained unattached? She was in her early twenties, twenty-two or three, at least. Did the rest of the men in town know something he didn't? Was she a shrew? Touched in the head?

He focused again on Catherine. He didn't want to miss anything else.

"Belinda has always been an odd sort," she said as if reading his mind. "The only man who ever tried to court her was Carl Rayburn, and she sent him down the pike with his tail between his legs. But Felicity..."

She looked at the door Felicity had just exited. "I thought for sure she'd find a good man to help her and Belinda run the business."

And there was the answer.

As obvious as the sun in the sky, though Catherine didn't seem to realize it. The sisters had proven they didn't need husbands to run a company they had already turned into a profitable success.

Catherine tilted her head to look up at him. "Maybe Felicity hasn't met the right man."

Ned picked up a folder from her desk and studied it as if it were of great importance. "Maybe not," he said noncommittally.

"Felicity is a busy young lady," Catherine went on. "Besides her position at the factory, she supports several worthy causes in the community. Her philanthropy seems more important to her than finding a husband. Pity. She's such a beautiful young woman. She should marry and have children and be happy."

Ned wouldn't suggest Felicity's philanthropy might bring her the same fulfillment a husband and children brought other women. He didn't want Catherine to think he cared one way or the other. But he did care. He liked knowing she had never married. He liked that she had a generous and giving heart. He couldn't deny he was intrigued by her and would like to get to know her better. But Catherine wouldn't get it out of him, no matter how many leading comments she made.

Without a word, he closed the file and returned it to the stack.

Chapter Three

E ven though Dr. Dutton had told Belinda to take it easy the first week, she had Shane create a lap desk so she could work with her injured leg propped on an ottoman in front of her.

After work, Felicity found her on the davenport going over accounts and making lists of tasks that needed her immediate attention.

"I thought the powder Lisette left with you was supposed to make you sleep all day," Felicity said as she stood over her sister and tried to read the closely written scrawl.

Belinda dismissively waved her hand. "I didn't take it. I can handle a little discomfort. What I can't handle is for Trego Leatherworks to fall apart while I'm sitting on my backside."

"Is that all the more you trust Mr. Hughes and me?"

"Don't take it personally. I don't trust anyone."

"It's my livelihood, too, Belinda. And Mr. Hughes'. He worked with Papa when you were a little girl. We won't let it flounder without you."

"You wouldn't intend to, but it could still happen."

She scratched her name onto the contract Felicity had brought and turned the paper around for Felicity's signature.

"First thing in the morning, tell Mr. Hughes I want to meet with him here at the house every afternoon," she said without looking up. "He came by this morning, but I figure we're going to need at least two hours a day. Tell him to bring one of the secretaries. Two p.m. will suffice. He can rearrange whatever he needs to on his schedule to make it work."

Felicity slid the signed document back into the heavy linen envelope. "Can't you and I take care of whatever business can't wait until you're back at the factory? I don't feel comfortable telling him what to do."

Belinda sighed. "Get used to it. Mr. Hughes works for us, not the other way around."

"Papa considered him a business partner, not an employee."

"That was Papa's error. I'll admit Mr. Hughes has been invaluable to our company through the years, but don't forget, it's our company, Felicity. I won't have any man pulling rank on me."

Felicity swallowed her frustration. She never stood up to Belinda. She also never had to work with her more than a few hours a week.

"I don't want that either. All day at the factory, I looked for ways I can assume a bigger role in the company. Every morning you can tell me what needs done and Mr. Hughes and I will take care of it."

"Oh, don't worry, I'm already working on that. But he still needs to be here every afternoon for at least two hours."

Belinda sank into the cushions and ground her teeth as her face etched with pain. "Blast this foot."

Felicity jumped up. "Are you all right? Is there anything I can get?"

"I need another dose of medicine, but I won't take it. It makes me sleep."

"Dr. Dutton said you need rest."

"What I need is to get back to work." Belinda lifted the lap desk and held it out for Felicity to take. "This is absolutely horrid. If only I hadn't been so clumsy."

Felicity carried the desk to the table. "You weren't clumsy. You should see this as a blessing. You're always moving and working.

You haven't spent a day away from the factory your entire life. Your body needs a break, Belinda. Take advantage of it."

"Where would this town be if I spent my time traveling the world or watching the flowers grow, disrespecting Papa's hard work. I can't trust Mr. Hughes to know what's best to keep the company running, and you don't know enough."

Felicity moved back to the couch. "Then teach me. I'll do whatever you need to help take some of the burden off you."

"This is what I need. Find someone to come in and help me. You're gone most of the day. I can't keep yelling for Johanna or Rhonda every time I need a pen or can't find a document."

"I wish you wouldn't yell at anyone. And you should've hired a personal secretary years ago."

"I won't spend money for something that's easier and faster for me to do myself."

"Papa had Mrs. Dawkins. She made his life so much easier and freed up his time to take care of more important matters. She could anticipate Papa's needs before he said a word."

Belinda sniffed. "I don't have the patience to train someone the way Papa did."

"It broke her heart when you let her go after Papa died."

"I didn't let her go. Her services were no longer required. She understood. She was old herself and ready to stop working."

Felicity straightened the papers on the desk. "Working for Papa gave her something to do after her husband died. She only lived a few months after she lost her position with us."

"Wasn't it nice she was able to enjoy that last summer without working like a dog in a stuffy old factory all day?"

"She didn't think it was nice. She grieved herself to death."

Belinda opened a financial journal she received every week from New York City. "You don't know that."

Felicity knew there was no point in debating Mrs. Dawkins' happiness the last year of her life. She went to the window and pulled back the curtain to let in the afternoon sunshine.

Across the street the elm trees that shielded the Lundy mansion were beginning to lose their leaves. In another few weeks she would be able to see the top of the mansion though the stone wall successfully concealed most of the property from passersby.

Felicity had only seen Ellie Lundy a few times since the night her father was killed on the shale driveway in front of his big house. She and Belinda had been summoned that night to stay with Ellie and her cousin Harper until the doctor and sheriff arrived.

Felicity shivered in the warm patch of sunshine. She saw Harper occasionally in town. Harper had married Logan Kinski, and the two lived in the mansion with Ellie. Harper never said much about how Ellie was dealing with her father's death and his involvement in the disappearance of her beau Matthew Dunleavy, and Felicity didn't want to pry by asking. But like everyone else in town, she was curious about what would happen to Ellie Lundy now that she had lost both the men in her life.

She glanced toward the ten-foot-high gate farther up the street. When Mr. Lundy was alive, the gate was always closed. Today it stood open. She supposed it was a good sign. She was confident one day soon she would see Ellie stroll out of the gate and get back to her life.

"What are you doing over there, Felicity?" Belinda asked. "Close the window. The sun hurts my eyes."

Felicity groaned inwardly as she pulled the drapes together. "I met Mr. Yates today."

"Um." Belinda turned a page in the paper.

"Why didn't you tell me there was a new attorney at the firm?"

"It wasn't relevant."

"Not relevant?" Felicity plopped onto the chair next to the davenport. "It would've saved me from embarrassing myself when Catherine told me Mr. Yates had written the contract. I thought the old Mr. Yates had risen from the grave."

Belinda didn't lift her gaze from the journal. "Who cares what that nosy Catherine Murphy thinks?"

"You might've told me how handsome he is," Felicity persisted.

For the first time Belinda looked up. "That is even more irrelevant," she said icily.

Felicity and Belinda never talked about men. They never talked about much of anything except how to keep the company making money. Belinda had no interest in frivolity. Sometimes Felicity did. Sometimes she would like to chat with Belinda like regular sisters instead of business partners.

"He is handsome," she pressed. "Don't tell me you didn't notice."

Belinda's lips drew into a narrow line. "It will do you well to get Mr. Yates, and every other man in the county, out of your head. Papa made his wishes clear."

Felicity's heart sank. "Yes, very."

When Papa died, she was too young to think about romance or husbands or anything beyond the tragedy of losing him. She hadn't questioned his motives when Belinda told her a stipulation in the will forbade them from marrying.

Not forbade exactly since he couldn't physically stop them. But the day either sister married, they would be written out of the will. They would lose every dime of inheritance and interest in the company. They would be sent from the house, with only the clothes on their backs.

Even nine years later, Felicity seldom thought about Papa's conditions. She was happy with her life. She stayed busy at the church and with her friends. She had her philanthropic activities and her responsibilities—small and inconsequential as they were—at the factory.

Lately, though, that had begun to change. She wanted a family of her own. She wanted a husband to share her life with. A child to hold to her breast. She appreciated Johanna and Shane, and she loved Belinda, but she didn't think it would satisfy her through old age. Meeting Ned Yates today only brought those desires bubbling to the surface.

"Why do you think Papa made that decision, Belinda? He always talked about grandchildren. I don't understand why he would want us to live here alone until we got old and brittle."

"Papa talked about grandchildren while he was here to enjoy them. Once he realized he wouldn't be around much longer, everything changed. He didn't want a son-in-law coming into this house, taking over the family business. He worked too hard for someone motivated by greed and selfish ambition to take advantage of his hard work and run the company into the ground."

Felicity stared at the pattern of the Oriental rug. Papa had always been able to see down the road. She knew how much the company meant to him. But his daughters' happiness had meant more. Surely, he trusted them enough not to give the company away to a charlatan who only married them for money.

"What happens to the company after we're gone?"

Belinda lowered the paper and looked at Felicity over the top of the newsprint. "What do you mean?"

"Neither of us will live forever. What then? Think what will happen to the town if the factory goes out of business. Did Papa think of that?"

"Why do you think we have a board of directors?"

Do you mean the board whose advice you never take?

"In the meantime," Belinda went on, "don't question Papa's wishes. He knew exactly what he was doing. There was never a better businessman alive."

"Yes, but..."

Belinda's face turned white. "Surely you're not entertaining notions about that Mr. Yates."

Heat rushed to Felicity's face. "Belinda," she hissed, "I just met him."

Belinda's glare deepened. "Good, because I would hate to see you make a fool of yourself the way you did when that federal marshal Grayson Dutton came back to town."

Felicity wished she'd never started this conversation. "I didn't make a fool of myself. I had idolized him as a child. When he came home, so tall and dashing, I couldn't help imagining..."

Belinda slammed down the pen. "And I had to remind you of what Papa wanted. It's a good thing Grayson married Dr. Pelletier and you were able to remember your duty to me and the factory. Papa worked too hard for you to muddle your thinking with a man."

Felicity sighed. Now she remembered why she never talked to Belinda about anything but business. "I would never hand our company over to a man."

"Well, just in case one of us lost our heads, Papa wrote his will the way he did. You wouldn't only be letting Papa and me down if you did something foolhardy like fall in love. Think of those poor orphans you esteem so highly."

Smug satisfaction filled Belinda's eyes. "Those children depend on you. And that woman, Mrs..."

She knew the name as well as Felicity, but Felicity filled it in for her anyway. "Mrs. McClanahan."

"Yes, Mrs. McClanahan. What a selfless soul. Where would she be without you? Where would you be without what I, what this house..." She swept her arms around the room. "...What Papa's hard labors have afforded you? You have a generous heart, Felicity. I know you would never forsake those children to satisfy your own selfish desires."

Tears tickled Felicity's nose. Of course not. What sort of a monster would she be to put the dreams of marriage and a family of her own above those poor children?

"Now, fetch a pen and tablet and let's get to work." Belinda said. "We'll create a list of friends and neighbors who might know a young woman who can come and work for me while you're at the factory. Johanna might know someone in need of employment."

Felicity was sure Johanna did, but she doubted the housekeeper disliked anyone enough to trick them into going to work for a bedridden Belinda Trego.

Chapter Four

"I'm leaving, Mr. Yates," Catherine called from the front office.

Ned looked up in surprise at the clock on the corner of his desk. He hadn't realized it was so late. "Thank you, Catherine," he called. "Have a nice evening."

Instead of heading straight out the door as she ordinarily did, she appeared in his doorway. "I trust you won't work too late."

He smiled at the concern in her voice. She already knew his schedule and how he often worked many hours after everyone else had gone. Unlike Mr. Simonton, he didn't have a wife and children to go home to. He wasn't yet involved with any community organizations and he only attended church on Sundays. All he had in his life was work and sending every cent he earned to the creditors.

"About another hour is all. I want to put a few finishing touches on some projects before Mr. Simonton returns."

"He isn't due back until next month. Or even longer if the missus has her way. Any work on your desk can wait until tomorrow."

"I know." He needn't tell her he had no reason to rush to the boardinghouse. Mr. and Mrs. Crothers were kind and tried to make the place a home, but it only served to remind Ned of how alone he was.

"What you need is a good woman," Catherine said, as if reading his thoughts.

Felicity Trego flashed across his mind. It had been difficult to keep her out of his head all day. Those sparkling blue eyes and full lips had continued to interrupt his thoughts, as well as the dove gray dress she'd worn today and the way it accentuated her lithe form.

"A good woman would only scold me for working so late, the way you are now."

She chuckled. "If you had a good woman waiting at home for you, I wouldn't have to chase you out of here every night."

"I'll keep that in mind."

"Well then, I'll save the scolding for your future wife. Don't forget, my church is full of young ladies who would love to meet someone like you."

"I haven't forgotten the offer."

"I hope I don't need to remind you you're not getting any younger, and neither are they. They won't wait forever."

"I found a gray hair this morning to remind me of that."

Catherine slapped the door lintel. "Oh, pooh. You don't have gray hair. But you'll look like me before you know it if you don't get out of this office now and then and notice the beauty God's provided."

Felicity Trego immediately jumped back into his mind at the thought of God's beautiful creation. He gave Catherine a parting smile and dipped his head back over his work. If she could read his thoughts, she'd never give him a moment's peace.

The front door closed behind her, and the lock clicked shut. Most of the shops were closed by this time of day. There was no need for her to lock the door. Anyone who walked in would bring business. Her mothering and kindness, though, reminded him of Dorena Yates, his true mother though she hadn't given birth to him.

Ned spent his early years looking after himself and staying out of reach of whichever of his biological mother's friends happened to be within striking distance. His first memory of her had been with a bottle in her hand. When she was at home, which wasn't often, she was still absent of mind. He didn't remember her ever pulling him into her arms or onto her lap for a hug or even ruffling his hair in passing. Her physical contact was limited to a slap or ear yank when he didn't respond quickly enough to a command.

Her lack of nurturing had been nothing compared to the torment he endured from the various men she invited into the house. Ned learned young to avoid them, even the ones who treated him with kindness. They were often the worst. He quickly recognized the predators from the looks they gave him after they'd drunk too much or Ma passed out.

It had been one of those occasions that sent him out of the house for the last time. He was nearly ten years old with nowhere to go and no money in his pocket or food in his belly. Hal had been watching him closely all evening with a desperate look, laughing too loud and reaching out to grab his arm every chance he got. When Ma began to snore in her chair, Ned knew his night was about to get very ugly. Hal drained the whiskey bottle and dropped it in the sink with a clatter. He unbuttoned his fly and stepped out back to relieve himself. Ned grabbed the bag he kept stashed behind the stove for such occasions and ran out the front door of the tiny, dilapidated shack.

He ran blindly for about six blocks. Hal would be furious when he came back inside and found Ned gone. Fortunately, he was too lazy to chase anyone farther than a few feet. Ned knew he could never go back. Hal would hang around for a few weeks, at least. If he saw Ned again, he'd beat him to within an inch of his life before doing what he'd planned to do tonight.

Eventually Ned's panic subsided and weariness forced him to slow down. Where to go? He thought of the relatives and Ma's friend Betty who had taken him in before. Not because they wanted to, but because they liked the free labor or they felt too guilty to let him sleep in an alley. But they'd send him home in a day or two, and he'd be right back in the same boat.

He clutched at the stitch in his side and wished he'd taken the time to grab Hal's wallet. There would've been at least a dollar or two inside. But if Hal ever got his hands on him after he stole his wallet, well, there'd be no walking away from that beating.

Ahead he saw the steeple of a church rising out of the predawn fog. He headed that way. Their doors were seldom locked, and he could get inside out of the cold. By the time the priest found him tucked under a pew, it would be morning and he could maybe find work in a stable somewhere. He might get lucky and they'd feed him before sending him out. He wouldn't get his hopes up though. He wasn't the only hungry boy in the city.

He waited in the shadows until a hostler's wagon passed and then darted across the street toward the church. Just as he took hold of the ornate handle, praying the whole time it was unlocked, the door swung open in front of him. A severe, scowling nun glared down at him. "What are you doing out here this time of night, boy? Looking to rob the offering plate? We've lost money to your kind twice already this week."

"No, ma'am...um...Sister. I wasn't."

"Go on then, get on with you." She pulled an object from the folds of her heavy flannel gown and lunged for him.

Ned didn't wait long enough to see what sort of club she bore before racing back down the stairs and into the street.

After a few more blocks, the skies opened and it began to rain, a cold drizzling rain that soon soaked him to the skin. He walked with his head down against it until his feet ached, and he shivered so hard he could barely stand upright. He would've cried, but he was too tired and cold. He hadn't thought to put on his heavy coat, and his thin jacket was soaked through.

He stopped under the shelter of a pine tree and looked around to get his bearings. He didn't recognize the neighborhood and couldn't see a street sign. He thought of sitting down right where he was under the huge tree and going to sleep. If he was lucky, he would die and wake up in Heaven. According to the ladies at the church where he'd gone a few times, Heaven was bright and warm. He didn't think anyone would make grabs for him there or try to hit him with clubs after taking him for a thief. He wondered briefly if they had food in Heaven. He'd never seen a picture of an angel eating a bowl of beans, but he remembered something about a wedding supper of the Lamb. He wasn't sure what that meant, but any kind of supper sounded good right now.

Rain began to seep through the branches. He would never get to sleep here, especially with his stomach cramping for food. He'd sneaked a few bites from the larder earlier in the day while Ma and Hal talked and laughed in the sitting room. Ma never thought of food when she was drinking. She seldom thought of it when she wasn't and acted put upon if Ned mentioned his hunger.

He stepped out from under the tree and trudged in the direction of some houses. He was outside the congested area of town and the houses sat farther off the street. Down an alley, he heard snuffling and movement of horses inside a shed. At least it would be drier and warmer in there. He might find an old blanket or mound of hay to sleep in before the owner woke up and ran him off.

As expected, the door was unlocked. He pushed it open on rusty hinges just wide enough to slip inside. The barn was decidedly warmer with two horses packed inside the small space.

Ned moved between the two horses and pressed his body against the bigger one. The mare swung her big head around to see if he was offering food. When she saw he was empty handed, she went back to dozing. After he stopped shivering, Ned moved around the small enclosure until he found a small rug used to protect horses under the harnesses. He propped against the wall facing the door so he could see whoever came in before they saw him. He put his wet bag with the change of clothes behind his head for a pillow, pulled the rug over him as best he could, and fell instantly asleep.

Ned capped his pen and closed the ledger. He might as well go home early. He wasn't accomplishing anything tonight anyway except stirring restless memories.

He seldom thought of those years so long ago. He didn't give time to self-pity. He hadn't been the only kid hungry and alone on the streets. He only thought of those days when he remembered how the Lord had brought him out of the situation. Things were good now. That night had been the last he spent with his mother and the last time he experienced the physical ache of hunger.

He put on his suit jacket and headed toward the front door. The boardinghouse was only two blocks away so he walked to work. He didn't want to spend money on a livery or a horse when he was close enough to walk. He had put out feelers for a house, but he wasn't yet making much money at the firm. When Mr. Simonton asked him to join the firm, he had hinted he would soon retire. Ned had been here a year, and so far, the older litigator hadn't made any actual plans for retirement. Ned didn't need a house now anyway since it was only him. Mrs. Crothers' cooking satisfied and the price was right. Still, he didn't want to live there forever.

As he walked, he thought of Catherine's words about finding a good woman. Ned had thought the same thing over the years, but he was always too busy to do anything about it.

For a moment he wondered if Felicity Trego could be that woman. He immediately dismissed the notion. There had to be a reason she hadn't yet married. She was obviously waiting for a certain type of someone. A successful man established in his field who could keep her in the fashion in which she'd been raised. That would probably never be him.

Still, he hadn't been able to keep her lovely face out of his mind for long today. Now, without the crush of paperwork and Catherine interrupting every ten minutes with more to add to his workload, he could relive the few moments he spent with her.

Those captivating sapphire eyes had seemed to pierce right through him. Her bright blond hair reminded him of the princess in a fairy tale, not that he'd read many fairy tales. He wondered if it felt as silky soft as it looked. He thought again of what Catherine said about the sisters not marrying.

He couldn't imagine two sisters more different than Felicity and the older Belinda who seemed to have no interest in anything other than business. His brief interaction with Felicity today hadn't been enough to prove she wasn't the same. The sisters' differences could be in physical appearance only. Ned hoped he'd get the chance to find out.

Chapter Five

The next morning Felicity left the house with a thick packet of papers and her head swimming with instructions from Belinda.

Belinda's foot might have slowed her down, but her mind was working overtime to make up for it. Shane and Richard, another of the stable hands, had brought a small bed down from an upstairs bedroom to replace the sofa next to the window. The rest of their day would be spent creating an office around the narrow bed so Belinda could work without getting up and down.

Felicity and Johanna tried to convince her to follow the doctor's orders and take the week off to let her body rest and deal with the pain.

They may as well have suggested she carry the bank vault to the top of a mountain, open the door, and let the wind carry their money all the way to the Pacific Ocean.

Belinda's last command as Felicity walked out the door was to find her a secretary/nurse. Johanna followed Felicity onto the veranda and pulled the door shut behind her.

"You better find us a new maid today as well." She looked at the door to make sure Belinda hadn't followed them out. "As soon as I walked through the door this morning, she started barking orders. Said I needed to get her dressed and ready to begin work. Well, I didn't have time for that, so I had Kerry help her. Poor girl must've made fifteen trips up and down those stairs fetching everything your sister said she couldn't survive the day without. She couldn't fix Belinda's hair to suit her, and Belinda was none too shy telling her about it either."

"Oh, Johanna, I'm so sorry."

Johanna nodded. "Kerry was in tears by the time she came to the kitchen for Belinda's breakfast. I don't know which one of the girls I can strongarm into fetching for her all day. Don't be surprised if the entire staff has run for the hills by the end of the week." She squared her shoulders. "Including me."

Felicity put her hand on the older woman's arm. "I'll see what I can do. And I'll talk to

Belinda. At the factory when she gives a command, people jump to obey. She's used to being in charge."

"Not here, she isn't. Your pappy put me in charge of running this household before Belinda needed a brassiere, and I've done a right fine job of it all these years. I may just remind her of that."

Felicity was used to Johanna's indelicate comments. "Maybe you should. I'll see what I can do about getting more help."

"I don't know if anybody's desperate enough for work to come into this house as long as Belinda has commandeered the parlor."

Felicity didn't tell her she'd been thinking the same thing. She climbed into the carriage Richard had waiting in the drive and headed for the factory. She had enough on her mind already learning the intricacies of day-to-day operations without finding her sister a valet/nurse/assistant she wouldn't reduce to tears the first day. How was she supposed to complete her own work while doing Belinda's as well? Fortunately, most of her own work wasn't important or difficult. She could assign it to someone who knew as much as she did about business—like one of the livery hands—while she took over Belinda's workload.

Her first order of the day was to find Mr. Hughes. She found the thin balding man at his desk sorting through invoices. She didn't expect him to stop at her appearance. He didn't.

"Here are Belinda's instructions for the day," she said without greeting. "These projects are of utmost importance and should be seen to as soon as possible."

The top of Mr. Hughes' head reddened. A white ring of hair circled his skull above his ears, making it look even brighter. He had always reminded Felicity of a skeleton. Now she noticed his thin shoulders drooped and his spine had developed a curve that showed through his suit coat. When had he gotten so old?

"I don't need anyone telling me what projects are important and which ones can wait." Even as he spoke, he pulled the folders across the desk and began looking through them.

"Belinda has only broken her ankle, Mr. Hughes. There's nothing wrong with her head." *Unfortunately,* she whispered to herself.

"She intends to do as much as she can from the house." She swallowed to gather her nerve. "She wants all meetings that are usually done with her in attendance held at the house for the time being. She refuses to miss a one. She wants you there at two o'clock to spend the rest of the afternoon, keeping her abreast of all business matters."

His head darkened further. Felicity hated talking to him like an employee. He had worked well with Papa, but he didn't agree with many of Belinda's implementations, even though she was usually proven right in the long run.

"That won't work," he huffed. "I have business here that needs my attention. Your sister isn't the only one who keeps this place running."

Felicity wanted to tell him she agreed, but her loyalty was to Belinda. She pushed away her doubts that made it hard to maintain eye contact. "I'm here to oversee operations when you're with Belinda. The foremen keep the machines on the floor running. Any problems they have, they can bring to me."

His scraggly eyebrows shot toward the top of his head. "You? No offense, Miss Trego, but you've never worked the floor. As far as I know, you've never even been there. How could you possibly answer questions or resolve issues?"

"The department heads and foremen will have to teach me. You're here most of the day if I have questions. I plan to learn everything my sister knows and become a more integral part of the company. It's long overdue."

"Begging your pardon, *Felicity*, but how do you suppose the men will react when you walk onto the floor?"

Felicity balked at her first name on his lips. She knew what he was intimating. Her looks might help her convince Willow Wood's business owners to donate money and goods to the foundlings' home, but they would be a hindrance when it came to telling people how to do their jobs on the factory floor. She didn't exactly exude confidence the way Belinda did. But she was still a Trego. She owned the place.

"They will show me the same respect and deference they show you and Belinda, or they will be shown the door. My sister isn't coming back for at least two months. Probably longer. This is how the company will be run during that time. Every person under this roof will do well to accept it."

He glared, and she very nearly looked away. Her first memory of the man was him coming to the little house on Buckskin Street to discuss business with Papa.

Oftentimes, she sat on Papa's lap during the meetings and pretended to read the graphs and charts spread across the table. Back then, both men worked nearly around the clock, building up the company. Without Mr. Hughes, she wasn't sure Papa would've been as successful. He deserved her respect and patience. But she deserved his. It was up to her to prove she was competent and up to the task.

"Whatever you say, Miss Trego."

She softened her stance. "Thank you, Mr. Hughes. This transition will be an adjustment for all of us. I'll need your expertise and experience to help me through. I don't want to let you or Belinda or any of our employees down."

Her humility didn't warm the steel in his gray eyes. "I'll do my best," he said flatly.

She watched him for a moment, her satchel slippery in her clammy hands. "I'm meeting with the other department heads this morning. If you need me, I'll be with Mr. Iverson until around ten learning how to decipher the fiscal reports."

"Yes, Miss Trego." His expression told her she needn't expect him to come looking for her.

She managed to keep her head up as she left the office. Inside she was quaking. The rest of her morning didn't go much smoother. She moved from office to office, passing on Belinda's instructions as if they were her own.

She wanted to maintain a working relationship with each department, but she couldn't let people see her as Belinda's pretty, empty-headed, incompetent lackey who didn't know the first thing about running the factory. Even if it was true.

Chapter Six

When the noon whistle split the air, Felicity nearly jumped out of her chair. She had been so absorbed in the last twelve months of fiscal reports and trying to remember everything Mr. Iverson had told her so she wouldn't have to ask for clarification, she hadn't realized the morning was gone.

She rested her head in her hands for a moment and prayed. She was a nervous wreck. How did Belinda do this every day? Though her stomach was empty, she couldn't imagine swallowing a bite. Still, she would give her favorite silk hat to get out of this office for an hour.

Belinda usually took her lunch at her desk or worked through the break without eating at all. Felicity couldn't.

Her head spun from the order and invoice numbers and all the information presented to her this morning by the various departments. She wished she had taken the initiative to learn how the company operated in the two years since coming home from the university.

Instead she only did what Belinda and Mr. Hughes allowed, with no interest in expanding her duties. Now she had to learn everything in one day.

The noise level on the street below rose in intensity and volume as the factory's workforce left the interior for the picnic grounds outside for their noon meal.

As anxious as she was to leave the confines of her office, Felicity decided to wait until everyone went back inside before she made her own lunch plans. She could drive home and have a cup of tea and perhaps some toast there, but that would mean answering a hundred questions from Belinda. If she couldn't face the factory force outside on the grounds, she surely couldn't face her sister.

Despite the headache behind her eyes, she kept working until she heard the workers filing back inside the plant. As expected, the street was quiet when she went to the livery behind the factory to fetch her carriage.

She could easily eat at the café across the street, but she had an errand to run after lunch. She might as well go downtown and eat at the restaurant inside the hotel. At least there, no judgmental eyes from the factory's management staff would watch her every move. She hoped.

Mrs. Ward, the owner of the hotel met her as she walked through the hotel lobby. "Good afternoon, Felicity. I heard about what happened to Belinda. Poor thing."

Felicity couldn't tell if she was talking about her or Belinda.

"I'll tell her you sent your best wishes," Felicity said.

Mrs. Ward smiled knowingly. "Please do." She kept hold of Felicity's arm as she escorted her into the dining room.

The large area was half filled with businessmen who tended to linger over their cigars after the rest of the town had gone back to work. On the other side of the room, it looked like Hershel List had just finished his usual meal of T-bone steak and cooked vegetables. He leaned back in his chair and clenched his teeth around a cigar as he smiled at whatever the man across the table had said to him.

Since last month when his business partner Hugh Lundy, Felicity and Belinda's former neighbor, had been killed, Mr. List was busier than ever. Last year Mr. List's daughter Ada had left town with a rail worker. As far as Felicity knew, no one had heard anything from her. Felicity tried to ignore the stories cooked up by Willow Wood's rumor mills about where Ada was and what she was doing. It was nearly impossible in a town so small. She wondered if Mr. List was more concerned about what would become of the Lundy-List holdings without Hugh Lundy than what happened to his adventure-seeking daughter.

"It's a good thing you didn't come in earlier," Mrs. Ward said. "We were very busy. Typical for the first of the week. The businessmen love to catch up on the news and compare battle scars. You won't mind terribly, dear..." she said as she whisked Felicity through the dining room to the tables near the window. "Mr. Yates just got here, too."

Felicity realized what was happening. "Oh, no, I couldn't..."

Mrs. Ward tightened her grip, picked up her pace, and talked even faster. "We're shorthanded in the kitchen today. You know how it is. Always when you need help the most."

She brought Felicity to a stop at a table for two. "Counselor, do you know Miss Trego?" Before he could respond, she rushed on. "I know it's an imposition, but would you mind sharing your table? My staff is just stretched to the limit."

Ned pushed out his chair and hastened to his feet. He looked as dumbstruck as Felicity felt. "No, uh, of course not."

Warmth filled her cheeks. He must surely think she orchestrated the whole thing. When this humiliation was over, she would tell Mrs. Ward what she thought of foisting her on an unsuspecting man like a prize heifer.

"I'm so sorry," Mrs. Ward went on, sounding not the least bit repentant. "Like I was telling Miss Trego, we're short staffed. It would help all of us out if you two shared a table since the lunch hour is nearly over."

Felicity watched Ned glance around the dining room where a full staff waited tables and bussed the empty ones. "If it's an inconvenience..." she began.

"No, I don't mind." Ned stepped around the table and pulled back the chair across from his. "I'd be pleased to share the table, Miss Trego."

Mrs. Ward released her vise-like grip on Felicity's arm. "Splendid." She snatched a menu off a neighboring table and plunked it down in front of Felicity, though Felicity knew it by heart. "Rachel will bring you some water in a moment and take your orders."

Felicity shot her a warning look, which she ignored as she bustled off toward the kitchen.

As Ned pushed her chair in and circled the table back to his seat, Felicity fiddled with the place setting.

When he sat, she exhaled loudly. "I'm so sorry about that. I hope I'm not intruding."

Ned's smile seemed sincere. "Not at all. I couldn't get away earlier for lunch, so I appreciate the company."

She realized she appreciated it too. This morning had been so stressful, she was thankful for an opportunity to talk about something other than how unqualified she was to fill Belinda's shoes. She should be annoyed at Mrs. Ward's obvious finagling to get her and Ned together. Instead, all she felt was pleasure and gratitude.

"Do you eat here often?" she asked. She ate here at least once a week and had never seen him. She was sure she would've noticed him.

"When I have a chance to get out of the office. Mrs. Crothers at the boardinghouse fixes my lunch most days. I try to discourage her. She has enough to do already, but she tends to mother us bachelors. I think she worries we'll starve between the breakfast and dinners she cooks."

"I am sure of that. When her son married and left town a few years ago he weighed nearly three hundred pounds."

Ned feigned a shudder. "I think that's what she plans for me."

Felicity laughed out loud. She couldn't imagine the tall, trim attorney turning to fat. She pressed her lips together to rein in her humor when she saw the waitress approaching the table. She set down two frosty glasses of water and took their orders.

"Mrs. Crothers is a very nice lady," Ned said when the waitress moved away. "I hope I didn't sound unappreciative of all she does."

Felicity took a sip of her water to cool the warmth in her cheeks. "No, no, it was my fault. I shouldn't have laughed. I was..."

Her voice trailed off. She couldn't tell him she'd been thinking of his athletic physique.

"Belinda and I love this restaurant. Papa brought me here at least once a week when I was little. I would walk from school to his office and if he could get away, we'd come here together."

She grew wistful at the memory. "He was always so busy I didn't see him as often as I wanted. He did his best to make time for Belinda and me. He was very close to Belinda. She's several years older than me, as you know, so she started working at the factory with Papa when I was still in primary school. She and Papa had a lot in common. The factory reminds her of him more than anything. This..." She motioned around the dining room. "...is where my memories are."

She pushed the bittersweet emotions aside.

Ned gave her a moment to collect herself before he spoke. "What about your mother? Did she ever join the two of you for lunch?"

The waitress appeared with their plates. Felicity used the distraction to take a deep breath and consider how much to tell him and how to do it. Best to jump right in and get it over with.

"My mother passed away when I was small."

Ned froze. "I'm so sorry."

"That's all right. You couldn't know. Besides, it was a long time ago. I was only four when she died. My life has always been Papa, Belinda, and me. They took wonderful care of me and made sure I had the best upbringing one can have without the benefit of a mother's love."

Ned's jaw tightened. Felicity wondered if she had said something wrong or if he was commiserating with her A moment passed before he gave her a sympathetic smile. "Do you mind if I bless the food?" Felicity bowed her head and smiled into her lap. A man who believed in prayer. What a nice development.

After a short prayer they began to eat. She was hungrier than she thought now that her stomach wasn't in knots over work. She couldn't dawdle over lunch, though, since she had an errand before going back to the plant. This wasn't like the old days when she could waltz out of the factory, free as a bird, and stay gone the rest of the day with no one missing her. Now, all the responsibility sat squarely on her shoulders.

"Have you found a nice church to attend?" she asked, hoping she wouldn't offend. There were only a few churches in town, and she had never seen him at hers.

He nodded as he swallowed his food. "Mr. and Mrs. Simonton invited me to theirs when I first moved to town." He took another small bite and chewed thoughtfully. Felicity could tell he wanted to say more on the matter so she didn't interrupt.

"I appreciate all they've done to welcome me to Willow Wood. I wouldn't want to offend either of them, but lately, well, I've taken to staying at the boardinghouse Sunday mornings and working on briefs. That's most of my job.

"After all those years in college I spend my days at my desk, reading huge books and writing briefs. By my second year of grammar school, I had a tolerable skill at reading and writing. If this is all there is to practicing law, I could've started back then."

Felicity laughed. Ned's eyes lit up. She took a bite of her pot roast to quell the laugh. She had seen that look in men's eyes before. Their egos appreciated the approval and attention of a woman. Sometimes it made them think the woman was interested in them. Not in her case.

Well, she *was* interested. She would like nothing more than to spend the rest of her day getting to know him. But it was out of the question. Even if Papa hadn't included the stipulation in his will that she would lose her inheritance if she married, she had enough on her plate running the factory during Belinda's convalescence. Not to mention her other obligations.

"Perhaps you would like to attend my church sometime. Reverend Sanders is very down-to-earth. He's earnest, to say the least, and he makes Scripture come alive like nothing I've ever heard."

"That sounds nice. I'll consider the invitation."

"How is everything at the factory without your sister?" he asked conversationally after a few moments of eating in silence.

"It's different, I must say. I've never played an integral role there before. I didn't really need to with Belinda at the helm. I almost didn't recognize the place when I came home from the university in Boise two years ago. She's very innovative. She made a lot of changes Papa would be proud of. She has more in store, I believe, if she can convince shareholders and Mr. Hughes to give her enough lead."

Ned nodded around a bite of food. "Doesn't the factory belong to you?"

"Well, theoretically. But we're women." She blushed at the obviousness of her statement. "Most people don't believe women have the constitution to run a company as big and prosperous as Trego Leatherworks. Of course, those people have never met Belinda."

Ned laughed.

Felicity couldn't help chuckling herself. She hadn't enjoyed lunch this much in a long time. She took another small bite of her sautéed potatoes. They were too salty for her taste, but she needed to do something to keep from looking into his olive green eyes. She could very nearly get lost in them.

"How do you like Willow Wood? Is your family still in Omaha?"

A shadow crossed his face. "I don't have much family. My parents are both gone. One of my sisters lives in Indiana with her husband. He's a State Representative. The other keeps busy with various civic organizations and charities."

"Um." Felicity didn't know what to say. It didn't sound like he was close to his family and she didn't want to force him to talk about a topic he'd rather not.

"I don't plan to stay at the boardinghouse much longer," he said, saving her from further comment on his family situation. "I never thought I'd stay this long, but it has helped me save money."

"Do you plan to stay at the law office with Mr. Simonton?"

"I would like to. When he found out I was seeking a position, he was eager to bring me here. He doesn't have children of his own and was happy to hear a Yates was willing to take over someday. He may retire soon. Mrs. Simonton misses being close to their grown children."

After a few more minutes, Felicity finished the rest of her lunch. She checked the watch on her bodice. "I must go. Mr. Hughes is going to the house to spend the afternoon with Belinda and I need to give him a report first." She pushed back her plate and prepared to stand.

Ned got to his feet first. "Allow me," he said as she signaled to the waitress.

"No," she nearly snapped and then softened her voice. "I must insist I take care of my order." She didn't want to give him the wrong impression by allowing him to pay for her lunch.

After paying, they stepped outside. "Thank you again for allowing me to share your table. I'm sorry about Mrs. Ward thrusting me upon you."

"Oh, no, think nothing of it."

Again, Felicity got the feeling he was as pleased with the way lunch turned out as she was.

He tipped his hat. "Have a nice afternoon, Miss Trego."

"You as well, Mr. Yates."

Side by side, they stepped off the sidewalk into the street. Felicity looked at Ned. He looked back.

"Are you..." they said at the same time, and laughed again.

"I have an errand at the general store," Felicity said.

At the same time Ned said, "I'm going to the post office."

An American flag flapped in the wind over the entrance of Endicott's General Store, indicating the post office within.

"Then, shall we walk together?" Ned offered his arm.

Felicity had no choice but to take it. Her heart soared, despite knowing Belinda would throw a fit when she discovered Felicity had crossed the street arm in arm with an eligible man in plain sight of all of Willow Wood.

Worse was knowing she would never enjoy anything with Ned Yates beyond lunch and a pleasant afternoon.

Chapter Seven

Felicity hoped she wouldn't run into anyone from the factory inside the store. Though the store was busy, most of the office workers from the factory were back behind their desks by now. The news of her entering the store with Ned would get back to Belinda eventually; she just preferred it didn't happen within the next five minutes.

Jessa Hammersmith was cutting a length of fabric from a bolt for a customer. She looked up and smiled in greeting. "I'll be right with you," she called. Her gaze landed on Ned, and her eyebrows rose in question.

Felicity moved to the counter to wait. She wanted to explain she was only with Ned because they happened to be going to the same place at the same time, but an explanation would only make the situation bigger than it was.

Jessa was the Endicott's oldest daughter. Felicity didn't see her much since she married Rodney Hammersmith at the first of the year. When Jessa finished with the customer and moved awkwardly between the aisles to the front of the store, Felicity noted her time was drawing near. In another month or two, the little bundle would arrive and she would have no time for helping her parents at the store.

A pang of jealousy jolted Felicity, surprising her with its intensity. She loved Jessa and was happy for her and her new husband. But the choice had been made for her years ago that she would never experience the same joys.

"Good afternoon, Felicity. Mr. Yates."

Felicity glanced at Ned waiting beside her, and realized what had stirred the emotions she could usually push aside. She stepped forward and clasped Jessa's hands and kissed her cheek. Her friend's protruding belly remained between them, reminding Felicity of what she couldn't have.

"Good afternoon," Ned said. "Is Mrs. Endicott at the postal counter?"

Jessa nodded. "She sure is."

He headed in that direction.

Jessa looked back at Felicity. "I heard about Belinda. How is she? Do you two need anything?"

"No, we're fine. Well, as fine as we can be with Belinda flat on her back, barking orders and scaring the life out of the staff who's used to not dealing with her all day."

Jessa laughed. "She might find she likes a slower pace."

Felicity tilted her head, skeptically. "I wouldn't count on it." She glanced at Jessa's expanding middle. "What about you? I didn't know if I'd see you here today."

Jessa put her hand on her stomach. Her face softened in contentment. "I work with Mama a few hours every afternoon so she can stay ahead of the post office paperwork. In a few weeks I'll be too busy for even that."

"How is Rodney?"

"He's fine. Busy at the office."

Love glowed on her face. Felicity glanced down the aisle to the postal counter where Ned talked with Mrs. Endicott. She forced her gaze away and hoped Jessa hadn't noticed.

She stepped closer to Jessa. "How is Mr. List handling the railroad and mining companies now that Hugh Lundy is gone? I keep wondering who will take his place. I haven't seen any indication that Ellie plans to."

Jessa glanced around to make sure no other customers were within earshot. "She isn't. I'm sure you know Ellie's cousin Harper and her husband Logan still live at the estate. Rodney and Mr. List have gone there a couple of times to update Ellie on company matters. Every time, she makes sure Harper and Logan are with her for moral support. But they can't do anything in her place unless she takes some kind of legal action. So far, she hasn't shown much interest. Patience has never been a strong suit of Mr. List, but he knows he has to take his time with her. She deserves a proper mourning period, but eventually she'll have to make a definitive move. At least assign someone to manage her interests."

She looked past Felicity to where Ned was chatting with Mrs. Endicott. *Simonton, Yates* was the only law firm in town. Felicity doubted either of the attorneys were equipped to handle holdings as large as what Ellie now solely owned.

Jessa leaned even closer. "She may not realize it yet, but Rodney says she's the richest woman west of the Mississippi."

Felicity's eyes widened. "Oh, my, you're right. I never even considered that. She's had quite the challenge thrust upon her."

She felt overwhelmed by her new position at the factory, but it paled in comparison to what Ellie Lundy faced. Which reminded her, she needed to complete her errand and get back to work. She had responsibilities now, besides what she really wanted to do.

"Is your father here? He was going to put together an order for me today."

"Oh, yes. I nearly forgot. He got called away, but everything's waiting at the back door. I can't help you load it," she said with her hand at the small of her back, "but if you can wait a little while, he'll be back soon."

"I'm afraid I can't wait. I suppose I could load it myself."

Jessa glanced down at Felicity's clothes. "Some of the things are very heavy. A barrel of pickles came in with a broken lid. He said you could take them if you want."

"Pickles!" Felicity exclaimed. "A whole barrel. How wonderful."

"But you can't load it. Even if I was able to help, I don't know if the two of us could wrestle it—"

Ned came back up the aisle. "Do you need help with something?"

Felicity gave Ned's suit the same look Jessa had given her. "Oh, no, I couldn't ask you to—"

"Jessa, are you nearly finished?" a customer called. "I need some help back here."

Jessa smiled apologetically at Felicity and Ned. "Of course, Mrs. Smith. You can always wait for Daddy," she told Felicity as she moved away.

Felicity thought of the ticking clock. "I really can't..." She stopped talking when she realized she was talking to Jessa's back. She looked at Ned.

"Don't let the clothes fool you," he said. "I'm strong as an ox under this broadcloth." He flexed his arms.

Felicity barked out a laugh. She quickly recovered before anyone else overheard.

"You can drive the carriage down the alley. I'll wait by the back door. I have a few minutes if you need me to ride along to deliver it."

Her chest swelled with unexpected pleasure, and not only because she wouldn't have to wait for Mr. Endicott. "Are you sure? The pickle barrel probably leaks."

"Nothing that can't wash off. Now, let's hurry before they miss you at the factory."

Law and tarnation. She'd nearly forgotten the factory. She spun on her heel and hurried outside and back across the street where she had left her buggy in front of the hotel. She had forgotten to ask Jessa about someone to come to the house to work for Belinda, too. That situation would have to wait.

Chapter Eight

"I didn't realize the Trego sisters had such an affinity for pickles."

Ned brushed his hands together to remove the dust and splinters after loading the barrel. He was pretty sure Felicity hadn't stopped at the store to pick up her own grocery order. Nor was it likely she was taking the barrel of pickles to the factory for the workers. Even less likely was the ten pounds of flour and fifty pounds of potatoes he'd loaded into the back of the rig.

"They're not for..." She snagged her bottom lip with the whitest set of teeth Ned had ever seen. Or maybe it was the blush on her cheeks that made her teeth look so white and her eyes so blue. He forced his gaze away.

"We do love pickles," she finished, her eyes gleaming.

She hopped into the buggy without giving him a chance to help her. He sure wouldn't have minded taking her hand and helping her up.

Once settled, she grasped the reins and waited for him to circle the buggy and climb aboard. "Are you sure you don't mind helping with my delivery?" Before he could answer, she gasped.

"I didn't properly thank the Endicotts for the order. They are so generous."

"Generous?" Had Trego Leatherworks fallen on hard times and the family had taken to asking for food donations?

"Mr. and Mrs. Endicott donate more things to the foundlings' home than any other business in town. Oh, I don't mean the others don't contribute. But sometimes, well, occasionally I have to use a little charm." She arched her pale eyebrows. "And more than a little guilt to get some of them to do the Christian thing."

He studied her. "I've been here a year and I didn't know Willow Wood had an orphanage."

"It's not an actual orphanage. Just a very dear, compassionate widow woman, Beulah McClanahan, who opened her home to children who didn't have anywhere else to go. I don't know how she finds the children or how they hear of her.

"Every now and then, there'll be a different face or two around the table while another disappears. I've never had the nerve to ask her how the whole situation works. I suppose she'll tell me if I ever need to know."

"How did you get involved?"

"I'm not involved. Well, I do my best to encourage local businesses and residents to support the children. Mrs. McClanahan makes the true sacrifice. I would be dishonoring the gifts God has given me if I stood back and didn't do my best to ease the burdens of widows and orphans."

Her lips were slightly parted at the passion behind her words. Her cheeks flushed, and her eyes shone bright. He'd never seen a more beautiful woman, yet she seemed so authentic.

Her eyes widened. "I'm sorry. I hope that didn't sound prideful."

Ned realized he had been staring. How could he not? "No, I never thought... What I meant to ask was, how many children live at the orphans' home?"

"Nine as of right now. There might be more by the time we get there." She laughed and it sounded like music in the crisp October air.

"The most I've seen are twelve. It's really hard for Mrs. McClanahan to care for so many on her own. She's ill equipped to take care of the ones she has. There aren't enough beds, for one, and the boys sleep on the floor in the kitchen next to the stove."

"How did Mrs. McClanahan get started taking children into her home?"

Felicity clicked her tongue and flicked the reins to spur the horse into a canter after leaving a congested street.

"Her sister had four children. She passed away and her husband didn't think he could take care of them on his own. He planned to parcel the children out to different relatives. Mrs. McClanahan couldn't bear them being separated after losing their mama. She and her husband took them in and finished raising them. Now her husband's gone, and she's doing the best she can on her own." She sighed. "I wish I could do more."

"I am sure she is thankful for all you do." He motioned to the ham in the brown paper wrapping at their feet.

"Their bellies need filled. But what I'd really like to do is find homes for each and every one of them."

"Most families have enough trouble feeding their own without taking more children in. If they do, it's for free labor."

Her eyes widened. Ned hadn't meant to say the words out loud. He avoided talking about his past to most people. Even the Simontons didn't know he wasn't Mr. and Mrs. Yates' biological son. He wasn't ashamed of where he came from; he just didn't want sympathy or for people to think of him according to who he used to be.

"I suppose that's true," she said, her voice etched in sadness. "It just breaks my heart to see a child suffer."

Ned merely nodded in reply. It broke his heart, too, but his experiences were a world apart from Felicity Trego's. She had lost her mother early, but she had a supportive family to love her and raise her. She could never understand how a boy would disappear from his home and his mother not waste an ounce of energy looking for him.

He didn't think often of his mother, except when the Holy Spirit prompted him to lift her up in prayer, wherever she was.

Sometimes—like now, on his way to a home for other unwanted children—the rejection of the woman who should have loved him more than life itself reared its ugly head.

They rode in silence until she turned onto a street barely wide enough for two buggies to pass.

Debris-filled ditches lined the thoroughfare and scraggly overgrown trees crowded each other for sunlight. "This is it," Felicity said as a sprawling, unpainted house came into view through the trees.

The horse apparently knew the way and turned into the lane with no discernible command from Felicity. No tall, forgotten weeds lined the drive to the house. The ditches were clear of trash. The lopsided house didn't look like it had ever known whitewash, but the porch and path were swept clean, and the grass cut back to make a clear approach.

Felicity's countenance brightened the closer they drew to the side of the house.

Ned's heart warmed at the love on her face. It was obvious she cared for these forgotten children. Some in her position would occasionally give to a foundlings' home to make themselves feel better. It looked like she truly cared about the children they were about to see.

She guided the buggy around the side of the house and drew to a stop in the shade of an overhang. She hopped down, again without waiting for help, and circled the back of the carriage.

Before she reached the door, it burst open and a girl about twelve years old stepped out. A faded calico dress that reached to mid-calf exposed bare feet. Her brown hair was coming loose from a thin braid. Her face, forearms, and hands were smudged with dirt.

"Miss Trego. We weren't expecting you today." The light in her eyes turned suspicious at the sight of Ned.

"Hello, Frannie, this is my friend, Mr. Yates. Mr. Yates, this is Frannie. Why aren't you in school?" she asked the girl.

Frannie held up her hands and turned them back and forth to show the grime on both sides. "There was a leak in the kitchen roof last night and part of the ceiling came down. We older kids stayed home to help clean up."

"Oh, no." Felicity started past the girl to go inside and survey the damage. She stopped and looked back at her loaded carriage. "Could you help Mr. Yates bring the things in. I'll send the big boys out to help."

The girl's eyes lit up at the sight of boxes and bags behind the seat.

Felicity smiled at Ned over the girl's brown head. "Hurry now. I can't stay but a minute."

Ned wrapped an arm around the flour sack and grabbed the ham with his free hand. He knew the butcher in town. The man didn't seem to have a generous bone in his body. Ned figured it was difficult for even the most tight-fisted to remain so when looking into Felicity Trego's beseeching blue eyes.

In the kitchen, Felicity and a thin woman in a stained apron over a plain brown dress stared up at the broken plaster in the ceiling. A girl, who looked to be in her late teens, was washing out cleaning rags at the sink.

"Oh, Ned," Felicity said at the sight of him, "can you believe what happened?"

Yes, he could believe it, though he didn't say so. From the sorry shape of the patched ceiling, he was more surprised the whole thing hadn't completely fallen in on their heads. He looked around the kitchen. The woman and children had managed to clean up the worst of the damage.

A boy in his mid-teens entered the room carrying a step-ladder. Another, about the same age, with the same crooked haircut and wary expression, followed with a roll of brown paper.

Felicity and the woman stepped out of the center of the floor to make room for the ladder. "Ned, this is Beulah McClanahan. Mrs. McClanahan, this is my friend Ned. He works at the law office with Mr. Simonton."

Ned hastily deposited the sack of flour and ham on the crowded kitchen table. Mrs. McClanahan stepped forward to shake his hand. "Ah, yes. I know Mr. Yates," the woman said. Her face was lined and tired, but her eyes were warm. "I ran into you a time or two at the postal counter."

"Yes, of course." Ned clapped his hands together to remove the flour and then grasped hers. "When Felicity was telling me about you, I didn't make the connection. Looks like a bad spot of luck you had there."

"Not luck, son. Rain. But you didn't come here to listen to my woes." She set her hand on the ham. "Ah, Felicity. You are a godsend, child. What would we do without you?"

"Don't thank me," Felicity said quickly. "It was Mr. Beals at the butcher shop."

Mrs. McClanahan looked at Ned and smirked. "That man wouldn't give a skinny chicken to his own mother without charging her full price. But who can resist our beautiful Felicity?"

Ned was thinking the same thing. "There's more outside."

Felicity gasped. "Oh, yes, I nearly forgot. Tim, Malachi, could you run out and grab the rest of the food? There's a barrel of pickles with a busted lid so you'll have to be careful."

"Pickles!" one of the boys exclaimed. "A whole barrel!"

"All for you, Malachi." She laughed as both boys rushed out the door. She looked apologetically at Mrs. McClanahan. "It isn't much. I've been so busy with the factory now that Belinda's indisposed. And I really must get back to town. I've already been gone too long."

Mrs. McClanahan put her hand on Felicity's arm. "Please don't fret. We appreciate everything you do. It means more than you realize."

Ned went to the stepladder and climbed up. He gazed into the hole and then backed down. He shook his head at the women. "A patch job on the ceiling isn't going to do you much good."

Mrs. McClanahan nodded solemnly. "I know. I had hoped to get one more winter out of the roof. But now..."

Felicity gazed anxiously at the ceiling. "What does that mean? She needs an entire roof?"

"Not entirely."

Ned and the women stepped aside as the boys wrestled in the barrel of pickles. Frannie came in behind them, dragging the bag of potatoes.

"Pickles, Mum," Malachi exclaimed, using the term the children used for Mrs. McClanahan. "The fat dill ones they sell at the general store. Can we have one?"

"Of course, but only one apiece for now." Mrs. McClanahan turned expectantly back to Ned.

"I believe if you replace the section over this end of the house, the rest will make it until Spring."

"But that's so expensive," Felicity said over the sound of the youngsters fighting for space around the tub in the corner to wash their hands.

"Can't be helped, dear," Mrs. McClanahan said. "The Lord always provides. We'll figure something out."

Ned looked out the back window facing the shed. "Looks like you've got some useable lumber out there. If your patch can last until Saturday, the boys and I can go out there and see if we can scrounge up enough for a proper repair."

"Oh, Ned, do you mean it?" Felicity asked.

Mrs. McClanahan set her hands on her hips and regarded his gray suit. "I don't know, young man. I won't turn down help, but it's a mighty big job. I'd never forgive myself if you slid off the roof and tore a hole in them britches."

Ned laughed at the teasing gleam in her eye. "Then I'll wear my roof-sitting britches." He straightened the collar of his shirt. "I may dress like a dandy, but I've busted my share of knuckles on a saw and a hammer."

"Well then, we'll see you Saturday."

"I'll come too."

Ned's heart nearly leaped for joy at the sound of Felicity's voice. He'd hoped she'd say that. She blushed when he and Mrs. McClanahan looked at her.

"I mean, if I won't get in the way."

"I'm sure we can find something for you to do," Mrs. McClanahan told her. "Men working on a roof need a hearty lunch. Isn't that right, Mr. Yates? It's a good thing Mr. Beals gave us this here ham."

"Then we'll both see you bright and early Saturday morning," Ned said.

He and Felicity bid their hasty goodbyes to Mrs. McClanahan and the children.

Felicity turned the buggy back toward the road. She kept glancing at him all the way back to the road.

"What?" Ned asked after another of her approving glances.

"I'm just...surprised is all."

He feigned outrage. "Surprised that I offered to help someone who needed it?"

"I didn't mean that. I just meant..." She tilted her head and looked into his eyes. She shifted the reins to one hand and laid the other on his arm. "Thank you, Ned. This means the world to Mrs. McClanahan and the children. And to me."

Ned smiled back. He meant to tell her no thanks were necessary. He was honored to pitch in. Instead he couldn't form a word with the weight of her hand on his arm.

Chapter Nine

"What took you so long?"

Felicity suppressed a sigh as she removed her coat and hung it on the hook near the front door.

She carried her satchel and bags into the front parlor where Belinda waited on one of the settees next to her bed with her foot propped on an ottoman. "I thought you'd never get here. Johanna held dinner for you."

Felicity emptied her arms onto the sofa table. "I'm so sorry. I had errands to run after lunch, so that put me behind schedule at the office. I wanted to finish everything before I came home."

"By errands, do you mean carting free stuff out to the foundlings' home?"

Felicity's stomach tightened. All the way home she had rehearsed what she would say when Belinda confronted her about cavorting around town with Mr. Yates.

Belinda had been on the sofa all day with only the maids and Mr. Hughes to talk to. Apparently, someone had told her about Felicity going to Mrs. McClanahan's. Time would tell if she knew Ned had accompanied her.

"Belinda, if you mean helping Mrs. McClanahan feed those poor homeless children, then yes, that's what I was doing."

"You know I don't mind you spending our money on those children or badgering the other businesses in town to help out. But I don't see why you need to take the things all the way over there yourself. You don't have free time the way you used to. Now that you have me and so many people depending on you, you'll have to learn to delegate."

Now wasn't the time to tell Belinda she planned to spend her entire Saturday helping fix Mrs. McClanahan's roof.

She leaned forward and kissed her sister's forehead. "I'm sorry I made you wait. I just want to do a good job for you."

Belinda softened. "I have no doubt that you will. Mr. Hughes says you're doing a great job, considering how little experience you have."

Felicity smirked. "High praise, I suppose, coming from that man. I was trained by the best."

Belinda smiled appreciatively. "I'm sorry I'm so gruff. It's a long day sitting here, thinking about all the things I should be doing and can't."

Felicity shuffled through her satchel to find the paperwork Belinda was waiting for. "There's no need to worry. The rest of us know what we're doing. Well, everyone else knows, and I'm learning."

She pulled the stool up to the settee so she and Belinda could go over the papers in her satchel. She was tired and would rather go upstairs for a rest, but Belinda would want to hear every detail from her day.

Belinda fanned the paperwork out on the makeshift desk across her lap. "I'm proud of you, Sister, for stepping up like you have and taking over at the factory for me. You just need to watch that no one takes advantage of you."

Felicity stiffened. Had she heard about Ned riding with her to the orphanage? Did she think he was taking advantage of her?

"Advantage? Who would take advantage of me?"

"I mean those children. Your heart is too soft for your own good. I know you care about them, but you must watch that they don't use your generosity against you."

"That isn't possible, Belinda. I take the donations out there myself because I want to. The children mean so much to me. If they come to expect it, I don't mind. They have so little."

"Our family started out with little, too," Belinda reminded her. Belinda liked reminding anyone who would listen that Papa had started with nothing but a love for crafting leather items that made people's lives easier. He never got a hand up. Why should they give one to those less motivated to build their own success?

"We provide a good living to nearly half this town," she said, reciting an argument Felicity had heard a thousand times. "That's enough charity, if you ask me."

Felicity wanted to remind her she hadn't asked. The only thing that separated her and Belinda from the children at the factory was the condition of their birth. They had built on Papa's idea, but they hadn't created anything out of nothing.

The Trego sisters were not responsible for the situation in which they found themselves, just like the children at Mrs. McClanahan weren't responsible for theirs. But she didn't want to spend the evening discussing a subject that would only lead to frustration for both of them.

Seeking any type of diversion, she reached past the papers she had put on Belinda's lap desk and picked up a crude drawing.

"What's this?"

A satisfied smile spread across Belinda's face.

"It's a project that's been in my mind for years. You know how difficult it is for women or children to hitch buggies with our small hands. I've always wanted to design a coupling device that works just as well but is small enough for a woman or child to operate."

Felicity studied the drawing. "This is brilliant. I always thought dealing with harnessing attachments was something a person with small hands just had to struggle with."

"It always has been. Until now. I'm going to design a hitch anyone old enough to handle a horse can easily attach with one hand, the way men do. Once I work out the kinks, I'll apply for a patent, and we're going to make them at Trego Leatherworks."

"But we...do we have the equipment? The manpower? We would have to build a whole new work area. We're full to the gills now."

Belinda squared her shoulders. "Then that's what we'll do. It's our factory. We can build whatever we want. I have to design the molds for the parts. I'll patent those too. When another company wants to produce the same thing, they'll have to apply to me to use my copyrights."

"Or copy the design and make them themselves."

"I'm not worried about that. Every step you take from the original loses quality."

"Creating a production line like this will cost a fortune. What does Mr. Hughes say?"

"Oh, pooh on Mr. Hughes. He doesn't say anything because I haven't told him. Nor do I plan to. Not until I have the patent in my hand. Don't you breathe a word of this either, Sister. The only other people who'll know anything about our plans is Mr. Simonton and that other fellow."

"Ned Yates," Felicity provided.

Belinda looked up sharply. "Yes, Mr. Yates. They'll have to submit the patent for me, but no one else must know a thing."

"I won't say anything. This is so exciting."

"You're going to have to help me. Tomorrow I need you to check out Building Four on the west side of the property. It has the largest yard area for loading and unloading from the rail line. Part of the building might have to come down in order to make room for a forge to make the molds. We'll need a constant supply of clay and sand to feed it. And ore, of course, for the metal castings."

Felicity sat back in the chair. "Sister, stop. You're making my head hurt. I don't know what you want me to do. I can't go in there tomorrow and start tearing down walls."

"Yes, don't do that. People would get suspicious. All I need at this point is an inventory of the equipment housed there so I can figure out how best to incorporate it into other parts of the plant when the time comes.

"I also need a roster of personnel and each department where they work. I need to determine the best candidates for working the foundry. I'm sure a few already have experience so we won't have to train them from the ground up."

"How will this happen without anyone finding out? What about Mr. Hughes? He's our business partner."

"He's our partner, but this is Papa's life's work. My life's work. Last year I suggested expanding the factory to him, but he said it wasn't prudent. It was too big of a risk."

"Maybe—"

Belinda's eyes flashed. "Law and tarnation, Felicity. I won't let that old stick-in-the-mud keep me from making this work. This invention is going to improve the lives of women on the frontier. Don't you want that?"

"Of course."

"Then don't worry. We're a team, you and I. After I finish my design and get it patented, we'll discuss how to proceed with the implementation. If you don't agree it's the best way to move the company forward, we won't do it."

Felicity stared at her. "Do you mean that? You trust me to help you make a decision of that magnitude?"

"We're all each other has. We have to be there for the other, no matter what."

Chapter Ten

On her way out the door the next morning Belinda reminded her to keep up the search for an assistant.

Felicity didn't tell her the matter had completely slipped her mind. She had enough to do already, learning her position at the factory without anyone realizing she was about to sink under the weight of it. Now she had to inventory the equipment and employees, again with no one realizing what she was doing. Finding an assistant for Belinda wasn't high on her list of priorities.

The one bright spot of her morning was today was Friday. Tomorrow she was going to the orphanage to help replace the roof. With Ned.

Belinda wouldn't be happy when she learned Felicity wasn't going to work. Saturdays were another work day for Belinda. She hadn't missed one since three years ago when Christmas Day fell on a Saturday and she was forced to close the factory and let the workers off—with pay, after much guilt from Felicity and Mr. Hughes, who thought it was the right thing to do.

She had complained until Easter about how much doing the *right thing* had cost her.

Felicity had spent more hours at the factory this week than she usually did in an entire month. She was ready for a break and had no intention of changing her plans because Belinda didn't realize there was a world outside the gray factory walls.

She drove straight through town instead of turning for the factory. Even she could tell the small pile of odds and ends of lumber next to Mrs. McClanahan's shed would not be enough to replace the section of roof over the kitchen.

As she drew abreast of Simonton, Yates Esq., she considered stopping to ask Ned what supplies he thought she should order at the lumber mill. Stopping, though, was only an excuse to see him again. Mr. Abbott at the mill would know the supplies were needed to complete the job without Ned's input.

She needed to stop seeking out ways to spend time with the man. Not out of fear of what Belinda would say when she found out—and she would find out—but to spare her own heart. It was bad enough she was spending the entire day with him tomorrow. After each encounter, she liked him more and wanted to know him better.

To what end? There could never be anything more between them than benign friendship. Her heart had already decided that wasn't enough.

If she had any brains at all, she would ride her horse into the mountains tomorrow and stay as far away from Ned Yates as possible.

After reminding Mr. Abbott at the mill of how much Trego Leatherworks appreciated his help with their many building projects in the past, Felicity procured a price for the lumber for Mrs. McClanahan's roof for thirty percent below market value. He assured her the lumber would be waiting in the side yard when she and Ned arrived in the morning.

She had nearly reached the factory when a carriage pulled abreast of her. As soon as she recognized the couple, she knew she had no choice but to stop and chat, though she was already running late. Again.

Bob Milstead, the owner of the bank and a senior member of the factory's board, tipped his hat and smiled his usual stern, businesslike smile. He was the only man Felicity had ever met who could make a smile look like a threat.

"Felicity Trego," his pretentious wife, Barbara crooned. "How lovely to see you. How is your sister?" She pinched her mouth into an expression of sympathy.

"Very well, thank you. She stays busy despite the pain and inconvenience."

"As expected, I'm sure," Bob said. "It'll take more than a busted foot to slow down Belinda Trego."

"Indeed," Felicity said. She thought of Belinda's drawings of the coupling mechanism. Mr. Milstead would be the staunchest opponent to changing anything in the factory.

Money was already rolling in and lining his pockets. He wouldn't want to risk one dime of profit on a project that could prove unmarketable.

"I trust the factory is running smoothly without her." His brows pulled together as he studied Felicity.

She knew just what he was thinking. How could the beautiful, empty-headed sister possibly take the place of the shrewd, intelligent one?

"Everything is running fine, as you'll see at next month's board meeting. Nothing will change without Belinda in her office."

Both looked surprised at the confidence in her voice. Felicity was a little surprised herself.

"Of course," Barbara said. "We have no doubts about your capabilities."

The horse snorted at the front of the carriage. "I really must go. It was nice seeing... Oh, I nearly forgot. Belinda is looking for someone to come to the house to work for her. Or work with her, I should say. A young woman who can see to her personal needs, as well as help with office work. Fetching things for her inside the house. Delivering messages to the office. Filing. Clerical work. That sort of thing."

Barbara's eyes lit up. She started to speak. Bob's stiffened beside her and shot her a warning look. "I'm afraid we can't help you."

Felicity looked from one to the other. "She only needs someone a few hours a day. If it's compensation, Belinda will pay a fair wage for the work."

They exchanged glances again as if Felicity should've figured out the reason herself. "Some people are...difficult to work for," Barbara said.

Bob adjusted his derby hat. "We couldn't, in good conscience, send a young woman into your house to work one on one with Belinda."

Though Felicity knew finding someone to work for Belinda was a tall order, she didn't appreciate hearing it from the banker.

"I know Belinda is a hard taskmaster. It's only because she expects things done a certain way."

"*Her* way," the banker clarified.

"What's wrong with that?"

Especially if she's paying for the help.

"There's nothing wrong with it," Barbara said, with a wary look at her husband. "Workers should serve without complaint. But it's the responsibility of the employer to teach with kindness and patience."

Felicity bristled. No one knew better than her how resolute and hard to work for Belinda was. But as far as Felicity knew, she was never unfair or unreasonable. She felt she needed to defend her sister.

"I am certain whoever takes the job will learn valuable skills to make them more employable in their next job search."

"I'm sure," Barbara said kindly. Mr. Milstead stared straight ahead.

Felicity looked past him to his wife. "Well, if you think of anyone..." She let the sentiment trail off. They knew what she needed. "It was good seeing you. Have a nice day."

She clicked her tongue and tapped the reins against the horse's flank.

"Give our regards to Belinda," Barbara called as their carriage moved in the opposite direction.

Felicity urged her horse faster. The Milsteads hadn't told her anything she didn't already know, but it seemed like they were leaving something out. Surely it wasn't impossible to fill a temporary position, even if it meant working for Belinda Trego.

Jobs for single women weren't exactly in abundance in Willow Wood. She would think running errands and bringing lunch for the stern businesswoman would be preferable over washing laundry or dishes for the miners. Her day hadn't even started, and she already felt like her head would burst with all the things inside it demanding her immediate attention.

She pushed her encounter with the Milsteads out of her mind. She didn't have an ounce of energy to spare on the perception of one prominent couple in town.

She left the horse and carriage with Mark at the livery and hurried up the stairs to the office entrance.

With her satchel in one hand and a bundle of journals and tablets clutched to her chest with her other arm, she leaned forward to reach for the door handle with her fingertips. Just as she managed a tenuous grasp, the door swung outward against her. The door hit her left side, knocking the journals and files out from under her arm and to the concrete landing.

Law and tarnation, she growled in her throat as the journals flapped open and a breeze scattered the loose papers at her feet.

Ned Yates grabbed hold of the door to stop its outward trajectory. "Felicity, I'm so sorry. I didn't see you."

Felicity nearly gasped aloud. Ned! What was he doing here?

Business, she was sure. His presence had nothing to do with her, but she couldn't keep her heart from soaring as the smell of his pine-scented soap filled her nose.

She dropped down to gather the scattering papers, thankful for the opportunity to catch her breath and hide her excitement at seeing him.

Ned knelt beside her. The two of them scrambled to grab the papers before the wind carried them back down the stairs. "It's not your fault," she said, her eyes on her hands. "Someone should put glass in the door so we can see who's on the other side."

"Perhaps you can put a bug in the owner's ear to take care of that for you."

She smiled. "I'll see what I can do." Her shoulder brushed his as they scooped up the last of the papers. She put her mind on the right person to call about putting a pane of glass in the door instead of Ned's nearness.

He grabbed the last of the papers in one hand and a few folders in the other. Their eyes locked and held. Felicity's breath caught. He was so close she could nearly count the tiny flecks of amber in his smoldering green eyes.

For a brief scandalous moment, she imagined those eyes looking up at her out the face of a baby of her own.

She started to rise and tripped over her skirts. Ned reached out to steady her. She fell against him, barely hanging onto her satchel and papers.

"Oh, my, I'm so sorry," she said, still picturing those green eyes in a baby's face. She could only imagine what Belinda would say if she knew the thoughts racing through Felicity's head.

Once she was steady enough for Ned to release his hold on her, he straightened the papers and slid them into a folder. "Can I carry these to your office?"

She should tell him no. He had been on his way out of the factory, his business apparently complete. He had no reason to follow her back inside. Still, she nodded, not trusting her voice. The heavy door swung shut behind them.

The clicking of her hard-soled shoes echoed along the corridor as she picked up her pace to stay ahead of his long strides so he wouldn't see how flustered she was.

"In here," she said at her office door. She dumped the satchel and the tablets she carried on the desk and motioned for him to do the same. "Thank you so much, Ned."

He rocked back on his heels and looped his thumbs in the red suspenders over his crisp white shirt. "I had to make it up to you. You wouldn't have dropped them if I hadn't pushed the door into you."

She laughed, pushing out the last of her nervousness. "That's true. Would you like a drink? Mrs. Jennings always keeps fresh water in the offices."

She glanced at the corner, hoping Mrs. Jennings hadn't let her down this morning. A frosty pewter pitcher stood on a metal tray with four glasses beside it turned upside down. Felicity never understood the need for four glasses. Every day she only used one. Mrs. Jennings must anticipate meetings in Felicity's office the same as all the department heads. So far, none of the meetings she conducted lasted long enough to require refreshment.

"No, thank you. I have an appointment this morning."

"Did you need to see me?" she asked.

He shook his head. "I came to get the government contracts you and Belinda signed earlier in the week."

"Oh, dear, I forgot all about them. I don't—
"

He nodded, finishing her thought. "I stopped at the house to get them from Belinda, but she had given them to Mr. Hughes yesterday." He chuckled. "She was rather annoyed that she doesn't have an assistant to run things like that back and forth for her."

The encounter with the Milsteads rushed back to Felicity's mind. "Papa always had a secretary. Belinda never wanted to bother training someone. Now she's in a bind."

"I suppose I can see her point. I run a lot of my own errands, but it isn't the most efficient way to get things done."

"Do you by any chance..."

He looked back at her expectantly. For a moment, Felicity wished she had the nerve to ask why he really came to Willow Wood. He was intelligent and seemed like a capable attorney. Why wasn't he making more money working for a firm in Omaha? Why didn't he already have a wife? Did he think about marrying? Had he ever been in love? Did he ever imagine a child looking back at him with those same green eyes?

Of course not. Men didn't think on those things. He probably wasn't married because he had no money. He had already told her as much when he explained why he was still at the boardinghouse.

She would never ask her questions. It was none of her business, and his personal life would never affect her in any way.

"You must meet a lot of people in your line of work," she said instead. "Have you heard of a young woman in need of employment? Someone bright and motivated, and hopefully with a strong enough constitution to put up with my sister every day?"

He looked like he wanted to laugh. "I'm afraid I don't. Perhaps Catherine does. I'll ask her."

"Thank you. I almost wish you didn't have to tell her the job was with Belinda until she found an applicant."

"I'm sure that won't have any bearing on someone looking for work."

"I hope you're right," she said, though she wasn't so sure.

"I'll leave you to your work, then." He stopped at the door. "I plan to be at the foundlings' home by eight tomorrow morning. Are you still coming?"

"I'm looking forward to it." It took effort to keep from smiling. "A load of lumber and supplies will be delivered and waiting on us."

"Lumber, eh? That will certainly help out."

"One thing I've learned from my sister, when you want things done, you don't stand around and wait for someone else to do them."

Ned stared as though impressed, but not by any lessons Belinda had imparted.

"I can pick you up at the boardinghouse if you need a ride." She hoped he didn't hear the hope in her voice. "Unless you have a horse."

"I don't own a horse. As long as you don't mind, it'll certainly get me there faster."

"I don't mind at all."

She definitely did not.

Chapter Eleven

"**M**iss Trego! Miss Trego!"
Felicity braced herself for
impact as the little girls ran full
tilt into her.

Jane, one year and two months older than
Hazel, reached her two strides quicker, but
Hazel wouldn't be left behind. Felicity leaned
over and caught Jane in a one-armed hug, and
waited for Hazel to jump into her a second later,
her little feet coming completely off the
ground.

The front door of the plain house opened,
and Mrs. McClanahan stepped onto the porch.
She wiped her hands on her apron. "Girls," she
called, but it was too late.

Jane grabbed hold of Felicity's hand. "Come see what we're making."

"It's paper dolls! It's paper dolls!" Hazel exclaimed, grabbing her other hand.

Felicity smiled at Ned over the children's heads. He had been waiting at the end of the lane outside the boardinghouse when she arrived fifteen minutes earlier.

As they crossed town, they chatted about the sunny skies and cooperative temperatures for climbing onto a roof. October was Felicity's favorite month of the year with its changing colors, brisk mornings, and mild evenings. Sharing a ride in the peaceful Saturday quiet with Ned Yates made it even better.

He reached behind the buggy seat to get the leather bag he'd brought containing two hammers, a few clamps, and a handsaw he borrowed from Mr. Crothers at the boardinghouse.

Jane bounced up and down beside Felicity, taking her focus off Ned and back to the little girls clutching her hands. "Mum brought some newspapers from the store. They were throwing them out. Lucy's showing us how to color clothes and cut them out."

"But my scissors don't work," Hazel said.

Jane looked down her pert nose at the younger girl. "It's cause you don't know how to use them."

"I do so. Come see, Miss Trego."

Mrs. McClanahan reached the three in the shade of the elm tree. "Girls, girls, for goodness sake. Where are your manners? Miss Trego came here to help us today with a very big job. She doesn't need you pulling at her."

They immediately dropped Felicity's hands and gazed adoringly up at her.

"I would love to see your paper dolls, but first I need to see if Mrs. McClanahan has thought of anything else we might need before the men get started on the roof."

Mrs. McClanahan crossed her arms over her narrow frame. She jerked her chin at a stack of freshly sawn lumber stacked near the back of the house. Two boys were on top of the stack, sword fighting with long sticks

"I didn't know what to think when two deliverymen from the sawmill delivered that load last night just before dark. It wasn't necessary, Felicity. We could've made do with what we had."

"I know, but there was no need, especially when Mr. Abbott practically gave me the lumber and nails for nothing."

Mrs. McClanahan tilted her head. "I'm sure if Mr. Yates or I had placed the order, we'd've paid full price. Isn't that right, Mr. Yates?"

Ned smiled at her and gave Felicity an appraising look. "I'm sure of it."

Felicity looked away, but not before noticing his appreciative look. She tossed her head. "Well, we'll never know."

"I suppose not." Mrs. McClanahan turned her gaze to Ned. "Just set that bag right there, young man. We'll get you a drink while I round up the older boys. I can tell you they're most excited to have you teach them a thing or two."

Ned and Felicity fell into step behind her. "I don't know how much I can teach them, but we'll get the roof in shipshape for you."

Inside two teenage boys were finishing their breakfast, while Mary worked at the sink.

"Have you eaten?" Mrs. McClanahan asked. "I can't put you up on that roof with an empty stomach."

"Mrs. Crothers makes sure I have a hearty breakfast every morning whether I want it or not."

"Yes, I imagine she would. Tim, Malachi, hurry up now. Mr. Yates is ready to get started. I'll send Mary out with a jug of water in a little while."

After the door closed behind Ned and the boys, she turned to Felicity. "My, my, my. That's one fine looking man. If I was ten years younger..."

"Mrs. McClanahan," Felicity cried.

"All right. Twenty years. Or thirty."

Felicity shook her head. She let Jane and Hazel pull her to the table where they'd been fashioning paper dolls and clothes. Mrs. McClanahan wasn't about to let the issue of Ned drop so easily.

"Makes a body wonder why a fine specimen like that is still hanging on the vine."

Felicity didn't tell her she'd spent plenty of time already wondering the same thing.

Mary left the sink and joined them at the table. "Maybe he's a widower. How tragic to lose his wife so young. Is he a widower?"

"I don't..."

Jane rested the tip of her scissors against her cheek. "If his wife is lost, we could help him find her."

"Maybe she's in the woods," Hazel said. "Lots of folks get lost in the woods. We can go look for her right now."

Mrs. McClanahan pulled Jane's hand away from her face. "Be careful, girl. You'll poke your eye out with those scissors. I don't think Mr. Yates's wife is in the woods. I don't think he ever had a wife. You girls go ahead and clear your things off the table. Those fellas will be back in here hollering for lunch before we know it."

"Yes, Mum." The little girls scooped up their crayons and scraps of paper.

"Find Frannie and Lucy. I need the four of you to pick some apples so we can have cooked apples with our lunch."

They squealed with delight and hurried from the room. Mary gathered the last of the dishes and carried them to the sink. Her gaze drifted toward the window.

Felicity knew without looking who she was watching for. Ned's voice calling instructions came through the thin walls, but she couldn't make out the words. The ladder scraped against the side of the house.

"Why aren't you married, Miss Trego?"

Felicity managed a smile she hoped would disguise the pain in her heart. "Why aren't you?"

"I'm too young."

"You're seventeen. I know girls your age who already have children."

"Then that means you're too old."

Mrs. McClanahan gasped. "Mary! You know better than to talk that way to your elders."

Mary sobered. "I'm sorry, Mum. I'm sorry, Miss Trego."

Felicity laughed. "No, no, it was my fault. I was only teasing. You are too young to marry. Besides, I don't think I like being called your elder."

She exaggerated a scowl at Mrs. McClanahan. The three women laughed.

Mrs. McClanahan clasped her hands in front of her. "I'm sure Felicity will marry when she meets the right man."

"Like Mr. Yates?"

Felicity didn't mind the teasing, but it was starting to chafe. How could she tell them she could never marry? If she did, she would have no more money for lumber or pickles or anything else that made their lives easier. She would lose her influence over the other businessowners in town when gently convincing them to help support the children. She could not put her own wants and needs before everyone who depended on her.

"Mr. Yates seems like a fine young man," Mrs. McClanahan said. "But in matters of the heart, you have to let nature take its course. You'll discover that for yourself one day."

"Yes, Mum."

Felicity joined her at the sink. She squeezed Mary's elbow. "As pretty as you are, it'll be quicker than you think."

Mary didn't look so sure. "I don't think I'll ever have a man look at me the way Mr. Yates looks at you."

Felicity jerked her hand back. "He doesn't look at me any way. We...we only just met."

Mrs. McClanahan sighed wistfully. "Sometimes that's all it takes. My Paul said he fell in love with me the first time he saw me."

"I think Paul said that to woo you."

She laughed. "You're probably right. That man could charm the bumps off a toad."

Feet pounded down the stairs at the corner of the kitchen. "Girls," Mrs. McClanahan scolded. "I've told you a thousand times not to run on the stairs. Young ladies shouldn't run indoors at all."

Four pairs of feet immediately slowed. "Grab those bags there and head out to the apple trees. Pick enough for lunch and maybe a pie or two for tomorrow."

The rest of the morning flew by. Mrs. McClanahan and Felicity cleaned and diced the vegetables while Mary sliced the apples.

"It shouldn't take much longer after we put the vegetables in," Mrs. McClanahan said when Hazel and Jane asked if it was nearly time to eat. "Bring the basket of mending in here and we'll work while the vegetables finish up."

"We want to go outside and help on the roof," Hazel said.

Mrs. McClanahan's eyes widened at the thought of them scampering around on the roof. Even Ronan and Grant had been delegated to sawing and packing supplies without climbing a ladder.

"You two will be in the way. Did you finish the sweeping and dusting upstairs?"

Felicity smiled behind her hand as the two girls—one blond and fair, the other olive-skinned and dark-headed—exchanged guilty glances.

"Bring me the basket and go on back up there. It's not fair for the boys and the big girls to work outside all day, and then have to clean up after you two. When you're through, we'll all enjoy a wonderful meal under a patched roof."

"It's a beautiful Indian summer day out there," Felicity said. "Perhaps we can use the sawhorses for a picnic table and eat outside."

Hazel and Jane cheered. "Could we, Mum? Please."

"A picnic means a lot more work," Mrs. McClanahan reminded them.

"I'm sorry," Felicity said. "I didn't think of that."

At home, she never had to consider the work or inconvenience her schemes caused someone else. The staff saw to any unpleasant details of a picnic or cleaning up after a party with no concern from her on how it got done.

"We don't mind," Hazel said.

"We'll do all the work," Jane agreed.

"Well, if you're willing to tote the chairs outside and then bring them back in, I suppose a picnic would be right nice. We won't have many more suitable days." She winked at Felicity while the little girls cheered. "But first, finish your cleaning upstairs."

Jane set the basket of mending on the table, and she and Hazel scampered upstairs. Felicity smiled as she watched them go. A longing she didn't understand sat heavy in her chest.

Lord, help me accept this kind of life will never be mine, she prayed.

"You're so good at solving every problem," she told Mrs. McClanahan.

The older woman snorted. "A person learns how to be a parent by doing it. You'll see when your time comes."

Felicity looked into her lap. Her life was full enough already. She had no right to the discontent crowding her chest. She had God. She had her work. She had Belinda and the children here. She didn't need a husband or children of her own, especially when she knew she couldn't have them.

Her hand closed around the toe of a sock in the basket just as Mary grabbed the top. They smiled at each other. Felicity relinquished her hold.

Mrs. McClanahan was still staring at her. Felicity stirred through the basket. "Marriage isn't for everyone," she explained.

"No, I suppose it isn't. But when two young people are in love, it's exactly what God designed."

"Oh, I'm not in love, and I don't plan to be."

"But I thought you and Mr.—" Mary began from her side of the table.

Mrs. McClanahan shook her head to shush the girl. Mary dipped her head over her darning.

Felicity grabbed a small dress from the basket. She turned it in her hands. The hem had come loose in a few places. She could repair a simple hem. Anything more complicated and she'd return it to the basket.

"Belinda and I are so busy running the factory," she said casually. "Now that she's laid up, I don't have time for anything else. Belinda says we're doing our duty to the town by providing jobs. Too many people depend on us for me to..."

She stopped talking when she noticed how Mary's eyebrows had slid together and Mrs. McClanahan's face was tensed in pity.

She stared into the basket. "Do you have any brown thread?"

Mary handed her a spool. "Well, I hope I marry," she said. "And I want to have ten children."

"Ten!" Felicity and Mrs. McClanahan exclaimed together. Felicity was thankful for the diversion.

"Yes, ten. Before I came here, I was all alone," she said as she threaded her needle.

Felicity listened with interest. Mrs. McClanahan surely knew Mary's story, but Felicity had never heard it.

Mary was here when she returned from the university in Boise, but she didn't know where the girl had come from or how she ended up here.

"I had two older sisters when Ma died," Mary continued. "Anita and June. Pa turned us out. Said he couldn't take care of three girls on his own, though, truth be told, we'd been taking care of him all along."

Felicity pricked her finger and clenched her teeth against the pain. What a tragic story. She couldn't imagine a pa turning his own children onto the streets. Mary couldn't have been more than twelve or thirteen at the time. What did the man expect three girls to do to provide for themselves? Even older women had few options, and less if they didn't want to turn to disreputable professions.

"I really miss my sisters," Mary went on. "That's why I want a lot of children. That way, they won't be alone if something happens to me. Not to mention, I would never marry a man who'd turn out his own kin."

"Where did you meet Mrs. McClanahan?" Felicity prodded gently.

Mary and Mrs. McClanahan exchanged glances. Mary nodded and reached for another sock.

Mrs. McClanahan took over the telling. "I heard about Mary from Rose Haney at the café." She reached over and patted the girl's hand.

"She had gone to Rose looking for work. Well, she was a little mite of a thing back then. Rose knew she couldn't put her to work and leave her to fend for herself the rest of the time. One of the miners said if Rose didn't have a place for her, he'd take her into his cabin. He wanted someone for laundry and housekeeping."

Her teeth clenched. The blood drained from Felicity's face.

"As soon as Rose heard that, she high-tailed it over here with Mary in the buggy beside her. Been here ever since."

Mary brushed the sock lint off her fingers and went to the stove to check the vegetables.

"What became of your sisters?" Felicity asked.

Mary kept her back to the table. "June took pneumonia that first winter. Anita married a miner. He took off with her to Utah. At least that's what somebody told me."

"How old was she?"

"Fifteen."

Felicity wanted to shout her outrage at the situation, but the people responsible weren't in the room.

Hazel and Jane thundered back into the kitchen. "We're finished. Can we start carrying out chairs now?"

Again, Felicity thanked God for the interruption. Life was sometimes so unfair. Young girls like Mary and her sisters forced out in the world before they were ready, while women like her had been given plenty but had no one with whom to share it.

Chapter Twelve

Within a few minutes the kitchen was bustling again. Mary strained milk for the meal, and Lucy supervised the oven to keep the younger girls safe.

Frannie showed Jane and Hazel how to roll biscuit dough and then helped them carry chairs and find wood planks to use as a table for the picnic. Felicity tried to help Mrs. McClanahan supervise and put the finishing touches on the meal while staying out of the way of her military precision. It took a lot of organization to run the home.

Ned and the four boys went to the back of the shed to clean up around a water barrel as the women carried everything outside. "What a fine idea this was, girls," Mrs. McClanahan announced.

When Felicity found herself seated next to Ned at the makeshift table, she figured it was Mrs. McClanahan's intention all along. Regardless of what she told Mary about love making its own way, she seemed determined to help it along.

After Ned blessed the food and the new roof, they all dug in, even Felicity. She had worked up quite an appetite talking and washing vegetables.

Tim handed her a large bowl of peas across the table. His left arm trembled from the effort. She waited until she secured the bowl in her own hands before she asked; "Did you hurt your arm?"

He barely glanced at her. "No, ma'am."

Felicity wasn't convinced. As the oldest boy, he usually laughed and teased the other children and tried to fill his role as big brother.

Today, she'd barely heard two words out of him. Now that she thought about it, he had been quiet and withdrawn earlier in the week when she brought the groceries.

He gave her a timid smile, though his face had tightened in pain. He bent his head over his plate and didn't look up again.

Felicity often helped the older children at the home find employment around the community. It helped them gain work experience and earn a little money while providing businesses and farmers with cheap labor.

They helped put in crops, swept stores, helped with a new baby, or picked apples. Tim had been working outside the home for about two years. He was amiable and quick learning, so employers asked for him again and again. Now, Felicity wondered what was bothering the usually gregarious teenager.

She didn't get the chance to pursue the subject further. The other boys bragged about their job on the roof, even the ones who kept their feet firmly on the ground the whole time.

Grant told of a hair-raising moment when it looked like Malachi might topple over the edge. Felicity's heart nearly stopped in her chest until she noticed Ned's smile and Mrs. McClanahan's calm demeanor.

All these years raising boys had made her immune to palpitations every time one of them ventured near grave injury.

The youngsters were full of questions about Ned's life in Nebraska. Felicity listened intently as well, as fascinated by his adventures as the children.

She noted none of his stories included his early years. He told them about two older sisters, who were already married and gone by the time his exploits began. But he had a lot of friends, and they managed to find enough adventure to make up for a houseful of children.

"How's come you don't have a wife?" Grant asked after a while. The children stopped eating and waited for his answer.

If Felicity didn't know better, she would think Mrs. McClanahan or Mary had prompted Grant to ask. She focused on her plate and hoped no one would realize how badly she wanted to hear the answer.

"I guess the Lord hasn't seen fit to give me one yet," he said.

Despite her best efforts, she glanced quickly at him. Fortunately, he wasn't looking back. She would've melted from embarrassment if he was.

"But you're old, though, right?" Ronan asked. "Shouldn't you have a wife by now?"

"Well, I don't think..."

"All right now, boys," Mrs. McClanahan broke in. "Let's be respectful and let Mr. Yates enjoy his meal."

"We was being respectful," Grant said. "We was just askin'."

"We *were* just asking."

"That's what I said."

The adults exchanged smiles. "How about somebody cut me a big wedge of the pie that's been torturing me the whole time I've been sitting here," Ned said.

Since Felicity was sitting closest, the task fell to her. "The pies were supposed to be for tomorrow, but the girls said so many apples were practically falling off the trees, there was enough for two pies now and two for tomorrow."

Ned applauded as he looked around the table at the girls, who glowed under his praise. Felicity set the plate in front of him. Her elbow brushed his sleeve as he clapped. Everyone at the table laughed at his display, except for Felicity.

He was so kind and generous and thoughtful she couldn't help respecting the man. Maybe even loving him if she hadn't been born an heir to Trego Leatherworks.

•••

Mrs. McClanahan thanked Ned and Felicity profusely for repairing the kitchen roof. She and the children stood in the yard and waved and called their thanks as Ned turned the buggy toward the road and headed off.

The sweetest thing about the day for Ned— even sweeter than the gratitude from the children and knowing how much a dry house meant to them—was the smile on Felicity Trego's face as they drove down the lane.

She had acquiesced when he asked if it was all right if he drove the buggy home. It was her buggy and her horse, but he felt rather useless watching her gentle hands do the driving when he was sitting right there beside her.

He rested his hand on his stomach. "I'm stuffed. I don't eat this much, even at Mrs. Crothers' table."

Felicity laughed a sweet, gentle laugh that warmed his insides. "You earned it. You did a hard day's work and didn't even take the whole day to do it."

He studied his free hand. "You're right. I think I made a couple of blisters. First time I've had those since I left home."

She laughed, louder this time. He looked directly at her. She pressed her full lips together, and a flush worked up her porcelain cheeks. She adjusted the angle on her oversized hat to keep the sun off the end of her nose.

Ned watched her another moment before forcing his gaze away. He had never seen a lovelier sight. She had to know she was beautiful as well, but she was the most unpretentious woman he'd ever met.

He couldn't imagine one of the young women in his family's circle of friends listening to two little girls prattle on about paper dolls and apple jelly and manage to look like she really cared about what they were saying.

She tilted her head and looked at him from under the brim of her hat. Ned's stomach gave a lurch at the sight.

"I wanted to properly thank you for giving the children your Saturday. It means a lot to them, especially the boys. They don't have many opportunities to spend time with men. Unless they're getting bossed around. You have a way of teaching that doesn't make them feel dumb or small."

He shrugged. "Not everyone has my gift."

The comment brought a smile to her face as he hoped it would. "Well, I appreciate it, and so does Mrs. McClanahan. I'm a little concerned about Tim, though. Did he seem all right to you today?"

"He's the oldest one, right? The redhead?"

She nodded.

"He was a little quiet. Seems to take himself more seriously than the others."

Worry lines appeared on her forehead. "That's just it. He usually doesn't. Normally, you wouldn't have been able to get a word in edgeways. He tries to make things easier for the younger children by kidding and clowning around. But the last few times I've seen him he's been very quiet. Gloomy, even. It's not like him."

Ned wanted to reach out and smooth her worry lines away. "I wouldn't worry about it. Boys that age don't usually announce to the world what's bothering them. Maybe he likes a girl who doesn't like him back. Or he's having a rough time with a subject at school. The next time you see him, he'll probably be back to his old self and you'll wish he'd be quiet for five minutes."

"Do you think so?"

"I'm sure that's all it is."

She smiled appreciatively. "I hope you're right."

"Of course, I'm right."

Her face softened. Ned marveled again at her beauty. Her heart-shaped face looked like it would fit right into his hands. And her full lips, so soft and tender... He jerked his gaze away and flicked the reins on the horse's flank, though he wanted this ride to last the rest of the day.

"I was thinking of that girl Mary."

Her brows slid together again. "Pardon?"

"Mary. The oldest one. You said Belinda needs someone to run office errands for her. What about Mary? Is she through with school?"

"Oh, my, what a wonderful idea. Yes, she graduated last year. I never even thought of her. It's the perfect solution for everyone."

"Do you think Mrs. McClanahan could spare her around the house?"

"Mrs. McClanahan's chief goal is to find placements for the children, either with jobs or good, Christian homes. She would never put one out, of course, and she's probably worried about what will become of Mary. The last few years have been hard on the girl." Her jaw clenched a moment, before her expression cleared and she rewarded him with a wide smile.

She squeezed his arm through his heavy coat. "Thank you so much, Ned. I can't wait to tell Belinda. She'll be thrilled. And thanks again for coming today. I don't know what we would've done without your help."

"And yours. You supplied the lumber."

She brushed aside the comment. "Paying for something is easy, especially when it isn't much of a sacrifice. It's a whole different matter when you're the one to get your hands dirty."

He studied her profile for a moment. "You're an interesting woman, Felicity Trego."

Her eyes narrowed. "What do you mean?"

"I don't mean anything ill. I just meant most women in your...situation would never notice a houseful of orphans. At least, the women in my experience."

"Do you have a lot of experience with women, Ned?"

"Why, no." He realized she was teasing.

"I don't have experience with women at all. My sisters were older than me, like I told the boys at dinner, so I didn't learn much from them about what women want or expect. They were married before I moved into the house."

Her sapphire eyes widened. "Before you moved into the house? What do you mean?"

Ned gave himself an inward kick. He hadn't meant to tell her the Yates weren't his real parents. Not like this. The last thing he wanted from her or anyone else was pity. Or a lot of questions he wasn't ready to answer.

He stared down the road for a moment. "Mr. and Mrs. Yates adopted me when I was fourteen."

"Oh. I...I didn't..."

He shrugged off her apology. "It's fine."

"Did your parents...die?"

"Not that I know of."

She clearly didn't know how to respond to his vague answer. He took a deep breath. She deserved some sort of explanation now that he opened this can of worms. And he wanted her to know. For the first time in longer than he remembered, he wanted to talk to someone about how his life started. He wanted to talk to *her.*

"I left my ma's home when I was around ten. I never met my father. I never even heard his name." He didn't tell her he doubted his mother remembered or realized which of the many men in and out of her bed had sired her only child.

"A family discovered me taking refuge from a storm in their shed. I stayed with them a while. The wife eventually sent me to live with an older couple she knew who didn't have childern. They needed someone to help with the chores. I needed to go to school, so it worked out for all of us."

Felicity's blue eyes glittered with compassion. Ned hadn't been merely flattering her when he said she was like no woman he'd ever met.

The Yates' friends and the well-off families he encountered in school were full of do-gooders who planned dinners and charity events to benefit the less fortunate. While he was sure they did some good, the events were more of an excuse to dress up and socialize and make themselves feel like they were doing something.

They talked a lot about making lives better for the orphans and street children of the city. But when it came to really making a change, they preferred to throw money at the problem. He couldn't imagine a one of them spending a Saturday in a hot, crowded kitchen on the wrong side of town, let alone breaking bread with the unfortunate souls they claimed to help.

He thought of the look of rapture on Felicity's face when those two barefoot little girls in their faded dresses leaped into her arms. His chest expanded.

No, he'd never met a woman like her.

"How did you meet the Yates?" Her voice was hoarse with emotion.

"I lived with the other couple for a few years until the wife got sick. The husband didn't know what to do with me. That's when a man from their church introduced me to the Yates."

He had never said this much out loud about his life before the Yates. It was too painful to remember, let alone talk about. She would never know about Ma's boyfriends who sometimes couldn't keep their hands to themselves.

He wouldn't tell her about the beatings from the man who discovered him in the shed the morning after he ran away from Hal, or the way the kids at school laughed at the way he ran because his boots were two sizes too small.

"Is that..." She twisted her mouth thoughtfully as if searching for a tactful way to ask what she wanted to know. "Is that why you're so good with the children? So understanding of orphans?"

He exhaled and studied the road a moment. "I don't think of myself as an orphan. The Yates never made me feel like one."

Except for their daughters, who still blamed him for what was discovered after they died.

"They loved me and taught me about God's grace. I had never known that before. They never introduced me as anything but their son. But I know what it's like to have nowhere to lay your head. To wonder if you'll ever matter to someone."

She laid her hand on his arm again. Ned looked down at her gloved hand on his jacket. She looked down at the same moment and jerked her hand back. Color rose in her cheeks again, but she didn't look away.

"I don't want you to feel sorry for me," he said quietly. His voice was hoarse but not for the reason she probably thought.

"I want you to know how much you matter to those kids, even if they don't tell you. How much their eyes light up when they talk about you."

She glanced away. "I don't do anything but spend a little money. My sacrifice is nothing compared to Mrs. McClanahan's. My heart breaks when I think of what would happen to them if she weren't around. Especially after what I heard about Mary today."

She shuddered. "I wish I could do more. Like make sure every one of them found good, loving homes."

"Those children know you love them. Believe me, as a kid who never knew if anyone cared if he lived or died, knowing you matter to someone is sometimes more important than food in your belly or shoes on your feet."

She stared at him for a moment. He looked from her gentle blue eyes to her lips and wondered how they tasted. Before he knew it, she was staring at his.

Ahead, a child called out to another. Somewhere in the distance, a door slammed. A gate screeched back and forth on rusty hinges in the afternoon breeze. A dog barked and another barked in reply.

Ned had intentionally steered the buggy around the more congested areas of town instead of driving straight through to the boardinghouse. He had wanted to prolong his time with Felicity without prying eyes infringing on their privacy.

He loosened his hold on the reins. The horse slowed its pace, but continued forward. Ned turned toward her in the seat. He cupped her chin with one hand and slowly drew her to him.

Felicity leaned into him. Her lips were warm and sweet. He moved a little closer. Her oversized hat banged against his forehead. She made a little sound of surprise and amusement and pulled back. She looked into his eyes. The smile on her lips died.

"I...I'm sorry," she murmured as she stuffed a pale blond lock of hair under the hat.

Ned didn't know what she had to be sorry for. He couldn't be happier. It was all he could do not to jump out of the buggy and dance a jig on the side of the road.

Chapter Thirteen

"How much longer, Rhonda?" Belinda's booming voice reverberated against the foyer's vaulted ceiling.

Felicity nearly stabbed herself with her hat pin as she reached up to remove it from her head. She shook aside the thought of Ned's lips on hers and aimed the hat toward the table inside the door. In her haste, she missed, and the hat toppled to the floor.

"I've been waiting for those files for ten minutes," Belinda's voice screeched from the front parlor. "Am I going to have to get up and get them myself?"

"If you want them any faster, I suppose you'll have to," the maid shot back.

Johanna appeared in the foyer doorway and retrieved Felicity's hat from the marble floor. "What's going on?" Felicity asked her.

Johanna pointed over her shoulder. She pulled the cloak off Felicity's shoulders. "Go see for yourself. If you dare."

Felicity stepped out of her coat and hurried into the parlor. Belinda sat red-faced and stone-jawed, her hands clutching the edges of the couch as if preparing to launch into the air.

The maid was in the center of the room at the desk Shane had moved in at the first of the week. She sorted through a pile of documents, many of which had slid to the floor.

"What's all the ruckus?" Felicity demanded. "I could hear you carrying on when I turned the corner at the bottom of the hill," she said, only slightly exaggerating.

"Well, look who finally decided to show her face. Where have you been all day?" Without waiting for an answer, Belinda jabbed her finger at Rhonda. "I asked for a simple document two hours ago, but she can't find it."

"And I've been trying to make her understand," Rhonda said with a jab of her own, "I can't stop what I'm doing every five minutes to come in here to fetch something that probably isn't in the house anyway."

Belinda turned her frustration on Felicity. "Where were you? I already know you weren't at work. Mr. Hughes said he hasn't seen you all day."

Felicity set her hands on her hips. "I told Mr. Hughes yesterday not to expect me, and I told you this morning I wasn't going to the factory. If you would stop shouting at people long enough to hear what they're telling you, you might remember."

"I can't be expected to remember where to hunt you down every minute of the day. I'm trying to run a company here. Where do you think we'd be if I took off every Saturday like some people?"

Felicity ignored the dig. Belinda hadn't missed a day at work since she wore pigtails. If she wanted to spend every day of her life inside the factory walls, it was her prerogative.

Felicity preferred feeling the October sun on her face. Among other things, she thought, thinking of Ned's lips.

Rhonda mumbled something about needing to finish her own work without taking on another position and stomped out of the room. Felicity watched her go and wished she could escape as easily.

"What is it you need so desperately, Sister, now that the whole neighborhood knows of your displeasure?"

Belinda seemed to forget Felicity hadn't explained where she'd been instead of going to work today.

"The licensing agreement for the equipment we bought last year. Mr. Hughes said the machine operators are already having trouble with some of the parts and I need to find out where to place a new order. I'm surprised you didn't tell me about it."

Felicity flinched. She'd been filling Belinda's shoes for a week, and she still hadn't gone down to the factory floor the way Belinda did once or twice a week.

"Surely that could've waited until Monday," she said. She began sorting through the stacks that were hopelessly out of order.

"Not everything can wait until Monday."

Felicity took a deep breath to hold her tongue. "Did you get any rest today? You look tired."

"Of course I'm tired. I haven't been outside all week. I have a pounding headache."

Felicity was too weary of the conversation to be compassionate. "Are you still refusing to take the medication Dr. Dutton gave you?"

"I take it at night."

There was no point in reminding Belinda she was supposed to take the medication throughout the day to give her body a chance to rest without pain. Her fingers closed around the invoice Belinda wanted. She carried it to her.

"I brought some good news home today."

Belinda's eyes narrowed.

"I may have found someone to help you around the house. Then you won't be chasing off our household staff."

"I thought you were at the orphanage today."

"So, you do remember where I was. There's a young woman there. Mary." She didn't know Mary's last name. She hoped Belinda wouldn't ask.

"What young woman? The only people who live there are children."

"She's seventeen."

"Seventeen?" Belinda sputtered.

"Nearly eighteen. Old enough to be trusted but young enough for you to train her the way you want. As long as your shouting doesn't run her out the door."

"I don't shout. I enunciate."

"Yes, and a prairie twister stirs up a little dust."

Belinda ignored the comment. "Is she smart? I need someone who can anticipate a problem and take care of it without me holding her hand the whole time. I don't have the patience to explain something over and over."

"She's very bright. And quick. Once she learns the way you like things done, she'll figure out what you need before you realize you need it."

Belinda looked toward the door where Rhonda had fled. "I suppose I don't have much choice."

"That's right. You don't. Now, if you don't need anything for a while I'm going upstairs to wash up. Please try not to shout at anyone while I'm gone."

She leaned over and kissed Belinda's forehead. "I love you, Sister."

Belinda snagged her hand and held onto it. "You didn't tell me who else was there today."

She never asked what went on at the orphans' home. She knew every visit cost the sisters money. Those were the only details she cared about. But today she was suspicious. Had one of the maids mentioned seeing Felicity riding with Ned? Had Mr. Hughes?

"Part of the kitchen ceiling fell in earlier this week. It needed repaired."

"I know. I heard you sent a load of lumber over there yesterday."

Felicity exhaled with relief. Hopefully, Belinda was worried over nothing more than the expense and Felicity's time away from the factory.

"I'll pay for it out of my earnings this week." Felicity wasn't sure how much money she actually earned at the factory. Belinda regularly deposited money into an account for her. She bought what she wanted and never paid attention to how much was left.

Belinda released her hand, but her gaze continued to search Felicity's face. "No need. I don't mind the money you spend over there. I care about the plight of orphans in this town, too."

"Really?"

"Of course. If we do our part to keep them off the streets, citizens don't have to worry about crime."

Felicity clenched her teeth. "I'll be upstairs if you need me. Just yell. We all know you can do that."

•••

Felicity sat in her chemise and studied her reflection in the mirror. She had brushed out her long hair, and it hung like satin around her slim shoulders. She put her fingers to her lips.

What had she done?

Belinda had succeeded in putting all thoughts of Ned and their kiss out of her head for a while, but now she could think of little else.

She shouldn't have let him kiss her. She shouldn't have wanted his kiss so badly. But being close to him, especially after Mary asked her why she wasn't married, had been on her mind all day.

When Mrs. McClanahan said sometimes you knew the instant you saw a person he was the one you wanted to spend the rest of your life with, she had known she wanted Ned.

It wasn't as simple as knowing. She had responsibilities. Too many people depended on her. The children. Mrs. McClanahan. Belinda.

She couldn't have both. She couldn't help the people who depended on her and have a future with Ned Yates at the same time. Her life was in this house. It was sending lumber to the orphanage to patch a roof. Finding work for the boys and a job for Mary.

The sooner she stopped thinking about Ned Yates, the better off everyone would be.

Ned Yates.

The name tasted good on her lips. Simple. Honest. Genuine. Just like him. She thought of what he said this afternoon about growing up not knowing if anyone cared if he lived or died.

The children at Mrs. McClanahan's were probably plagued with the same feelings, even as Mrs. McClanahan tucked them in at night and make sure a solid roof was over their heads. No one took the place of a loving parent.

Felicity knew it well. She barely remembered her mother. The memories she cherished were probably not hers but transferred through Belinda's stories and the pictures on the wall.

She still missed Papa as if he'd gone yesterday. Her heart ached when she thought of his laugh or his gentleness or worry over his daughters.

Belinda said his love and concern were the reasons he put the stipulation in his will that neither girl could marry. It sometimes seemed unreasonable or intrusive, but he only wanted to protect them.

She turned her face toward the ceiling. "You should've trusted us, Papa. You raised us to be strong and to think for ourselves. You may not have trusted a man with unbridled access to the company you built. But you could've trusted me."

Chapter Fourteen

The next two weeks flew by for Felicity, as they dragged for Belinda.

The pain in her foot subsided by degrees. Instead of a blessing, though, it made her more impatient and irritable than usual that she couldn't jump and run to do whatever she wanted without asking for help.

Mary was at the house every morning by seven o'clock. Some days she went to the factory with Felicity to pick up ledgers or files Belinda couldn't live without or to get signatures from Mr. Hughes or other department heads.

She was thick-skinned enough that Belinda's gruff manner didn't seem to bother her. Within days Belinda developed a grudging respect for the girl and soon asked her opinion on matters.

At the end of the first week Belinda told Shane to select a horse from the family's stable for Mary to use.

"It takes too long for her to walk back and forth across town," Belinda explained when Felicity nearly fell out of her chair in shock. "She's exhausted by the time she gets here."

"A horse is expensive to keep," Felicity reminded her. "Mrs. McClanahan doesn't have fodder to feed it overnight."

"Law and tarnation, Felicity, do I have to think of everything? Have the girl stop at the livery and tell Mr. Waugh to deliver whatever she'll need out to the orphanage."

"That's very generous of you, Belinda."

Belinda sniffed. "Generosity has nothing to do with it. I need her here, and if a horse is part of fulfilling that need, so be it."

Felicity smiled to herself. Belinda could pretend it was all business, but it was obvious she liked Mary and wanted to make her life easier.

Felicity and the rest of the household were just as happy at how much Belinda liked having Mary around. It was still strange with Belinda home all day, but life settled into a workable routine.

Every evening after Mary went home, Felicity and Belinda discussed the invention and patent. Belinda made adjustments and calculations throughout the day. She and Felicity went over the logistics of production at night.

Felicity got more and more excited about the expansion of the plant. Not only would it change the business, it would benefit Willow Wood's economy and make life easier for frontier women who would use the coupling device for years to come.

She avoided Ned Yates. When Belinda needed her to drop something off or pick something up at the law office, she had Mary do it.

She didn't know what she'd do when she saw his face again. He obviously had feelings for her. She couldn't deny her feelings for him. The only way to keep him out of her mind was to stay busy. It wasn't always easy.

His kiss came to mind at the most inopportune times. It hadn't been deep or passionate; just enough to let her know she wanted to kiss him again. As often as he'd allow.

She didn't know what she'd say when she saw him again. He deserved to know there could never be anything between them before his heart got involved. If it hadn't already. She hadn't been fair to him. She needed to explain she didn't have any right to kiss him, no matter how much she wanted to.

It was full dark outside Friday evening by the time Felicity looked up from her ledger. She arched her back and rotated her head a few times to work out the stiffness. She wanted to finish before going home. Though she had no plans at the orphanage for tomorrow, she still planned not to come to work.

Last Sunday was the only day she'd taken off in the last two weeks, and she was ready for some fresh air and sunshine. The weather looked favorable for a long ride in the mountains. She wondered briefly about asking Ellie Lundy to accompany her. Ellie was a year and a half older than Felicity, but they had grown up as neighbors and were both accomplished riders.

Felicity hadn't seen Ellie since her father's funeral. She would like to rekindle their friendship. She suspected Ellie might want it too.

The fire in the grate had died to a few glowing embers. November was only a few days away, and the day's warmth faded quickly once the sun slid behind the mountains.

She stirred the embers and added a small chunk of wood. She wouldn't build the fire up much; just enough to brew a pot of coffee.

The factory floor had gone quiet two hours ago as everyone else went home. While she worked, she listened to the building's groans and sighs she didn't notice during the day.

The quiet of the cavernous empty building was unsettling. She didn't know how Belinda stood being the last person to walk out of the factory nearly every night.

She set the coffeepot on the stove and went back to work. She would hurry. She didn't want to worry Belinda more than she already had, and truth be told, she wanted to hear someone else's voice. She flexed her fingers and reached for her pen.

A knock echoed through the empty hallway. Felicity jumped in her seat. She had no meetings scheduled. Surely someone hadn't locked himself out. She put her hand over her heart and willed it to return to its normal rhythm. It was probably a maintenance worker or Mark from the livery inquiring how much longer she planned to work. He couldn't leave as long as a horse remained in his charge, and he was probably anxious to head home.

The door squealed on its hinges. A man's voice called out. "Hello? Anyone here?"

Felicity stiffened. It wasn't Mark. She realized the size of the building and all the shadowy corners and looming spaces. And she was completely alone.

This was nonsense. Belinda worked alone here all the time. Papa had done it. Mr. Hughes did it, and he was a frail old man.

She shook aside her cowardice and strode around the corner of her desk. She was the boss while Belinda recovered. It was time she acted like it.

"In here," she called, sounded more assured than she felt. "May I help you?"

In the doorway, she saw the form of a man coming up the short flight of stairs from the street. The only distinguishable details were wide shoulders and a confident, masculine gait. Almost immediately, she recognized those long legs. Her shoulders sagged with relief. And anticipation.

"Ned," she said in careful nonchalance. "What are you doing here this late in the evening?"

His face softened into a warm smile. She thought he glanced at her lips as she did his, but she couldn't tell for sure in the dim glow of the gas lamps.

"I could ask you the same question. I thought the boss was the first one out the door on Friday evenings."

"Not around here." She wanted to ask something personal. She wanted to ask how he'd been since she saw him last. Since he'd kissed her and awakened emotions in her breast she didn't know were there.

"Is there something I can do for you?"

He held up a leather folder. "I had some contracts to go over with Mr. Hughes. I didn't realize how late it was until I saw the building was dark. I figured if the door was unlocked, someone must still be here."

"Only me. Mr. Hughes never came back after meeting with Belinda at the house this afternoon. I fear this situation with her is distressing him. I think he's aged five years in the last three weeks."

"Do you know how much longer she'll be recovering?"

"Close to two months at least. Mary is working out wonderfully. Thank you so much for the suggestion. Maybe her rough life up to this point prepared her for working with my sister."

He laughed, a deep throaty sound that made her heart echo against her ribcage. She backed into the office. "Can I help you since Mr. Hughes isn't here?"

He followed her inside and glanced around the large room. It was utilitarian at best. A large window, high ceilings, and the small stove in the corner did nothing to brighten a person's work day.

One filing cabinet stood on the wall, indicating how insignificant she was to the success of the company. Filing cabinets lined the walls in Belinda's office. She had thought about installing a bookcase or putting up curtains but hadn't got past the thinking stage yet. Even a painting on the wall would go far in dispelling some of the gloom.

Ned handed over the folder. "It should be secured for the night. Do you have a locked drawer?"

"Certainly." She circled the desk and opened the center drawer to look for the key. She still didn't know her way around the office as well as she should. "I just put the kettle on for coffee. Would you like a cup?"

"Don't mind if I do," he said, smiling. As an afterthought, he looked at the papers on her desk. "You look busy, though. I should go."

"No, don't," she said much too quickly. "I was planning to take a break when I heard you come in. I missed lunch. I have some bread and cheese. I know it isn't much..."

Now was a good time to tell him that while she thought a lot of him, she couldn't grant him permission to court her, if that's what he was looking for.

Courting was out of the question. He needed to know before she said or did anything that made him think she was interested in him.

She didn't say any of it. She looked into his eyes, the color of dark jade, and willed him to accept her invitation to share her simple dinner.

"If you're sure I'm not in your way."

She moved a stack of dusty ledgers from the chair across from her desk that no one had ever sat in. "Of course not. I've been in here all afternoon trying to get ahead of a few things for

Belinda. Instead, I think I found more work for both of us."

He stepped forward and brushed off the dusty seat. "I'm sure she won't mind."

Felicity chuckled. "You're probably right."

She found the key for the deep desk drawer and stowed the folder of papers to give Mr. Hughes on Monday. She took a knife from a drawer of the secretary and unwrapped the cheese and sausages from the wax paper. She cut thin slices and arranged them on a plate.

While she unwrapped the crackers, Ned touched the side of the coffeepot to see if it was hot enough to drink. Satisfied, he found two cups and filled them and carried them to the desk. Felicity was glad she had something to keep her hands busy. She had never had a man pour her a cup of coffee before.

It felt...different. Nice.

When the simple meal was prepared, she carried everything back to the desk.

"Do you mind?" Ned asked and clasped his hands.

Felicity barely heard the simple prayer of thanks. All she could do was wonder how she would swallow any food with her stomach fluttering at his close proximity.

"It's late for you to be working, too," she observed as she put a few pieces of food on a napkin and drew it toward her.

"I usually work late. There's not much for me to do at the boardinghouse. Most of the residents gather in the parlor after dinner and smoke cigars and talk about old times. I've been there so long I know all their stories."

Felicity took a bite of the sausage. It was just salty and spicy enough to satisfy her rumbling stomach.

"At the house Belinda and I spend our evenings in the parlor. It's usually very quiet. I read or knit or play the piano. Belinda goes over contracts or invoices. Sometimes she'll allow me to draw her into conversation. Most of the time, I think I just distract her."

"It must get lonely for you."

She chewed thoughtfully. "It does sometimes, but I don't often think of it that way. When I was younger, I missed having a large family. In school most of my friends had several brothers and sisters. I just had Belinda. She was so much older than me, she was more like an aunt or even a mother. All children without brothers and sisters probably wish for them, while those from large families dream of peace and quiet."

They ate a few moments in silence. "What about you? Did you wish for brothers and sisters?"

She regretted the words as soon as they were out of her mouth. He had told her enough about his childhood to know he had more immediate needs in mind, like food and clothing, to wish for brothers and sisters.

"I'm sorry. That was inconsiderate of me." He shook his head. "Don't worry about offending me. Not many people know the Yates weren't my real parents. It isn't because I'm ashamed of where I came from. The Bible says the sins of the parents are visited upon the children. I guess I'm the perfect example of that. My parents sinned and gave me life. My mother didn't know how to love me—or she chose not to—so I couldn't stay in her house.

"Those events were through no fault of mine, but they led me to the Yates where I learned love and grace and patience. Oh, they weren't perfect. Far from it. But God used them to shape me into the man I am.

"Every event that ever happened to me contributed to who I became. I learned a long time ago I could let those events defeat me if I wanted. I could waste away in self-pity and resent those who had an easier life."

He paused, and Felicity wondered if he was thinking of her. No one in Willow Wood had an easier life than she did, with her big house and thriving business created by the sweat of Papa and Mr. Hughes, and now Belinda.

He brought his gaze back to her. "In the Yates' house I learned God knew before He laid the foundation of the earth, every sequence of events that would lead to you and me sitting here in this office tonight. He knew I would need the Yates and you would need Belinda. He set it all in order. You could let the grief from losing your mother so young blind you to the pain of others. I could stay mad at what my mother did or her boyfriends..."

He shook his head as if he realized some words didn't need to be spoken aloud. "I could let it destroy any chance I had at peace. Or I could use those circumstances to understand other hurting people and help ease their pain."

"Ned, that's...amazing," Felicity said around the lump in her throat. She shook her head afraid he would misunderstand. "I feel like I've been in church."

He smiled sheepishly and took another bite of sausage.

"I think that's why I want to help the children at Mrs. McClanahan's," she said. "I've been given so much. Too much really. The least I can do is use it to help others."

He reached across the desk and laid his hand on her arm. "You don't do it to pay a penance, Felicity. You do it because you have a compassionate and gentle spirit."

She blinked in surprise at the intensity in his gaze.

"God has touched you. He is using you to do great things. You may think you're only buying pickles and lumber from your surplus. But you are showing those children there is good in a world where they don't see it very often."

Tears blurred her vision. She wasn't good. Oh, she tried to be. She prayed to be. But she thought of herself as selfish and reckless and vain.

She thought too much about dresses and hats. She spent too much time in front of the mirror trying to wrangle her hair into an attractive style. She did the things she liked instead of working hard every day, day after day, like Belinda.

He must've seen the doubt in her eyes. "Don't minimize what you do, Felicity. You'll never know this side of heaven all the ways God is touching lives through you."

He squeezed her arm before withdrawing his hand.

She sniffed away the tickle of tears in her nose. "Thank you, Ned. Sometimes I think I'll never be...enough."

He nodded in understanding. "We all battle those thoughts. But one person's *enough* is not the same as another's. All we can do is strive to please God in our individual situations. To touch the people He puts in front of us so they can see Him, too."

For a long moment she didn't know what to say. She couldn't even think.

"You don't talk like anyone I ever met."

"It's my accent. We all talk like this in Omaha." He ducked his head and grinned.

She slapped his hand and laughed. "Oh, you."

She looked into his smoky jade eyes. Her gaze slid to his lips. She wanted to kiss him. More than she'd ever wanted anything.

She couldn't. Even after everything he said about not helping the children out of obligation but out of a gentle spirt, she knew helping others required resources.

Resources she wouldn't have if she gave in to her selfish desires to love the man in front of her. What kind of person would disregard the needs of so many to satisfy a carnal need of her own?

She reached across the table and began gathering the napkins and remaining pieces of food. "I really should get back to work. I have just a few things to finish up before..."

She looked up and could see he knew what she was doing.

He stood. She mirrored his action on her side of the desk. "Would you like me to wait and walk you out?"

"No." She took a deep breath to calm the feelings raging inside her. "No, thank you. My buggy is in the livery. There's always someone there. I won't be alone."

She stuffed the wrappers into her lunch basket and sat back down.

"Thank you for the company, Miss Trego. You saved me from another lonely evening at the boardinghouse."

"And you saved me..."

She didn't know how to finish. He hadn't saved her. He had reminded her of the things she would never have.

She would never know a man's embrace. A wedding with all her friends watching and wishing her well. A child of her own wrapping its pudgy fingers around hers. Someone to sit beside her and stroke her hand as she prepared to pass from this world to the next.

She was sure of only one thing. She was better off before Ned Yates came into her life and forced her to recognize how empty her life was.

Chapter Fifteen

Felicity didn't go for a ride on Saturday. She didn't walk across the street to rekindle her friendship with Ellie Lundy. Instead of enjoying the sunshine and warmer temperatures before November pushed them aside, she stayed in her suite and tried to read.

For the first time in a long time she wished she could talk to Papa. She would ask him why he didn't trust her or Belinda to choose a man who wouldn't pretend to love them in order to get his hands on the factory.

The Papa she remembered was reasonable and fair. He never distrusted a man until he'd been given a reason. Or many reasons.

She was sure if she could talk to Papa, she could make him understand that Ned Yates wasn't like other men. Like Papa, he had integrity. He loved God. He saw the best in people, even when he had no reason to.

Her worrying and fretting were for naught. The situation wouldn't change. Papa wasn't here. She couldn't convince him to change his will. Not that it would matter if she did. Ned hadn't given her a reason to think he wanted the things she did.

One kiss and a few thought-provoking conversations were all she'd ever have with him. That was the end of it. Like he said, her purpose was to help the people God put in her life and point them to Him. A wedding, a husband, a family; they would never be hers. All she could do was create a fulfilling, contented life without those things.

•••

Monday morning started like the last three Mondays. No more sleeping late or leaving troubling situations for the competent Belinda to handle.

She no longer had the luxury of dawdling in front of the mirror or filling her calendar with things she wanted to do instead of what had to be done.

At the livery she handed off her carriage to Mark and hurried around the building to the stairwell, her mind and satchel bursting with things that needed her immediate attention. Would she ever get ahead of them?

An image of Ned coming up those very steps Friday night temporarily crowded work duties out of her head. She couldn't think of him now. She couldn't think of him at all. It wasn't fair to him, and it wasn't fair to her heart.

At the corner of the building she noticed activity in the alley. Three older boys were gathered around something in the gutter. One of the boys looked familiar. She studied the trio and realized two of them were Malachi and Tim. She stepped away from the corner of the stairwell.

"Boys, hello. Over here." They stopped what they were doing and looked in her direction. She waved with her free hand.

"Miss Trego," Malachi cried. All three headed her way, Tim bringing up the rear, which was strange for the usually exuberant teen.

"Why aren't you in school?" she asked when they were within earshot.

"We still have fifteen minutes," Malachi answered for all of them. "We can cut through the alleys and be there in no time."

The boy Felicity didn't know nodded in agreement. Tim stood behind the others.

Obviously the oldest, he stood nearly a head taller than the other boy and half a head taller than Malachi.

Tim had been at the orphans' home nearly as long as Felicity had been going there. She remembered him five years ago as a shy, nervous ten-year-old with a crooked ear Mrs. McClanahan said he earned at the hand of an abusive stepfather. Today, the ear reminded her of Ned and what he had gone through growing up.

"What are you doing on this street so far from the school?" She directed the question at Tim since he was going to great lengths to hide behind the others.

"We followed a dog," the unknown boy piped up. "It only had three legs. We saw a man from one of the shops give it a kick in the ribs. We wanted to make sure it was okay."

Felicity gritted her teeth against the anger at the shopkeeper. It was nothing short of a miracle the children could still feel empathy for a mistreated animal after everything they'd suffered themselves.

"Did you find it? Was he okay?"

The younger boys nodded. "We went behind the market and found some old bread they threw out and gave it to him."

"I'm going to ask my pa if I can take him home," the unknown boy said.

"It looks to me like you need to get to school first. Don't fret about that old dog. He's probably pretty scrappy and will figure out how to make his own way."

"Yes, ma'am."

"Just don't forget the best way to best a bully who would kick a dog is not to become one yourselves."

"Yes, ma'am."

The boys turned to head back toward the alley that cut through town to the schoolhouse. Felicity caught hold of Tim's arm. "Tim, could I talk..."

Tim yelped and shrank away from her hand on his arm. Instead of letting go, Felicity jerked up his shirtsleeve with her free hand.

She gasped in shock and horror. Angry red welts lay in perfectly laid strips across the pale skin.

Her eyes narrowed. "What happened to you?"

"Nothing."

"Mr. Harrison hit him."

"Shut up, Malachi," Tim said through clenched teeth.

The other boy gaped at the wounds.

Black dots of rage blurred Felicity's vision. "Mr. Harrison did this? Why?" Not that a reason mattered.

Tim pulled free. He smoothed his shirtsleeve down over the welts.

"It's okay, Miss Trego. Sometimes I'm slow. Sometimes I drop things. A few weeks ago, I was pouring flour into a tin in the kitchen and it slipped and I spilled it all over the floor. I wasted a sack of flour and caused Mrs. Harrison a lot of work cleaning up my mess."

"He did *that* over a sack of flour?"

Felicity's jaw was clenched so tight, a headache began to form. She took a deep breath. "I'm not mad at you for keeping this a secret. I'm mad at Mr. Harrison for hurting you. He has no right."

Malachi stepped forward. "It's not a big deal, Miss Trego. Some men get real mad real easy if we don't work to suit 'em. They cuff us on the ear or cock us on top the head with the end of a buggy whip."

Felicity's knees nearly buckled. She thought of Tim's crooked ear that had already taken abuse from his stepfather.

If she wasn't so mad, she'd burst into tears. "What? That's unacceptable! Is that what Mr. Harrison has been doing to you, Tim?"

Tim looked at his feet and shook his head. "He slaps me with the leather strap that hangs by the door in the barn. I just need to learn to work better. I lost my grip on the flour because my arm hurt and I couldn't hang onto it."

"He hit you over something that was his fault for hurting you?"

"Mr. Harrison don't see it that way," Malachi said.

Felicity realized she was trembling from head to toe. "Tim, this is all my fault. I'm sorry I ever got you that job. You're not going back. No one has a right to slap you with a leather strap because he thinks you're slow."

"I have to go back, Miss Trego. I need the money."

"I'll find you something else."

"You can't. Mr. Harrison will tell everyone I'm a thief or lazy and no one else will hire me. That's why I didn't want you to find out. I knew it would cost me."

He looked close to tears. He turned and hurried up the alley. Malachi and the other boy watched him go. Malachi looked at her. "What you gonna do, Miss Trego?"

"I'm going to the sheriff."

"Please don't do that. Tim'll never get another job if you make him out as a troublemaker."

"He's not the troublemaker here, Malachi. Mr. Harrison can't get away with abusing you boys because he's impatient or unreasonable."

"It's all right. It happens all the time. We know to expect it going in."

Felicity watched the two boys hurry to catch up with Tim, worry over the three-legged dog forgotten.

Regardless if she ruined Tim's chances for future employment, she wasn't about to let Wes Harrison get away with beating a child.

She circled the building and hurried back to the livery. Mark saw her coming and rushed out to meet her. "Miss Trego?"

"I'm sorry, Mark. Can you bring my buggy out to me? I have an errand that can't wait."

Chapter Sixteen

As she pulled into the Harrison barnyard, Felicity wondered if she should've brought someone with her. If Wes Harrison would lay stripes on a boy's arm, what would he do to a nosy woman?

She assured herself he only hurt youngsters he could bully into compliance. Youngsters who didn't have anyone to defend them.

Flo Harrison stepped onto the porch as Felicity brought the buggy to a stop next to the two-story farmhouse. Flo wiped her hands on her apron.

"Why, hello, Miss Trego. Lovely morning for a ride," she said pleasantly.

Felicity had barely taken the time to notice. She unclenched her jaw. It wouldn't do to take her anger out on Mrs. Harrison. "Yes, it is."

"Well, climb down from there and come in and set a spell. Tell me about your poor sister. How's she been since her accident?"

"She's right well, Mrs. Harrison. Actually, I need to speak with your husband if I may. I only have a moment before I need to get back to the factory. It's about one of the boys from the orphans' home in his employ."

Mrs. Harrison's eyes widened as she cast a furtive glance toward the barn.

Law and tarnation, Felicity thought. She knew. The woman knew her husband had been abusing Tim, and she had let him get away with it.

In the next instant, she wondered if Mrs. Harrison was a victim herself of her husband's unreasonable expectations. Even if she wasn't, there probably wasn't a lot she could do if he chose to push someone around. It was the way things were, whether she wanted to accept it or not.

"Is he in the barn?"

"I..." Another glance in that direction. "I'm not sure. Maybe the workshop. You're not going to make trouble for him, are you, Miss Trego? It's just a misunderstanding. Those boys do more loafing than working, and Wes don't have no patience for lollygagging."

If Felicity thought for one minute Mrs. Harrison wasn't also a victim of Wes's abuses, she would unload on the woman.

"I'll speak with Mr. Harrison about it," she said as evenly as her voice would allow.

She clicked her tongue and tapped the horse's backside with the reins. She drove the buggy to the side of the barn where a closed-in lean-to comprised Mr. Harrison's tack shop.

She heard the ringing of tools against metal as she climbed down from the carriage. Her heart pounded in her chest. She tried to sort her thoughts so she wouldn't start yelling uncontrollably as soon as she entered the shed.

It wouldn't do any good to lose her temper, but she didn't know how she could prevent it either.

The door was open as expected since foundry work was hot work even on cool mornings like today.

Even though she was seething with rage, deeply ingrained decorum made Felicity pause and knock on the door lintel before she stuck her head inside the dim interior.

Mr. Harrison saw her at the same instant she made out his shadowy figure holding a pair of metal tongs over a scythe he was sharpening.

"Good morning, Miss Trego. What brings you out?" He didn't stop swinging the hammer against the scythe.

Felicity stepped inside the shed. "I've come to discuss Tim."

He kept working. "What about him?"

"I saw the strap marks on his arm."

Finally, Mr. Harrison stopped swinging. He lowered the hammer but didn't let go of it. In the sudden stillness, Felicity wondered again if she was safe.

"It had to be done, Miss Trego. A boy's got to learn the proper way to do things."

"By stripes across his arm?"

"It was all right for my pa. Some boys' heads are harder'n others. Ain't no other way to get through to 'em."

"There are always other ways, Mr. Harrison. You could tell him not to come back if you weren't satisfied with his work."

Mr. Harrison shook his head. "I can't afford a proper farmhand. I didn't have a rich pappy die and leave me a prosperous business."

Felicity clenched and unclenched her fist. If she thought it would do any good, she would whack him on the head with a whip handle the way Malachi said some of the men did to the boys. But that would make her no better than him.

"It's not my fault they never been taught nothing," he continued. "I have to spend half my time explaining the simplest chore. I was doing the boy a favor."

"By flogging him?"

Now Mr. Harrison just looked impatient. "No, by educating him. What with him not having no pa, I'm trying to teach him how to do a job right. I can see now, you with your delicate sensibilities, wouldn't understand. You may never have had to learn things the hard way, but Tim will. He didn't have another man to show him how things were, so I did my best. If you don't want him to come back—"

"Oh, he won't be back," Felicity interjected. "I'll do my best to make sure you won't find any other young person to work for you."

For the first time Mr. Harrison looked close to losing his temper. "You need to keep your pretty little nose out of my business unless you want to take a chance at losing it."

Felicity stepped deeper into the shed, forgetting her fear for her personal safety. "Is that a threat, Mr. Harrison?"

"It's not a threat." He stepped forward until he was towering over her. "It's the way things are. I can't run this farm myself, and I can't afford nothin' but them boys. It wouldn't do you any good to meddle in my business."

Felicity couldn't decide if she was angry or terrified of the man.

"It won't do you any good, Mr. Harrison, to bully me. I'm not as easily frightened as these children."

"And I'm not impressed with your money or the way you walk around town with your nose in the air."

"I do not—"

He wasn't finished. "Just because you own half the town doesn't give you the right to tell the rest of us how to live."

"Mr. Harrison, that has never been my intention. All I care about is protecting those children. I will not let you or anyone else flog them or whack them with buggy whip handles to teach a lesson you think they should learn."

"Then keep those brats away from my farm."

"Don't worry. You'll never see another one."

•••

All the way back to town, Felicity wondered if she had overreacted about the entire situation.

Tim and Malachi didn't seem to think being flogged by a disapproving employer was worth losing one's position.

Wes Harrison claimed he was doing Tim a favor by teaching him the hard way how to complete a task. Tim would be upset when he learned he wasn't going back to the farm to work. Mr. Harrison was angry he had lost his source of cheap labor and could cause trouble down the road for Tim.

Perhaps they were all right, and she was too sensitive to appreciate the way things worked outside her insulated existence. Belinda was always reminding her it was a man's world. Maybe this was part of what she meant.

Regardless, she would never get to sleep tonight until she had done everything she could to make sure the children of Willow Wood were protected from Wes Harrison and his ilk.

At the factory, Mr. Hughes was probably pacing the floor, wondering where she was. She glanced at the timepiece on her bodice. She was already late; what was a few more minutes? She needed to finish what she started.

She brought the buggy to a stop outside the sheriff's office. She had only met the new sheriff a time or two around town. Burl Hansen, the former sheriff had kept the peace in Willow Wood since Felicity was a girl. Last year he retired to a small farm on the edge of town where he grew tomatoes and beans and entertained like-minded men with plenty of time on their hands with much-exaggerated stories of his exploits on the frontier.

Apprehension rose in her belly as she entered the jail. She'd feel a lot more comfortable if she was talking to Burl Hanson.

Sheriff Deavers was seated behind the desk, his head bent over a ledger. He looked up. He was thin and rangy with a wide forehead and eyes too small for his face. He had always reminded Felicity of a scarecrow with some of its stuffing gone. His severe expression softened at the sight of her.

"Good morning, Miss Trego. No trouble over at the factory, I hope."

"No, sir." She swallowed, remembering Mr. Harrison's reaction to her accusation.

"I'm here about one of the boys at the orphans' home. He was abused by one of the farmers who give the boys work sometimes. Wes Harrison. He flogged the boy."

Sheriff Deavers didn't flinch. "The boy tell you that, did he?"

Felicity stiffened. "No, he didn't tell me. I saw the marks on his arm. Every time he makes a mistake, he gets a few undeserved lashes across the inside of his arm where no one will see."

"Then I suggest you counsel him to stop making mistakes."

Felicity nearly fell over at the man's flippant remark.

"Sheriff, this isn't a laughing matter. I'm the one who found Tim the job with Mr. Harrison. I wanted him to learn the value of a hard day's work and hopefully earn a little money. I didn't send him out there to get knocked around."

The sheriff slowly came to his feet. He hitched up his gun belt over his narrow hips and perched on the edge of the desk. "I'm sure you didn't, Miss Trego. I'm sure you only meant to do good by the boy. But some folks have a stricter code of ethics than others."

"I assure you, Sheriff, I am as ethical as the next person. My papa also taught me a fair wage for a hard day's work. I don't believe he meant getting lashes for dropping a bag of flour."

"Miss Trego, I can talk to Wes if that makes you feel better. Remind him of patience and the Good Book's words on how to treat a servant. But if a man's got a willing employee, he can pretty much do whatever he wants to make sure he gets what he expects for his wages."

"We're talking about children here."

"Orphans. We're talking about orphans. You or I might believe we have a better way to teach a young person how to do a job. But I'm not qualified to tell another man how to run his farm. If something more grievous than a few lashes were to occur, then I would have the authority to step in."

"You mean if he kills the boy."

Sheriff uncrossed his arms and blew out a long puff of air. "Miss Trego, I suggest you not get worked up over this. Wes is a good man. I've known him for years. I would hate to see his reputation tarnished over a few lashes to a boy who's probably better off for it."

Chapter Seventeen

Felicity stormed out of the sheriff's office, black dots of fury flashing before her eyes.

The injustices facing the children at the orphanage were nearly more than she could bear. If Tim was part of a prominent family in the community, the sheriff would at least investigate her claims. Since he was an orphan, he needed to take his lumps and appreciate the lessons learned.

She had been too angry to give the sheriff a piece of her mind. By the time she reached the board walk outside his office, she realized the real blame lay with her.

She was the one who had set up Tim to become Wes Harrison's whipping boy. She had been so anxious to find jobs for the children, she hadn't spent sufficient time vetting prospective employers. She was so determined to prove her employment program a success, she sent the older children into homes of anyone willing to take them.

For two years she had cajoled and begged farmers and businessmen to find work for the children. Young girls had gone into homes to cook, do laundry, and help mothers with small children. Boys had gone to farms, the blacksmith shop and livery, and even the railyards to serve as hostlers.

All with Felicity's blessing.

Had the girls been safe? Some were as young as thirteen. If someone hurt or mistreated them, would they have been brave enough to speak out? Or had they believed—as Malachi told her this morning—it was the way things were? Felicity's skin crawled at the thought of what may've happened to a naïve young girl trying to earn money for shoes or a warm coat.

Breakfast roiled in her stomach at the possibilities. She hurried past where her buggy waited and stepped into an alley just in time to throw up into the dirt.

When she finished, she slumped against the rough side of a building and fumbled in her sleeve for a handkerchief.

Long, tanned fingers thrust a man's linen handkerchief under her nose. Her heart sank at the sight of a monogrammed Y.

"Here you are."

Soap and aftershave assailed her nose. While pleasant, the smell so soon after emptying her stomach, coupled with embarrassment of being caught, almost made her heave again.

Ignoring the offered handkerchief, she snatched her own from her sleeve and held it to her mouth.

"Thank you, Ned."

He stepped back to give her air, his features chiseled in alarm. "Are you all right?"

She nodded weakly and breathed inside her handkerchief to make sure her stomach was through embarrassing her. "I'm fine."

She swallowed a few times as her stomach slowly settled. "I recently received some distressing news."

"Allow me." Ned took her arm and led her to an overturned barrel resting against the building opposite where they stood.

Felicity sat down gingerly. After making sure the barrel wouldn't roll out from under her, she relaxed and took another steadying breath. "Thank you. I'm feeling better now."

"Could I get you some water? Tea?"

Felicity shook her head. Water or tea sounded heavenly, but she didn't want to involve him. Nor did she have time to indulge her disgust with herself. "I'll be fine as soon as I get my feet under me. I need to get back to the factory. I had only planned to run a quick errand. Now I'm dreadfully late."

'Then allow me to escort you to your office."

She nodded over his shoulder. "I have my buggy."

"May I drive you? You still look out of sorts. Are you sure you're all right?"

She looked at his extended hand. "Actually, I'm not. I would appreciate you taking the reins."

She took his hand and allowed him to assist her into the carriage. Tongues would be wagging all over town at the sight. Surely the news would get back to Belinda. For once, Felicity didn't care.

"I hope your distressing news will be quickly reconciled," Ned said once the buggy got rolling.

"I don't think so. I fear there is no recourse for what happened."

"Is it something to do with the factory? Perhaps I can be of assistance."

"Had anything gone wrong at the factory, I need only let Belinda know, and she would make sure the situation was resolved satisfactorily and quickly."

He smiled and she smiled back.

"I might still be able to help, or at least advise," he said hopefully.

Felicity considered his offer. She wanted to confide in him. But if he shared the sheriff and Mr. Harrison's attitude about how to teach children the value of hard work, she would never be able to look at him again. Maybe every man in the world had the same attitudes toward children, and she was the one with unreasonable expectations.

She didn't want to lose her respect for Ned. At the same time, she wanted to know how he viewed the matter, even if it ended up breaking her heart.

"I fear I've put one of the children at the orphans' home into a dangerous situation. Tim. Remember how I told you he has been acting strangely? Well, it's worse than I thought. I hoped the sheriff could help me. It doesn't look like that will happen, unless...unless a severe crime is committed against the boy."

Ned studied her for a moment. "What exactly happened?"

Her heart ached, imagining the evil memories her words could bring back for him. "The last few years I've helped the older children find work around the community. Jobs that wouldn't interfere with their schoolwork. Today I found out Tim has been abused by one of his employers. The boys told me it isn't uncommon. They almost blame themselves.

Malachi told me they have to learn to work faster or—"

"Duck quicker," he finished.

Tears of anger filled her eyes. "This is all my fault. I sent him there to learn job skills, not how to duck."

Ned fixed his gaze on the road ahead of them.

"Am I the only person who doesn't know this happens to children who don't have parents to protect them?" Felicity demanded.

He reached over and clasped her hand. His comforting warmth seeped through her leather gloves.

"None of the children blame you."

"That's the problem. They trust me. The only lesson I taught them is adults can't be trusted. Even the kind ones can make life hard on them. I should've done more to protect them. Isn't that our duty? As a Christian, it's my obligation to see to the needs of orphans. Jesus commanded it. I failed that calling miserably."

He didn't respond until the sounds of the factory announced they were nearly there. She looked desperately at him. She wanted an answer before he pulled up in front of the livery.

"The fact that you're so distressed proves you are not to blame."

Felicity squeezed his hand in appreciation. "I just don't know what to do about Tim. He isn't going to be happy when I tell him he can't go back to Mr. Harrison's. Maybe I can find him work at the factory."

He looked doubtful. "I don't know if a factory is a suitable place for employment for a youngster. He seems responsible, but I've heard of too many accidents that befall young people around machinery and the fast pace."

She exhaled. "I'm sure Belinda would say the same thing."

He squeezed her hand and let go. "Try not to worry, Felicity. Everything will work out."

She smiled up at him. She wanted to thank him again, but the words died on her lips at the intensity in his eyes. Her gaze dropped to his mouth. Her rational mind reminded her she could never kiss him again. But her heart—her reckless heart—nearly made her throw her arms around him and burrow into his warmth.

"Are you sure you're all right?" he said as he turned the rig around the back side of the building to the livery. "You still look a little green around the gills."

She shook her head. "I have a kettle in my office, remember?"

Mark stepped out of the livery's doorway.

"I'm so sorry," she told Ned. "Now you have to walk all the way back to town."

He leaped down from the rig and circled it to help her down before Mark reached them to do it for him. "I don't mind. It isn't far."

He put his hands on either side of her waist and swept her to the ground.

His hands remained there a moment longer than they needed to while Felicity kept her hands on his shoulders.

Their eyes locked. She touched her lip with the tip of her tongue. She breathed in the scent of him and marveled at the weight of his hands on her waist. She could stand here all day. Draw from his strength, his compassion.

With effort, she dropped her hands and stepped back. "I'm going to stop by Mrs. McClanahan's on my way home tonight. I want to tell Tim I spoke to Mr. Harrison. I hope I can make him see it's for his own good. Are you free to go with me?"

The slow smile she found so endearing spread across his face. "Mr. Altman will be disappointed if I miss our evening chess game, but I think he'll understand. I'll be at the law office until six."

Relief swept through her. Not only might it be easier to get through to Tim with Ned beside her, but she was thankful he would be there for *her*.

She knew it was wrong to encourage his interest in her and her interest in him. It wasn't wise to spend one moment alone with the man.

She also knew she could no longer deny her love for him another day.

Chapter Eighteen

Tim and Malachi were hammering boards together when Ned and Felicity rode into the side yard that evening.

Ronan and Grant were watching, and obviously awaiting their turn with the hammer. They called out a greeting and waved, then ran inside to tell everyone else they had company.

Ned climbed down and circled around to help Felicity. Though she didn't need the assistance, she waited, relishing the warmth of his hand on hers.

"It's getting too dark for hammering," Ned told the boys.

"We're building a frame for a new porch roof," Malachi explained. "We got the leftover lumber and shingles, and the overhang at the back door's about to cave in on us."

Felicity knew without looking he was right. She looked past the smiling Malachi to find Tim. He wasn't smiling. She figured he'd already heard he was out of a job.

Ned went to the frame they were building. Malachi stood it up, and Ned examined it. Felicity knew he was giving her time to talk to Tim alone.

She walked a few feet away from Ned and Malachi and motioned for Tim to join her.

"I couldn't let you keep working for Mr. Harrison. He may have believed he was teaching you, but he had no right. He could've caused severe injury."

His forehead puckered. "Begging your pardon, ma'am, but I can take care of myself."

"I know. You've been doing it for a long time. You shouldn't have to. There's no shame in having someone to watch out for you. You're not on your own."

"But I am, Miss Trego. I have Mum and all of you here. It's more than I ever had before. But all us kids know we're different. We always will be. I appreciate you wanting to look out for me, but I have to learn to protect myself from the Wes Harrisons of the world."

"Oh, Tim, I'm so sorry you have to. It was my fault you went to work for that man. I had to do something to make it right. Or at least I thought I did."

"I appreciate it. It's nice knowing somebody cares."

Felicity gave him a quick hug. She wished she could take away his pain. She wanted to rectify the situation for every homeless child on the frontier.

Before she could say anything else, the back door burst open and the children spilled out followed by Mrs. McClanahan.

"We have to tell Mrs. McClanahan why you aren't going back to Mr. Harrison's," she told Tim.

He frowned. "We can let her think he doesn't need me anymore."

"She may hear something in town. I don't want her to think it's your fault."

He didn't look convinced, but he followed her to the porch where the children had gathered around Ned, peppering him with questions.

Ned involved the other children in a game of tag while Felicity and Tim told Mrs. McClanahan about losing his job. The woman pulled him into her arms and fretted over him as his face darkened three shades.

"Don't ever keep something like this from me again," she scolded.

"I won't."

"I mean it, Tim. You don't need to think you can't bring any problem to me. If you can't talk to me, you have Miss Trego and Mr. Yates. You're not alone anymore."

"I know. I won't forget."

•••

"Do you feel better after talking to Tim?" Ned asked as he drove the buggy back onto the road.

"I do." As relieved as Felicity was about Tim being away from Mr. Harrison, she couldn't focus on anything but Ned's leg pressing against hers on the narrow buggy seat.

"How did he take it?"

"He told me I should've let him handle it."

"Sounds like he's growing up."

"He's only fifteen."

"Some of us have to grow up faster than others."

She gulped. "I'm sorry, Ned. I didn't mean to be insensitive."

He nudged her with his shoulder. "I'm not sensitive. I went to law school, remember?"

She smiled appreciatively. "I still don't want to dismiss what you've been through as if it wasn't difficult."

He looked at her head-on. "I don't think you have it in you."

"Maybe not intentionally, but look what happened to Tim. He got hurt because I didn't do my due diligence to make sure he was sent into a safe home."

He studied her for a moment in the near darkness. She could barely make out his expression. He edged the carriage to the side of the road and stopped. He set the brake and turned to face her.

Felicity's breath caught in her throat. She hadn't been this close to him since the day he kissed her. All around them, she heard sounds of civilization. But all she was aware of was Ned Yates' nearness.

"Felicity, you've done right by those kids. I want you to stop blaming yourself. Evil things happen in the world. None of us can avoid it as long as we're alive. The day will come when there'll be no lashes on a boy's arm or hungry children or parents who die and leave young ones to fend for themselves. But it won't be here on earth."

He tipped the brim of her hat up a little to put his face closer to hers. She couldn't see much in the darkness, and she knew he couldn't either. She got the feeling he wanted her to sense his resolve since she couldn't see it.

"Tim talked to me some when we were up on the roof a few weeks ago. He told me his pa died when he was eight. His ma died the next winter. An aunt took him in for a few months.

Then some folks she knew. He got passed around from one relative or neighbor to the next until there was nobody left."

Felicity put her hand to her mouth. "The poor boy."

Ned took hold of her hand and pulled it down. He didn't let go of it.

"It wasn't anybody's fault. It's just the way things happen. Tim knows that. He doesn't blame his parents or the relatives who couldn't keep him. Everybody tried their best. But..." He lifted a shoulder. "He didn't want to be a burden. Truth be told, he probably got tired of seeing that desperate look on hungry people's faces when they already don't have enough and then they're stuck with one more mouth to feed."

She shook her head as tears pressed at her eyes. "He was just a little boy. No child should know that look. I hate to think *you* know that look."

"There are worse things."

Still holding her hand, he looked past her shoulder. Felicity held her breath, wondering what he saw in the darkness.

"If I had stayed in my mother's house, I probably wouldn't have lived to see another birthday."

Felicity swallowed, determined not to interrupt, though she wanted to cry over what he'd been through.

"I told you about hiding in a family's shed to get out of the rain. They fed me. For the first time in my life I had plenty to eat. The missus treated me fair. Their son had left a few months earlier. She missed him something fierce, and I think I helped her get through that time."

He scratched the stubble on his chin as though the memory brought him discomfort, but like a bothersome scab, he knew he'd be better off getting rid of it.

"Her husband had a small smithy shop in the back yard. He made and sharpened hoe heads, shovels, saws, plows. Anything people were willing to pay him for. It was hard work for little money. Without their son, he needed another pair of hands. It was hard and heavy work for a skinny kid like me. I made a lot of mistakes."

He didn't speak for a moment.

"What does that mean?" she prodded, though she didn't want to hear the answer.

"Just like Tim and Malachi have done, I learned not to make mistakes."

She wanted to cry at the injustice of it all. She pressed her lips together to keep quiet. It was his story; she'd let him finish it.

"The man got used to having me around. I think he even warmed to me a little, but I don't think he knew how to be anything but heavy handed. The whole two and a half years I was there, their son didn't write or visit once. I didn't know where he went and I knew better than to ask.

"The man's temper didn't improve. Missus could see the situation was escalating. Maybe she didn't want the same thing to happen with me that happened to her son.

"One morning she rolled my few belongings into an old sheet and told me I was going to live with some people she sometimes worked for. I could go to school and I'd always have shoes that fit. She said I was worth more than working for food at a smithy shop. She kissed me for the first time and told me she loved me, but she never wanted me to come back. It was the kindest thing anyone ever did for me."

The clouds shifted to reveal a half moon. With his thumb, he wiped a tear from her cheek he hadn't seen in the darkness.

"I was scared to death. Life with that couple had been hard, but it was better than my mother's house. After that, I stayed with the older couple for a while until I ended up with the Yates. Every step I took brought me closer to them. Closer to you."

She hiccupped around her tears. "Closer to me?"

He took hold of her chin with his finger and thumb. "Life isn't fair. Sometimes it looks like someone else gets all the breaks while another only knows an empty belly and holes in his shoes. But if we trust God's sovereign will, He'll bring us through to something better."

Felicity wasn't sure what he was saying. Did he believe God had brought him here? She was his something better?

He smoothed a tendril of hair away from her face and tucked it behind her ear. He stared at her hair for a moment and then at her. "That's one question answered."

Was he wondering the same thing she was. "What question?"

"Your hair. I've been wondering since the day I met you if it was as soft as it looked. Just like your skin." He kissed one cheek and then the other. "And your lips."

Felicity's breath caught in her throat as she waited for his kiss. At the last moment he pulled back. He put his hands on either side of her face and wiped away the last vestiges of tears with his thumbs.

"I think I love you, Felicity Trego."

She shivered inside her cloak. Dampness had settled in with the night, but it wasn't the chill in the air that caused the shiver.

"Oh, Ned." Like a splash of cold water, she realized she loved him too. She had loved him since the moment she saw him climb down from Mrs. McClanahan's roof, covered in sawdust, his hair damp from sweat and curling around his shoulders.

She loved him. She loved his kindness and his humor and his faith. Though she knew it could never happen, she wanted to spend her life looking into those stormy-sea green eyes.

Ned's lips found hers in the darkness. A groan of desire sounded, and Felicity was surprised it came from her.

She wrapped her arms around him and pressed her body against his as the kiss deepened. Too soon, Ned loosened his arms. Her cloak had fallen off one shoulder. He lifted it back into place and attached the button at her throat.

Felicity was breathless and trembling. She wanted to say something. She wanted to tell him she loved him too. That she wanted him to kiss her again and never stop. Instead she put her hands on either side of his face and pulled it down to her.

The kiss was more tender and gentler than the last. More loving. Her heart expanded in her chest, crowding the rest of her until she could barely draw a breath.

Yes, she loved him. More deeply than she thought a person could love another.

She pulled away, needing to tell him. "Ned, I..."

She tilted her head and looked up at him. He was gazing down at her, waiting for her to finish, waiting for her to profess her love for him.

She wanted to. She wanted to tell him exactly how she felt, and of the battle raging within her right now. She wanted him to know she loved him more than anything, but she couldn't abandon the children. She couldn't let Belinda down. And Papa.

She lowered her chin and looked away. "Thank you for coming with me tonight. It's good for the children to have a strong man to talk to."

He kissed her again. "I didn't come only for them."

"I know. Thank you for that too."

Ned wrapped his arms around her and pulled her close again. The kiss was deep and long and passionate.

Every cell of Felicity's body was set ablaze. A hunger she had never known, never imagined, rose within her. anything She didn't want to ever be anywhere but in his arms.

How could she go back to life without him? How could she not let him kiss her and keep kissing her?

A tiny voice told her she wasn't being fair to Ned or to herself. She needed to get out of this man's arms and go home. She needed to remember who she was and what Papa wanted for her and Belinda.

With a resolve she didn't know she possessed, she pulled away. Her hat was askew and her hair had come loose from the pile pinned at the back of her head.

He trailed a finger along the side of her face and ended at her chin. He twirled a tendril of loose hair around his finger and studied it.

"I've never met anyone like you, Felicity."

Her throat was too dry to respond. She swallowed hard and pulled farther away. She smoothed her hair back from her face and replaced a few pins that had come loose. It wouldn't do good for Belinda to see her in this state.

"I've never met anyone like you, Ned Yates. You make me forget who I am."

He tilted his head. "Why would you want to forget?"

She ran her fingers around the brim of her hat before setting it back in place. "I have...responsibilities. People depend on me. I don't have time for..."

She looked into his eyes. It was hard to see his expression, but the furrow in his brow and set of his jaw were obvious.

She didn't want to tell him she didn't have time for him, but maybe it was exactly what she should say. Better for a small hurt now than a big hurt later. But was it too late for a small hurt? She already loved him. More than she ever dreamed possible. Nothing she said would make it easier.

She pulled completely out of his arms. "I really must go. Belinda will be worried. She may send someone looking for me."

"Yes, I wouldn't want to worry her."

Confusion and hurt echoed in his voice. She needed to apologize. She needed to tell him she shouldn't have allowed him to kiss her. She shouldn't have allowed him fall in love with her. She shouldn't have fallen in love with him.

Tonight was the last time they could be together. No matter how much it hurt, she had to say goodbye for both their sakes. She wanted to tell him she was sorry things had to end this way.

If she tried to form a word, she would burst into tears of loss and grief for the life they'd never share.

If he was right and God had set every sequence of events in motion to end up at this moment, she wanted it to last forever.

Chapter Nineteen

"Sister?"

Felicity tensed inside the door. She had brushed down the horse herself in the stable instead of letting Richard do it. She needed time for her hands to stop shaking and for the flush to leave her cheeks. If Belinda noticed her mussed hair and breathlessness, she could blame it on the horse.

She removed her hat and hung her cloak in the foyer. She wanted to go straight upstairs. She didn't want to talk to Belinda or anyone else.

She wanted to throw herself across her bed and give in to the grief ripping her chest open.

But there was no denying Belinda. She took a fortifying breath and walked into the parlor.

Belinda was pale and drawn, more so than she had been this morning. Felicity's heart lurched at the sight of her. Had she added to her sister's vexation by staying out so late this evening?

She hurried to her bedside. "I'm sorry I'm late. How are you? Have you eaten today? You've lost weight."

Belinda snorted. "I was beginning to think I could lose a hundred pounds before you took notice."

Felicity clasped Belinda's hands between hers and sank into the chair next to the bed.

"Oh, Belinda, I'm sorry. I've had so much on my mind lately. I'll never understand how you do it. The factory has always energized you. It overwhelms me. I'm looking forward to the day when you're back behind your desk. Can you believe I found a gray hair today?"

She parted her hair and leaned forward to show Belinda her scalp. "See? It's frightful. Blond hair is supposed to slowly fade to a soft silver, not go gray."

Belinda snorted even louder, but this time she laughed. "Oh, Sister, you're so vain."

Felicity was relieved to see a light appear in Belinda's eyes. "I know. I shall pray for absolution on Sunday. But I'm also going to pray that gray hair away."

They both laughed. The trepidation over Ned slid out of Felicity's shoulders, until Belinda spoke.

"Why are you so late? Mr. Hughes said you were late this morning. Is something going on I should know about?"

Not anymore, Felicity thought.

"I had an errand to take care of this morning."

She opened her satchel. It was usually the first thing Belinda asked to see. She pulled out a sheaf of papers and fanned them out on the desk. Hopefully, they would capture her sister's attention and she would lose interest in whatever had kept Felicity tonight.

No such luck.

Belinda watched her expectantly.

"I heard some distressing news about one of the children from the orphans' home," she said when Belinda wouldn't look away. "I needed to make sure all was well."

"Mary didn't say anything to me about any trouble."

"She may not know yet. It's Tim, the oldest boy. He's being abused by his employer. I went out to talk to the man and tell him Tim wouldn't be working for him anymore."

Belinda rolled her eyes. "Why would you use work time to insert yourself into something that's none of your business."

Felicity's jaw went slack. "But...it is my business. Anytime a child is mistreated, it's all our business. As human beings. As Christians."

Belinda pursed her lips. "I understand things like this upset you. You've always been sensitive. But your duties at the factory should come first."

Sensitive. There was that word again. How could caring for a child implicate weakness?

"I wasn't being sensitive. I was being the responsible adult in the situation."

"By chastising Wes Harrison? By running to the sheriff to lodge a complaint?"

Felicity couldn't decide which peeved her more; the sheriff tattling to her big sister, or that Belinda considered a boy being abused by a man who should've protected him beneath the sheriff's time.

"How did you know I talked to the sheriff? How did you know it was Mr. Harrison?"

"I'm still part of this town. I hear things. Especially something like this. Sheriff Deavers came by to ask me if I was aware of how you were spending your time instead of running the factory."

Felicity felt the blood drain from her face. It took a moment to find her voice. "He said I...I wasn't running the company?"

"Not in so many words. He knows I'm laid up. He knows how much the town depends on Trego Leatherworks. If something were to distract one of us from doing our job, well, who knows how it would affect Willow Wood?"

Again, Felicity couldn't decide who she was madder at; the sheriff or Belinda. "How dare the two of you sit in this room and accuse me of not doing my job when I'm not here to defend myself."

"That isn't what we were doing."

"It certainly sounds like it. Not one thing inside that factory has slipped without you there. I think that's the problem. You have dedicated your whole life to the business and it's running smoothly with me in your place. I think a small part of you hopes we'll lose money this quarter so you'll know how important you are to its success."

Belinda set a hand on her hip. "Oh, Felicity, be serious. I would never want to lose money to prove a point. I may be stubborn, but I'm not stupid."

"Then what is it? Nothing has distracted me from doing my job."

Belinda's expression darkened. "I think *someone* has distracted you."

Felicity clenched and unclenched her jaw. "I am working harder for this company than I ever have in my life. I never appreciated what you do more than I do every single day when I walk into those offices. To think you can't show me the same respect, that you think those children and my interests outside the factory would compromise my commitment to it—that breaks my heart.

"I know every person in this town sees me as Belinda Trego's pretty, vain, helpless little sister. I just never knew you see me the same way."

Belinda lunged forward and grabbed her hand. "Felicity, no. I don't see you like that."

She looked so sincere Felicity almost believed her.

"I love you and I trust you. It's just that I know you're a hopeless romantic. You want to save the world."

"What's wrong with that? It's better than believing the world is beyond saving."

"Of course, Sister. I love you for your pure, giving heart. But..." She squeezed Felicity's hand. "...That pure heart is sometimes too trusting. You've never had a nefarious thought about anyone, and you can't imagine anyone having a despicable intention toward you."

Felicity pulled her hands free and stood. "What exactly are we talking about here? The only despicable intention is those marks Wes Harrison laid on Tim's arms."

Belinda stared at her in that way she had of making Felicity think she could right through her.

"I'm talking about Mr. Yates."

"What about him?" Felicity managed to keep the quaver out of her voice. "He wanted to ride out with me when I told Mrs. McClanahan what Wes Harrison had done to Tim."

"Law and tarnation, Felicity. He wouldn't be the first man to feign interest in a cause to impress the woman he's wooing."

"He isn't..." Felicity cried. She stopped herself. Too much protestation would only give credence to Belinda's fears.

She started over. "Mr. Yates truly cares for those children. He grew up without his own parents. He understands the suffering of children in their position."

Belinda studied her from under her honey-colored brows. "Oh, Sister, how could you have let this happen?"

"Let what happen?"

"You're in love with the man."

"No..." Felicity began. She stopped at the knowing look in Belinda's eyes. She couldn't do it anyway. She couldn't lie to her sister. She couldn't lie to herself.

"You just met him," Belinda reminded her. "Yes, he's handsome and educated. I'm sure he's kind and charming, too, and knows all the right things to say. But he's still a man. They're all the same."

"Don't you dare say that. You don't know him. I do. You've never given any man a chance. They're nothing more than professional rivals to you. The only emotion I've seen you express toward a man is disdain."

Belinda pushed the tray aside and folded her arms over her chest. "I've dealt with them all my life. If my attitudes seem harsh it's because I want to protect you. I want to protect what Papa built."

Felicity tried to keep her anger in check. "Are you suggesting I don't? Ned is not after your precious factory."

"Does he know you can never get involved with a man? That you can never marry?"

Heat rose in Felicity's cheeks. She thought of his kisses. His embrace that made the blood pound in her veins, even now. "What do you expect me to do, Belinda? Tell every man I meet to keep his distance because my father's will forbids me to marry?"

"That would be the kindest thing." Belinda sighed heavily. "None of this is your fault. You're beautiful. And witty and warm. Every man in this town has probably dreamed of being the one to sweep you off your feet.

"No, you don't need to announce it from the town square, but it isn't fair to let them believe you would consider marrying one of them. Your duty is to our family. I know you haven't forgotten those children you love so much. Do you think it's fair to them? They depend on you. What would they have done if you hadn't supplied the lumber and supplies to fix the hole in the roof? The entire roof will probably need replaced by Spring. No one else in town is going to finance the project. I know you wouldn't leave Mrs. McClanahan high and dry."

Felicity stared at her feet. "I wouldn't dream of it," she murmured.

"Good," Belinda said as if the matter were settled. She patted Felicity's arm.

"I know the stipulation in Papa's will seems harsh and unreasonable, especially since you're still young and fanciful with dreams of weddings and a dashing young man. Trust me, those dreams will pass. Soon you'll understand Papa's way was best. He knew what was best for us. For this town. You have to trust him and get Mr. Yates out of your head."

Felicity wanted to burst into tears. How was she supposed to do that?

Belinda must've read the doubt in her eyes. "Mr. Yates isn't the first man you thought you loved. Doesn't that prove your heart can't be trusted?"

"I was younger then."

"Young and foolish. Had Papa not forbidden it, you may have pursued Sam Ogilvie. Remember him? I do. You were in *love* with him before I sent you away to school. You were sure he was the man you wanted to spend your life with."

Belinda snorted. "Then there was Marshal Dutton. Remember when he moved back to town to help his father run their ranch? It's a good thing I stopped that potentially humiliating situation before you did something that couldn't be undone."

"I wasn't going to pursue Grayson. I had looked up to him as a child. I realized right away I wasn't in love with the man, just the hero I had built him up to be. It was obvious he loved Lisette Pelletier. I'm very happy for them."

"I'm happy, too, that everything worked out for them. They have a beautiful family now, as God intended. That goes to show you Papa knew what he was doing. He knew he wouldn't be here to protect us, so he needed to protect us and his company from ourselves.

"He knew how easily an impressionable young woman can have her head turned. If I had allowed a man to sweet talk me out of my good sense, you would've been left with nothing. And the same for me if you let it happen with Mr. Yates or anyone else."

Felicity wanted to defend herself. She wasn't impressionable, and Ned wasn't a leech only after her money. She thought of his kisses and the way he had cradled her face in his hands. Her love for him wasn't a schoolgirl infatuation like it had been with Sam and Grayson.

This love was strong. Real. If she lived to be a hundred, she would never love another man. But Belinda was right. It didn't matter what kind of love they shared. It could never go beyond tonight.

"We don't know anything about him," Belinda continued. "He's a professional man and well thought of by Mr. Simonton. But can one ever trust a lawyer?"

She laughed. Felicity didn't join in.

"They say whatever it takes to sway opinion to their side. It's the nature of the profession. I'm sure he's an upstanding young man. But..." She shrugged. "Papa's will is clear. We can't undo it. If you can't think of a kind way to let Mr. Yates know it's pointless to pursue you, I'll do it for you."

Felicity gasped. "No. Don't say anything to him."

"If that's how you want it. Believe me, it's for the best. Papa knew this day would come and he wanted to protect his legacy. He wanted to protect us."

•••

Ned stared at the water-stained ceiling above his bed. He knew every stain in the ceiling and along the walls. Mrs. Crothers did her best to make the old house cheerful and homey. She whitewashed the ceilings and hung paper on the walls, but in places the stains still showed through.

That's how Ned felt tonight. He had papered over the holes in his heart, but tonight they showed through.

He hadn't intended to tell Felicity everything about himself. Once he got going, he couldn't stop. He wasn't sure if his need to talk about his childhood was brought on by what happened to Tim. Or if it was Felicity herself. Whatever the reason, he wanted her to understand who he was—what he was.

He had only known her a month. His practical nature balked at the idea of falling so deeply in love after such a short time. He couldn't know her well enough to love her. But he knew he did.

Looking back, he realized he had fallen in love with her the first day he saw her in his office. It hadn't been merely her outward beauty that drew him to her, though he had suspected as much at the time.

Even then—before he knew the first thing about her—he had sensed something in her that many people hadn't taken the time to see past the gilded wrapping.

Felicity Trego was so much more than her beauty. He winced in embarrassment at the way he had blurted out his love for her. She hadn't said she loved him back, but he saw it in her eyes.

She was a blessing God put in his life, and there was only one thing for him to do. He had to marry her. He wasn't sure how it would work. He had no money. He was still buried under the debt of his parents' estate.

He wasn't sure how a man went about marrying any woman, especially one like Felicity. He couldn't buy her a mansion to rival the one where she now lived. He couldn't buy her pretty hats or a fancy carriage to drive around town.

At the moment, none of it mattered. He'd work out the details somehow. All he knew tonight was he loved the most beautiful woman in the world, and she loved him back.

Chapter Twenty

Felicity spurred the horse faster as she passed the law office. She hadn't seen Ned since last week. When Belinda needed something dropped off at Simonton, Yates Esq, she sent Mary.

Felicity was sure Belinda was doing it on purpose, though the sisters never talked about it. Belinda wanted to keep her from seeing Ned. She needn't bother. Felicity wanted it too.

The week had passed in a despondent blur. She kept busy at the factory so she wouldn't have time to think about the wedding she'd never have. The babies she would never hold to her breast.

While Ned had not proposed, she believed he would if she gave him any encouragement.

When he did, she would have to turn him down. It wasn't fair. But she had no right to compare fairness when she compared her life to the children's. Or Ned's. Or practically anyone else's in town.

She had never had someone lay stripes across her arm for dropping a sack of flour. She had never sought refuge from a storm in a stranger's barn. She went to bed every single night of her life on clean sheets with a full belly.

She had so much to be thankful for. And she was. She knew God loved her and held her in the palm of His hand.

Today, though, it didn't soothe the discontent and loneliness in her heart.

This morning she had barely gotten through her meeting with the company's advertising staff. When Lou Chaney told her the department could complete next month's newspaper ads without her input, she snapped at him. The advertising department was the only place in the company where she believed she was qualified to contribute.

She had told Lou and each of the round-jawed men in the room that as soon as Belinda returned to work, she was revamping the department. If they weren't interested in her changes, they were welcome to transfer to another department or leave Trego's employ.

As soon as the noon whistle blew, she left her desk and went to the livery to have Mark saddle a horse. There was another man to whom she needed to give a piece of her mind, and she would reach him a lot faster on horseback than by buggy. She only hoped he was more receptive than Lou had been.

At the center of town, she turned onto a side street and began the climb to the cemetery above Willow Wood.

She hadn't been up here for nearly a year. Every Christmas she and Belinda brought holly wreaths to lay on Mama and Papa's graves. Belinda shared a few memories of Mama since Felicity barely remembered her. They talked a little about Papa—and depending on how cold the day—they shared a few moments of silent introspection.

Felicity always prayed, while Belinda stamped her feet against the cold and wished she'd hurry up.

The last few days had reminded everyone winter was coming. The first snow had fallen on Monday, but it hadn't stayed on the ground long.

A north wind blew on top the hill, but the temperature was tolerable enough under the pines.

Felicity slid off the horse and tied the reins to a pine branch. She pulled her hat down over her ears and held her heavy woolen cape together as she moved among the headstones.

Her parents' monument was the largest on this side of the hill. Belinda had seen to that.

Last Christmas's wreath against Mama's side of the headstone was dried and withered. As Felicity moved it aside to read Mama's name, it fell apart in her hand.

She brushed aside the remnants of dried holly and smoothed her fingers across the cold marble.

"I miss you, Mama."

As soon as she spoke the words, her throat clogged with tears. "I wish you were here. Belinda tries to take your place. She means well, but she doesn't have a mother's heart. She doesn't understand me. She never has."

Felicity sat back on her heels and wiped her eyes. "I'm sorry. I didn't come here to feel sorry for myself. I came here to talk to Papa."

She looked at her father's name. Instead of wiping the silt and cobwebs from his name, she clenched her hands in her lap.

"I'm angry with you, Papa. I'm hurt and angry. No one respects me the way they do Belinda. I own the company and I have to stamp my foot and raise my voice to get anyone to listen to me. They treat me like I don't know what I'm doing. Okay, maybe I don't, but I'm trying and I deserve respect."

She wiped her eyes again as anger pushed the tears aside.

"I'm used to it. It's been that way my whole life. But not you, Papa. You knew me better than anyone. You told me I was smart. You said you hoped I learned to trust myself. But you didn't mean it.

"I am smart, Papa. I'm becoming an astute businesswoman. I've been running the company this last month without Belinda, and doing a fine job of it, if I do say so myself.

"I knew more than I gave myself credit for. I always wanted to make you proud. And Mama too. But you're no different than the people in town who look at me and only see a pretty face. You don't respect me any more than Lou Chaney."

Despite her indignation, the tears started again. "You should know you can count on me to help the company. But I want a husband.

"I'm in love, Papa. With a fine man who understands how much the children at Mrs. McClanahan's mean to me. But you don't trust me to do the right thing. You think I'm so addle-brained I'd let a man talk me out of the shoes on my feet.

"How could you, Papa? You know me better than that. Belinda says you were trying to protect your legacy. I don't think so anymore. You thought I was too stupid to make good choices so you took my choices from me."

She stood and wiped the dust and decaying leaves from her skirt.

"I'm sorry, Mama. I don't mean to be disrespectful. I'll apologize to Papa later, but right now, an apology would be insincere. I love you both. I'll see you next month."

She turned back to the horse.

In the distance she saw a woman laboring up the hill. She immediately recognized Jessa Hammersmith. Even at a distance, Jessa's difficulty crossing the uneven ground was evident. It looked like her baby could arrive any moment. Hopefully not on top of the hill in front of Felicity.

She dried her face with the corner of her cloak before hurrying over to Jessa. She hoped Jessa hadn't seen her railing at her parents' headstone.

Jessa heard her coming a few moments before Felicity reached her. "Good afternoon, Felicity. I didn't expect to see you up here."

"Nor I you." Jessa's cheeks were red and she breathed heavily "Should you have come all the way up here alone?"

Jessa's smile was radiant. Felicity suspected all expectant mothers wore that look.

"Dr. Dutton says exercise is good for me as long as I don't tire myself out. Snow will bury the paths up here within a few weeks. This is probably my last chance to walk up here until Spring."

She pointed a few feet away to a group of small headstones. "My little brother and two sisters are buried there. I used to come up here as often as I could when I needed to be alone. Or when I wanted to remember."

Felicity nodded in understanding. "I suppose that's why I'm here. I don't come up here much. But today I had to...I needed to get away from the factory for a while."

Jessa looked past her to where Felicity had left the horse under the trees. "Are you getting used to your new role?"

Felicity glanced down the hill toward town. Willow Wood spread out below them. The American flag in front of Endicott's General Store flapped in the breeze. Though she couldn't see it from where she stood, Simonton, Yates Esq. law office was on the next block. She imagined Ned inside, perhaps wondering where she was and why she was avoiding him.

"It's not as bad as I thought it would be without Belinda. But..." She sighed and brought her gaze back to Jessa.

Jessa cocked her head and waited.

"I'm not like Belinda. I don't know if I'll be happy doing this the rest my life."

"Why do you think you have to?"

Felicity's eyes stole again to Jessa's expectant middle. "It's the way things are."

Jessa stepped up to her and snagged her hand. "Felicity, what's really the matter?"

Felicity shook her head at the futility of the situation. Mr. Simonton was probably the only person in town who knew Papa had forbidden her and Belinda from marrying.

"I have so much to be grateful for," she said. "The company's successful. Belinda is working on innovations that could make it even more so. I have no right to wish things were different."

Jessa stared at her. "I'm sorry, Felicity. I don't know what you're talking about."

"So many people in Willow Wood rely on Trego Leatherworks. I don't want to let anyone down."

"Do you worry you can't take Belinda's place?"

"Something like that." Jessa didn't understand her dilemma, but it felt nice to talk about it anyway. "I'll never be as naturally suited to business as Belinda."

Jessa chuckled. "I don't think there's a person in the state as suited to business as Belinda."

Her joke helped dispel Felicity's despair. "She's never wanted anything more."

"And you do?"

Felicity nodded. Tears filled her eyes, but she wouldn't let them fall. "I want to marry. I want to have children."

Jessa gasped and her eyes lit up. "Is it Mr. Yates?"

Felicity's jaw dropped. "How did you..." She clamped her lips together.

Jessa smiled gently. "I've seen the two of you together. What choice did the poor man have but to fall in love with you?"

Felicity grasped her hands. "Oh, he does, Jessa. He... I've never met anyone like him. But..."

"But what? If you love him and he loves you, what's the problem?"

"I can't..."

She couldn't tell Jessa what Papa had done, even though she was still angry with him. She couldn't betray him. He had done what he thought was best.

"Belinda needs me at the factory. I can't leave her alone."

"You wouldn't be leaving her alone. Just because you marry doesn't mean you can't be involved with the business. It would just be in a different capacity. Mama always worked with Papa in the store, even with three babies hanging off her. Belinda loves you. She wants you to be happy."

Felicity wasn't so sure. Jessa would never understand Belinda didn't have the time or patience for romantic love.

She understood one thing, and that was making Trego Leatherworks the most successful leather manufacturer in the West so she could rub its success in the noses of every man who ever doubted her abilities.

"A woman can't marry and run a business the size of the factory," she said instead. "Especially once babies come. It wouldn't be fair to Belinda. Or to Ned if he wanted to marry me."

"I don't agree," Jessa exclaimed. "It's more dishonest to your sister to not tell her how you feel. What you want. All that matters to her is your happiness."

Felicity pivoted the conversation to Jessa's baby and the Lundy List company where her husband Rodney was moving up through the ranks.

Rodney wanted to break ground for a new house for them on the outskirts of Willow Wood. Jessa was in no hurry. She wanted to stay in their little house on Spruce Street until she had time to adjust to motherhood.

Felicity was truly happy for her friend. She apologized for not bringing the carriage so she could drive Jessa home. Jessa laughed and told her the walk back down the hill was invigorating.

"You'll see when your time comes," she said with a smirk. "You'll have so much nervous energy you'll have no choice but to walk it off."

Felicity smiled in return, kissed her goodbye, and walked back to where her horse waited. Her time would never come. She would never need to worry about babies and nervous energy.

Forgive me, Lord, she prayed as she rode the horse down the hill. *Bless Jessa and Rodney and their little one. Help me overcome my petty jealousies. I have Belinda. I have a prosperous business where I've finally found my place. I don't need anything else but a closer relationship with You.*

It wouldn't be easy, but she would get over Ned Yates.

When he kissed her, she had felt like her feet would never touch the ground again. Then she talked to Belinda and had cruelly plunged back to earth. She needed to think of her responsibilities; of the needs of others.

The children at Mrs. McClanahan's needed her. Tim needed her to defend him against people like the sheriff and Wes Harrison.

Ned Yates was a grown man. He would get along without her. In time, she would forget him.

She hoped her sister was right.

Chapter Twenty-One

Ned pulled his chair closer to Belinda. He couldn't help but note the differences between the sisters, in appearance as well as temperament.

Not unlike the cloud of spun gold on Felicity's head, Belinda's blond hair was faded and lacked luster. Instead of being brushed to a brilliant sheen, she had combed it against her head in a severe, practical style.

Her blue eyes were nearly the same shade as Felicity's. They didn't shine with a passion for life, but were shrewd and piercing.

She was dressed in the same practical business attire as every other time Ned had seen her; a black serge skirt with a crisp white shirtwaist under a black vest.

He knew his judgments weren't fair. Belinda had been inside with her foot propped up for six weeks. She couldn't be expected to radiate vibrant health.

He pushed his unprofessional assessments aside to get down to business. Mary, the orphan girl who had become Belinda's assistant, had come to his office this morning and summoned him to the Trego house as soon as he could get away.

Ned had fought down the disappointment. An appointment at the house in the middle of the day meant it wasn't likely Felicity would be present.

He hadn't seen her since last week when they drove home from Mrs. McClanahan's. He was sure it had to do with his profession of love. She had looked shocked at the time but not distressed. Now that she had time to think about it, she might have realized she didn't return his feelings to the same intensity. He knew she liked him. Maybe even loved him. But she was right; she had responsibilities, and she might not know how he could fit into them.

Belinda sat at a desk in the center of the large room with her right leg straight out in front of her propped on a plush footstool.

"I'm ready to apply for the patent for my invention Felicity told you about a few weeks ago. We have inventoried the equipment and staff, and determined the most practical spot on the grounds to begin the production process."

She leveled a severe look at him. "You realize confidentiality is our utmost concern. I don't want anyone to know what we're doing until we're already doing it."

Ned looked up from the notebook where he'd been recording her instructions. "I realize you are accustomed to working with Mr. Simonton. I assure you, your privacy is the top priority of everyone at the firm and it always will be."

Her lips flattened as she studied him a long moment. "As long as we understand each other, Mr. Yates. I can't risk my plans or specifications getting into the wrong hands before the patent is registered."

"I wouldn't dream of compromising your invention."

She visibly relaxed. "Good. As I'm sure you can appreciate, I am anxious to complete this process so we can begin production. I began working on this design years ago when I had trouble hitching a horse on my own. Most work implements are designed to fit a man's hands. Not every woman has a man. Or wants one."

She gave him a challenging look, as if daring him to contradict her. He wouldn't dream of it. He doubted many men ever did.

She wagged her finger at him. "You're the only other person in the world who knows of this invention besides Felicity and myself. As you pointed out, you are not Mr. Simonton. It's hard for me to trust people, Mr. Yates. You're new in town. You don't know how things work around here."

Ned stared back at her. "I imagine they work the same as most everywhere else. There isn't an attorney in this country worth his salt who would break your confidence."

"Is there another frontier town with a factory run by women that employs nearly half the town?"

"Not that I'm aware."

"We have Mr. Hughes, of course." Her nose wrinkled in distaste. "He's the only person who believed in Papa in the beginning, so we're beholden to him, if you will. But Felicity and I do well on our own. We don't need anyone else."

Ned had a feeling she wasn't talking only about business. Had Felicity told her about their ride home last week? He doubted it, but from the way she look at him with those shrewd blue eyes, he imagined she could read every thought he ever had.

"Now that you know the direction of Trego Leatherworks, I feel it's only fair I tell you something else. Something you may not realize."

Ned resisted the urge to push his chair back to lengthen the distance between them.

"Anything you tell me will be kept in strictest confidence."

"I know you're in love with my sister."

Ned nearly fell out of the chair. Felicity hadn't told her. He was sure of it. She just knew, and that made it worse.

His mind couldn't fashion a suitable response so he said nothing.

"There's no point in denying it, Mr. Yates," she said evenly. "I saw it in the way you walked through the door a few minutes ago, looking all around, hoping she was here."

Perceptive as well. He wasn't surprised.

"All men fall in love with Felicity. It's been that way since she was little. Old, young, married, confirmed bachelors, it doesn't matter. Men can't resist her.

"She could get whatever she wanted from a man just by smiling in his direction. Don't worry. She isn't loose or anything, God forbid. I'm just telling you this to spare you the inevitable embarrassment that will come from knowing her. I'm sure you've wondered why a woman Felicity's age, with her beauty and wealth, isn't married."

Belinda glanced toward the door and then back, as if she were about to bestow a deep secret. She leaned toward him. "Felicity will never marry a poor man."

Ned's eyebrows slid together. Surely, he'd heard incorrectly. Felicity Trego didn't care about wealth and status. She had the sincerest heart he'd ever encountered. But did he really know her?

"I'm not suggesting you're poor," Belinda went on. "I'm sure you'll build up your practice and earn a comfortable living for yourself in Willow Wood just like Mr. Simonton has done. But comfortable isn't enough for Felicity. Even if it were, it could take years in a town this size. Should you decide to stay, you'll never procure the wealth required to appease my sister."

Ned found his voice. "I'm sorry, Miss Trego. I don't know why you're telling me this. Felicity and I have not made an arrangement about marriage. And if we had, she has never expressed an interest in money."

Her laugh set his teeth on edge.

"Why should she? She has plenty of it. After we begin production on the coupling device, she'll become incredibly wealthy. That's why she will never consider marriage to a man who isn't rich. She couldn't respect a husband who doesn't have as much as she has.

"She is devoted to me and the factory. She would resent a man who needed her financial support. She's told me many times she'll only marry a man wealthy and successful in his own right."

Ned wanted to dispute her words. Belinda wasn't describing the woman he knew. Felicity was honest and kind and hard-working.

She also hadn't spoken to him in a week. Not since the night he told her he loved her. She must know a profession of love was generally followed by a proposal of marriage. Was that why she started avoiding him? She cared enough about him to spare his feelings when she told him the truth.

No. She wasn't that way. He saw her with the children. Her love and compassion were genuine. It wasn't an act.

Yet who knew her better than her own sister? She wouldn't be the first woman who relished in the attention of men, even if she didn't consider them serious suitors.

"Felicity has a generous heart," Belinda continued, as though reading his mind. "But she has expensive tastes. You've seen how she dresses. She seldom wears the same hat and cape twice. You should see her suite upstairs. She has an entire room just for her clothes. One wall is nothing but mirrors. Of course, if I looked like Felicity, I'd love the mirror as well."

She laughed at the absurdity of it. "I've worked hard to rein in her extravagances. I can only do so much. I fear a husband would not be as strong. I almost pity the man Felicity sets her sights on. She's already run two men out of town who couldn't provide the life she demands."

Ned's shoulders slumped, striving unsuccessfully to hide his dismay from Belinda.

"I appreciate your candor, Miss Trego, but I don't think you need to worry about me."

"I hope not, Mr. Yates. Men take one look at my sister and believe they'll be the one to snare her and change her heart. You seem like a discerning fellow. Surely you know a leopard seldom changes its spots."

Chapter Twenty-Two

The next morning Felicity left the house without telling Belinda goodbye.

Last night she had barely spoken to her before retiring to her suite. She knew it wasn't fair to take her frustration out on her sister. Papa's provision had nothing to do with Belinda. It just irked her that it didn't seem to bother her independent-minded sister.

If only Belinda had fallen in love when she was young. Maybe then she wouldn't so easily take the situation in stride. If she had been in love, at least she could understand what Felicity was going through now, and they could commiserate together.

But Belinda didn't understand. Jessa didn't understand.

She couldn't even talk to Ned. How would she begin? She wondered what he'd think if she walked into his office this morning on her way to the factory and told him she loved him, but she couldn't marry because of Papa.

A copy of the will was stored in Mr. Simonton's office. Ned could read it for himself. Then he would understand why she couldn't see him again.

It was cruel to let him think she didn't care for him. He must already be hurt that she had been avoiding him for a week. She owed him an explanation. She couldn't let him think any of this was his fault.

Belinda believed it was better to walk away and let him get the picture on his own. Rip off the scab and let the bleeding cleanse the wound.

It didn't feel better to Felicity. But maybe this way was fair. Ned could find another love and get on with his life. Eventually she would learn to manage her pain, and she could forget Ned Yates had ever stepped into her life.

The morning passed quickly. Fortunately for her broken heart, business was brisk.

One of the machines had broken down at the end of yesterday's shift and an entire line was out of work until the part was repaired.

The advertising department complained about an impending deadline they couldn't meet because of Felicity's changes to the newspaper advertisements at yesterday's meeting. She wouldn't budge. She was in charge now, and they needed to get used to it.

She worked through the noon whistle and barely noticed when it blew the second time signaling everyone back to work. Despite her hunger she kept working. If she stopped, she would have time to think, and that was the last thing she wanted.

By the end of the day, her irritation toward Belinda had cooled. Though she and Belinda would never agree on the fairness of Papa's stipulation, and Belinda would never sympathize with her over losing out on a husband and family, she was nearly the only family Felicity had. She didn't want to cause a rift with her sister that might never be repaired.

Mr. Hughes was still in his office when she left for the day. At the livery, Mark's eyes widened in surprise when she got downstairs at only a little after four to pick up her rig. She thanked him and climbed into the carriage.

The scent of cinnamon and fresh-baked pastries on the crisp air reminded her she had missed lunch and had barely eaten more than a few bites of her dinner last night.

If her nose could be trusted, Mrs. Connagher had baked a batch of her popular apple tarts. She wouldn't get her hopes up, but there might be a few left on the bakery shelf.

Belinda loved them. It would be a nice treat for all of them.

"Good afternoon, Felicity," Mrs. Connagher called out, nearly before Felicity poked her head in the door.

"I was going to drive straight past, but my nose wouldn't allow it. Please tell me you have some apple tarts left."

The woman moved down the glass case that was nearly bare. "You're in luck. I have half a dozen."

"Box them up. Johanna and Rhonda have earned a treat, too, since they've been working so hard to make Belinda comfortable."

And they haven't killed her yet.

"That'll leave one for Mary, Belinda's assistant, and one for Shane."

Mrs. Connagher laughed as she boxed up the desserts. "You've thought of everyone. That's why this town thinks so highly of you. Felicity Trego puts everyone ahead of herself."

Felicity smiled at the compliment, though she didn't feel like it.

The sentiment was meant to make her feel good, but it had the opposite effect. She was tired of putting others first. All she wanted was what most women took for granted. A wedding in church. The reverend pronouncing her forever committed to the man she loved. The one thing she most wanted was the thing she could never have.

"Felicity? Is there something else?"

Felicity blinked. Mrs. Connagher was holding the box out to her, a look of confusion and concern on her face.

"Oh, no, I'm sorry. A lot on my mind these days."

"I would imagine so. Has the doctor told Belinda when she can go back to the factory?"

"Not definitively."

Felicity drew the money out of her reticule. She included a large gratuity the way she always did with the town's merchants since she asked them for a lot when collecting donations for the orphans.

"Probably after the first of the year, though Belinda is holding out hope it will be sooner."

Mrs. Connagher clicked her tongue. "Poor Belinda. She doesn't like anyone telling her what to do, even a broken foot. I wonder what she'll think when she goes back to the factory and realizes the place is running fine without her."

Felicity grimaced. She wondered the same thing. Belinda wanted the factory prosperous, but she liked thinking it couldn't happen without her.

"I'll be happy to relinquish my position," she said. She was eager to put her focus on the advertising department, but not in the way it had been before. Belinda was welcome to everything else.

She took the bakery box and stepped out into a brisk afternoon wind, heavy with the hint of snow. Maurice Levenson, the watchmaker, was washing the windows in front of his shop next door. "Miss Trego, I'm so glad I saw you. I have your papa's watch ready."

Felicity smiled in greeting. She had almost forgotten Papa's pocket watch Belinda had brought in to be fixed at the beginning of the summer. He dried his hands on the black apron around his waist and led her into the store.

"It completely slipped my mind," she said.

"Ah, I am so sorry for the delay. It took a while for me to find the problem. One tiny little spring causing the trouble. It had to come all the way from New York City."

"It's no problem," she assured him. "No one uses the watch anymore. It just sits on the bureau in Papa's room. Belinda and I like to go in and wind it and listen to it tick sometimes."

The small dark-haired man circled the counter and brought out a black velvet box. He opened it and removed the watch on a long chain for Felicity to inspect.

"The watch tells the story of the man, I always say."

Tears filled Felicity's eyes at the sight of it, surprising her. "That is so true. I never feel closer to Papa than I do when I open this watch."

Mr. Levenson waited quietly as she held it up to the light. She watched the second hand tick around the face for a moment before she gingerly closed it and handed it back to him. He boxed the watch and slid it across the counter to her. "I am pleased to have it back in its rightful place. I'm afraid the price is a bit high, but the mechanism..."

"Oh, no, Mr. Levenson. Whatever the cost, it's worth it to Belinda and me."

The bell over the door jangled as two ladies entered. "I will be right with you, ladies," the jeweler's voice was nearly reverent in the quiet of the shop.

Felicity looked over her shoulder. Barbara Milstead, the banker's wife bustled in with Margarite List, whose husband owned half of the Lundy List Railroad and Mining Corporation.

She hadn't seen Barbara since the day she met her and Mr. Milstead on the road and asked them about someone to come to the house to help Belinda.

She hadn't seen Mrs. List since before Ada List left town with a beau, whom she and her husband despised. She pasted an obligatory smile on her face as she turned to face them.

She left the bakery box and jeweler's box on the counter as she kissed their offered cheeks.

"Mrs. Milstead. Mrs. List. How lovely to see you?"

"And you, too, Felicity," Mrs. Milstead crooned.

"Felicity, you're looking as lovely as ever," Mrs. List followed. "How is your dear sister?"

Both women's mouths turned down in concern, though Felicity knew neither cared much for Belinda.

The sentiment went both ways since Belinda couldn't stand their pretentious backsides either. It didn't help that Mr. Milstead was one of Belinda's biggest opponents at the factory and Mr. List didn't have much regard for women who believed they could fill men's roles.

"She's doing well," Felicity trilled. "She's accomplishing quite a bit from home. A broken foot hasn't slowed her down for a minute."

Margarite snorted. Barbara frowned. "Give her our regards, darling," she said.

"I certainly will."

Felicity was tempted to asked Mrs. List about Ada. Like everyone else in Willow Wood, Felicity was bursting with curiosity. If any good news had been received, Ada's mother would be shouting it from the rooftops. Since she hadn't spoken publicly on the subject of Ada in the year since the young woman left town, polite society didn't ask questions but wildly speculated on the matter behind her back.

Instead, Felicity turned back to the watchmaker. He tucked the invoice into the black box and slid it toward Felicity.

"Oh, Margarite, look," Mrs. Milstead squealed.

Felicity turned with Mr. Levenson to see what she was carrying on about.

"Oh, my stars," Mrs. List gushed. "Felicity, have you ever seen anything so lovely?" She grabbed Felicity's elbow and pulled her away from the counter to a glass display along the wall. "Mr. Levenson, is this new? It's exquisite."

Most of Mr. Levenson's business was making and repairing watches and clocks, but he was also the only dealer of fine jewelry in the area. Felicity's eyes widened at the sight of a sapphire and diamond necklace. While she wasn't as excited over the necklace as the older ladies, she had to admit it was the most beautiful piece of jewelry she'd ever seen.

"Try it on, Felicity," Barbara urged. "You simply must. It's made for you."

Not wanting to disappoint his two best customers, Mr. Levenson stepped forward to open the case.

Margarite clasped her hands under her chin. "She's right, Felicity. Those sapphires will bring out your beautiful blue eyes. And the diamonds, oh my. What girl can say no to them?"

Warmth filled Felicity's cheeks at the thought of putting the masterpiece around her neck. She had nice jewelry at home, but nothing like this.

She was almost tempted to buy it. If Belinda and Papa wouldn't let her have a husband, she should at least be allowed to squander the equivalent of a small country's gross domestic product on a bauble.

She didn't have to wonder what Belinda would say. She would have a stroke and fall down dead, then rise up and throttle Felicity.

"I shouldn't," she said weakly, even as Mr. Levenson fastened the necklace around her neck. The weight of it settled into the hollow of her throat.

Margarite thrust a mirror in front of her. Both women squealed in delight.

Felicity gasped aloud herself. "Oh, my."

Mrs. List was right. The sapphires illuminated her eyes and seemed to make them double in size. She couldn't tell if the diamonds brought out the flush in her cheeks or the flush was from simply wearing it.

Her eyes found the jeweler's in the mirror. "It is incredible, Mr. Levenson. Can you imagine Reverend Sanders' face if I wore this into church Sunday morning?"

The older women laughed. "You would certainly inspire a lengthy sermon on vanity."

Felicity laughed. She pulled the loose tendrils of pale hair away from her face and turned this way and that to admire her reflection. "Oh, my." There were no other words to say. "Oh, my."

She couldn't keep from laughing as Barbara and Margarite applauded.

"I couldn't. It's too much."

"Nonsense," Margarite insisted. "Your slim neck is the perfect display for such a creation. Imagine if you should ever meet the queen."

Felicity laughed out loud. "The queen? In Willow Wood?"

"One never knows." Barbara elbowed Margarite, and they all laughed again.

Felicity blushed at the attention. If felt nice to think of something besides not having Ned in her life. She took one last long look at the necklace. "You should hire these two as salesladies, Mr. Levenson. They've almost convinced me."

He stepped forward to unclasp the necklace and replace it in the case.

The older ladies groaned. "Are you sure, Felicity? There's not another neck in the state worthy of such a necklace."

"I'm sure it will find a home. I really would have no place to wear it."

"What about a wedding?" Barbara exclaimed.

Margarite grabbed her arm. "Oh, Felicity, of course. You'll be the most beautiful bride in Willow Wood."

The color drained from Felicity's face. She stepped away from the mirror and nearly tripped over Mr. Levenson's foot. "I...um...I'm not..."

She hurried around the women and grabbed the bakery box and jeweler's box off the counter.

"Thank you, Mr. Levenson. I...um...have to go. Ladies." She tipped her head at them and practically ran out of the shop.

Chapter Twenty-Three

Ned couldn't get Belinda Trego's words out of his head. Felicity had never given him any indication she was only interested in wealth. He couldn't imagine her seeking out a rich husband. To think she needed a strong man to rein in her reckless spending was even more ludicrous.

It was clear Belinda didn't trust him. She had accurately deduced he was in love with Felicity. It was the only logical reason she would bring up Felicity's resolve to marry a man of wealth. But was it true?

He didn't typically take a person's word as truth without examining the evidence. After his anger at Belinda cooled, he considered what he knew about Felicity.

She was a wealthy, intelligent woman. It made sense that she would seek a man who shared the same values and goals as she did.

She was always impeccably dressed, even the day they went to the orphanage to fix the roof when she knew she would be in a steamy kitchen all day.

She wasn't reticent about spending money on the children and other charitable causes. As far as he could see, she wasn't shy about spending money on anything she wanted. Did that mean she would only marry a rich man? Like Belinda said, she had enough of her own if she chose to support every orphan in Idaho.

"I try to rein in her extravagances, but I can only do so much."

Did Felicity have reckless, extravagant tastes, and Ned had been too blinded by her beauty to notice?

Father hadn't seen those traits in Mother either, or if he had, he didn't act upon them until it was too late.

The Yateses didn't argue often, but when they did it was over money and how Mother couldn't control her spending. Ned would always believe her lavish tastes had driven a good man to an early grave.

So far, he only had Belinda's word on Felicity's attitude about money. He needed to talk to her.

He had wanted to talk to her since last week when he had kissed her. He loved her before the kiss.

After the kiss, he couldn't imagine not waking up next to her every morning. In fact, he spent far too much time thinking of that very thing. Kissing her. Touching her. Knowing every inch of her.

He shook his head to dispel the salacious thoughts. He loved her, and he wanted her in his life the way the Lord intended. But he couldn't watch a wife destroy his spirit and health the way Mother had done to Father. He had to know the truth.

He slid the folder containing a farmer's land deeds into the filing cabinet. The paperwork had kept him busy most of the afternoon. Now that he was finished, all he could think of was Felicity.

He gathered his briefcase and coat and headed out the door. With the threat of snow in the air, he had sent Catherine home an hour ago. Perhaps he could catch Felicity before she left her office at the factory. He couldn't talk to her at her house with Belinda standing guard.

A stiff wind grabbed at his coattails as he locked the office door behind him. He had only taken a few steps when he spotted Felicity's carriage and horse down the street in front of the bakery.

He picked up his pace. He hoped she had time for a cup of coffee or tea in the café or even dinner at the hotel's restaurant. Not only did he want to ask about what Belinda had told him, he wanted to see her again, touch her hand, hear her voice. His long, lonely evening suddenly looked promising.

He ducked his head under the awning and glanced inside the bakery window. It was empty except for the store owner cleaning up in the back. He looked around. If Felicity didn't step out of a store soon, he'd wait next to her carriage.

Familiar feminine laughter sounded next door. Ned moved to the watchmaker's window.

He smiled in relief. He could just see Felicity's profile and the top of her head past two older ladies blocking his view.

He immediately recognized them. Margarite List and Barbara Milstead, wives of two of the most powerful men in Willow Wood. The jeweler stood behind the women, and all of them were focused on something in the mirror.

Mrs. Milstead stepped aside, and Felicity came into full view. She wore a large jewel necklace that winked in the light. Even from across the store, Ned could tell the diamonds and blue stones—sapphires, he assumed—were authentic.

The only thing inside the shop that outshone the necklace was Felicity. Her eyes sparkled and her face glowed as she laughed and admired her reflection in the mirror.

She swept her hair up off her neck and preened for the other women. Ned couldn't make out what they were saying, but it was obvious the ladies were oohing and ahhing over how beautiful the necklace looked on her.

They weren't wrong.

Ned backed away from the window and off the sidewalk, nearly tripping over his own feet.

If he had a horse, he would ride as far and as fast out of town as he could. He hadn't ridden in nearly a year. Not even Mr. Simonton knew he'd been forced to sell the family's stock after Mother's death to pay the creditors.

He had sold everything. The house. The furnishings. Their clothes. Mother's piano. It all had to go, and still debt remained.

His adopted sisters had accused him of taking advantage of their mother's grief in the year following Father's death. Ned didn't waste his breath trying to convince them there had been nothing left to take advantage of.

If they had taken a moment to stop yelling at him and look around, they would've realized the truth.

Everything was gone. All the money Father had worked so hard to earn had run through Mother's hands. Her spendthrift habits hadn't begun during the last few years. His sisters weren't stupid. They must've recognized she had spent Father into the poorhouse.

Blinded by their grief and desire to find someone to blame for why no fortune remained, they chose Ned.

Felicity's flushed face admiring the necklace around her neck reminded him of his own helplessness over what eventually tore his parents apart.

He remembered the day he came home from the university. In his jacket pocket, he carried a letter from the admissions office. Swallowing his sense of betrayal since the letter was addressed to his father, he had carefully slit the seal and opened the letter before he got home.

If Father asked why the letter opened so easily, Ned would tell him the truth. He wasn't a child. It was his problem too. He figured, though, Father would be so distraught over the contents, he would forget to be angry.

The letter read that the family owed for three quarters of tuition. If the sum wasn't paid immediately, Ned would not return to school in the fall, and the debt would be sent to a collections' agency.

Ned never forgot the defeat on Father's face as he read the letter. His free hand swept through his thinning hair as realization of the situation dawned. He dropped the letter to the desk and stared at it as if trying to make sense of the words.

He was still sitting there, looking stunned and wounded, when Ned slipped from the room.

He spent that summer applying for grants and writing scholarship essays without his parents' knowledge. They had already done so much for him. He didn't want to see defeat so deeply etched on Father's face again.

He couldn't stop wondering how Father allowed Mother's spending to get so out of hand. Everyone knew she loved to shop. She always came home with new hats and dresses and hairpieces.

Father would kindly, gently—too gently as far as Ned was concerned since nothing ever changed—tell her they could no longer afford for her to shop with such abandon.

Hadn't she just bought a new dress? Did she really need a new hat for church or a simple outing when she had so many things in her closets?

Each time she dismissed his concerns and called him a skinflint. She couldn't understand why he didn't want her to enjoy the trappings of wealth like other men's wives. He worked hard. Wasn't it so his family could have nice things?

The fissure between them became a yawning divide. Father stood up to her less and less.

Mother didn't only spend money on her own wants. She was generous to a fault. She hosted a lavish dinner for the congregants of their church every Christmas with a special gift for each child. She financed arts shows at the girls' schools and was a member of the historical guild, which came with hefty membership fees.

Arguments occurred less often as Father gave up the fight, and Mother refused to concede an inch.

As Ned watched the lines of worry march across Father's face and the silver crowd out the brown on his head, he determined he would not be dismissed by a wife unwilling to be a helpmeet and respect his concerns.

Six weeks after Ned became an associate at his first firm in Omaha, Father passed away, and the gravity of the family's financial situation came to light to the community.

Making sense of the situation fell on Ned. Mother gave in to her grief and finally admitted her fault in the matter. It was too late.

Ned began selling everything he could to pay the family's creditors and taxes. The extra buggy and horses were the first to go, along with extraneous household staff.

Ned felt like the boy holding back the dam with his finger. After his mother's death a short ten months later, he barely had enough money for train fare to Willow Wood where Mr. Simonton had offered him a job.

He had stretched the truth some when he told Felicity he worked long hours because he didn't have anything to do at the boardinghouse.

In truth, he could barely afford to support himself. Even Mr. Simonton didn't know how financially strapped he was.

Eventually he would be in a position to live a comfortable life in Willow Wood. It would not be enough to suit a woman like Felicity who wore diamonds and owned a suite of rooms full of clothes and mirrors.

He could not provide any woman with more than a simple living until the remainder of his family's debts were paid off.

Nor could he live with a woman who saw him as a skinflint. He couldn't marry a woman who would grow to resent his tight-fisted ways, as he grew to resent her disrespect for him.

He knew Felicity had a loving, sincere heart. She truly cared for the orphans at Mrs. McClanahan's. Even if her reckless spending was motivated by love for needy children instead of herself, Ned wouldn't stand aside while she spent him into the poorhouse or caused him the grief his mother caused Father.

He thought of her soft lips and gentle manner. Had he misinterpreted what he saw in the jeweler's window? She seemed so genuine. Her heart was as big as any person's he'd ever met. He knew she loved the Lord and she loved those kids.

Mother had loved too. She loved Father and she loved Ned, the orphan boy she brought into her home and raised as her own.

At the same time, she loved money and the pleasures it bought. Maybe there was no woman who would love Ned the way he needed.

For the rest of the night he prayed for grace and strength to face life without the woman he loved.

Chapter Twenty-Four

Felicity closed the door a little louder than she intended as she fled the watchmaker's shop.

She glanced around to see if anyone on the street had noticed her less than graceful exit. What must Mrs. List and Mrs. Milstead think? They had to realize the casual comment about wearing the necklace to her wedding had hurt her feelings.

She pictured them exchanging looks of pity and curiosity, speculating over who in town had broken her heart and jaded her against marriage.

The question would keep their tongues wagging for, well, forever as they watched her grow into a faded, sad, reclusive spinster. She was stuck in Willow Wood and the factory with no hope for a husband and family.

She hurried toward the carriage, her gaze fixed straight ahead. Just as she clasped the tail of her long coat to climb aboard, she saw someone watching her out of the corner of her eye. Her heart leaped.

Ned.

Despite her determination to get him out of her head and her heart, the despair of a few moments ago dissipated into the cold air. She smiled and started toward him. He stood stock still in the center of the street as if looking for an escape. Her footsteps faltered. Did he wish to avoid her?

After a moment he started her way.

"Good afternoon, counselor."

He tipped his hat. "Miss Trego."

Even though she knew they could never be more than friends, she couldn't suppress the excitement of being close to him. "Did you get out of the office early?" she asked.

He nodded. "Looks like you did too."

"And just in time. I nabbed the last of Mrs. Connagher's apple tarts."

Instead of looking at her, his gaze fixed on the watchmaker's box and the bakery box in her hands. She expected him to offer to carry them to the carriage. He didn't.

"I'm sorry I didn't get a chance to see you this week," she said.

She wanted to tell him she hadn't been able to think of anything but his kiss. Reliving that night wasn't fair to either of them, and she didn't have the nerve to speak about it anyway.

She shifted the bulky bakery box to her other arm. "Could I give you a ride to the boardinghouse?"

"No, thank you. I have another stop I need to make." He looked past her and then back to the boxes. "I should go. I...I'm running late."

"Oh, of course. I'm sorry. Have a good evening."

"You too, Felicity." He tipped his hat and hurried off.

Felicity stood in the middle of the street watching after him for a few moments until she realized how pitiful and desperate she must look to Mrs. List or Mrs. Milstead if they were watching from Mr. Levenson's shop.

Without another glance in Ned's direction, she strode purposefully to her carriage and headed home.

•••

"The patent forms should be ready today," Belinda reminded Felicity. "Stop and pick them up on your way home and we can sign them and mail them out first thing Monday morning."

It had been a week since Felicity had seen Ned on the street outside Mr. Levenson's shop.

She had vowed to avoid him, and now it looked like he was avoiding her.

She had expected him to come up with an excuse to stop at her office to see her. He never came. It had been nearly two weeks since he told her he loved her. They hadn't had a real conversation since. Every night the noose around her heart pulled tighter and tighter.

"Aren't you afraid I'll run into Mr. Yates?" she asked caustically. "Why not have Mary pick them up?"

Belinda removed her reading glasses and glared at her. An ivory handled cane leaned against the desk beside her. She still sat with her foot propped up, but she was able to take a few mincing steps around the room if she needed something from a filing cabinet.

She wasn't as dependent on Mary or the household staff as she had been. Any day Felicity expected to see her standing at the door ready to walk out. If not for the long set of stone stairs outside the factory, she would probably already be back behind her desk.

"These papers are too sensitive for Mary or anyone else to handle. Besides you and me, the only other people who know anything about my invention are inside that law office. I plan to keep it that way."

Felicity slid the forms she and Belinda had worked on last night into her satchel. Belinda reached out and touched her hand.

"I'm not worried about Mr. Yates, Sister. I'm worried about you."

Felicity stiffened. She hadn't spoken much to Belinda in the last week either. She wasn't exactly mad. She just didn't have anything to say.

"Well, stop worrying. I'm fine."

Belinda tightened her hold on her arm. "You don't sound fine. You haven't been yourself the last few weeks. I feel it's the fault of that Mr. Yates. I knew this would happen. *Papa* knew it would happen. It's why he never wanted us to complicate our lives with matters of the heart. Now you've gone and fallen in love, and you're jeopardizing what we're building here."

Felicity snatched her arm away and stepped out of reach.

"I'm not jeopardizing your precious company. I go to that office every day. I do every blasted thing you tell me to do. You haven't heard any complaints, have you? The machines are still humming. Orders are being filled. Money is piling up at the bank, though I don't know what good it will ever do either of us."

Belinda's eyes went wide in alarm. Felicity didn't care. She grabbed the satchel off the desk and secured the double latches with two angry clicks.

"Felicity, please," Belinda said gently. "I didn't mean to offend you. I always look forward to a smile from you to begin our day. I fear Mr. Yates has hurt you."

"Ned isn't the one who hurt me," Felicity snapped, intentionally using his first name.

Belinda's gaze turned suspicious. "Have you spoken to him lately?"

"No," Felicity admitted before she could stop herself. She didn't want Belinda to know she had won. Tears welled in her eyes. She turned away so Belinda wouldn't see. "I haven't seen him in a week. It's been even longer since we've spoken."

Belinda sighed heavily.

Felicity spun around. "What's that supposed to mean?"

"I didn't say anything."

"No, but you were thinking something."

Belinda looked like she was about to cry. "I'm so sorry this happened to you. You are such a gentle, compassionate person. You deserve better than to be treated like this."

"What are you saying?"

Belinda sighed again. "Mr. Yates works at the law office. He has access to all our files, including Papa's will. He's probably discovered if he pursues you, you will be left penniless. I'm sure he cares deeply for you. He may even love you. Who wouldn't? But to marry a penniless girl when he has no money of his own. He's deeply in debt, Felicity."

"How do you know?"

"Mr. Simonton told me last year when he brought Mr. Yates into the firm. Oh, Mr. Yates tried to hide it. He's ashamed, I'm sure. His family made some reckless business decisions. I believe it's the real reason he left Omaha. To take a wife who has no money of her own while he's living in a boardinghouse would be beyond irresponsible." She shuddered.

"I know it doesn't feel like it now, but it's better that it happened this way, before you fall hopelessly in love with each other. It will spare you both grief down the road."

Felicity didn't feel spared. All she wanted to do was run back upstairs to her suite and never come back down.

Chapter Twenty-Five

All day Felicity dreaded stopping at the firm to pick up the patent application.

She had thought about doing it at lunch but couldn't work up the nerve. She thought about ignoring Belinda's concern for privacy and sending a lackey from the office.

Belinda would be furious if there was even a possibility someone found out about the patent before it was filed with the government. Felicity couldn't send a lackey, even if she wasn't worried about incurring Belinda's wrath. This was her job. She would do it. She couldn't put off seeing Ned another minute.

She never dreamed he was the kind of man to seek a wife based on her financial situation. It all made sense now, though, since Belinda brought it up.

He still lived in the boardinghouse after a year of working for Mr. Simonton. She didn't figure associate attorneys earned much money while building their practices, but they usually made enough for a proper roof over their heads.

If she got the chance, she would tell him she loved him. She didn't care if he was poor. And he shouldn't care that she would become so. She didn't care if they had to live in a shed behind the boardinghouse. If Belinda wouldn't give her a job as a seamstress or a clerk at the factory, she would wash sheets for Mrs. Crothers or clean stables at Mr. Waugh's livery. Whatever it took as long as they could be together.

She knew she'd never have the nerve to say any of it.

She left her office a little early to make sure she didn't miss Ned before he left for the day. Outside the law office door, she stopped herself just in time before tilting her hat at a becoming angle and pinching her cheeks for color even though the cool evening air had surely taken care of it for her.

She wouldn't make the effort for a man who couldn't even tell her the truth. She took a steadying breath and pushed her way inside.

"Good evening, Felicity," Catherine said. "My, it's getting cold out there. Can I fix you a cup of coffee?"

Felicity took another deep breath so Catherine wouldn't notice her nervousness. "No, thank you. I only have time to pick up the paperwork and get home. You're right. It's quite cold."

Catherine circled her desk and headed to the door that led to the offices. "Felicity Trego is here," she said into the hallway.

The door opened all the way and Vance Simonton stepped out. "Felicity, how good to see you."

Felicity blinked in surprise. "Mr. Simonton, you're back. It's good to see you, too, sir."

He rested one hand on his round stomach pushing at the buttons on his vest and motioned her through the door.

"Come on back. I'm afraid Mr. Yates is out of the office, but he explained your situation with me. I'm quite excited for you and Belinda. Going to set the industry on its ear, eh?"

Felicity chuckled without humor. "That's the plan, sir."

Part of her was relieved she wouldn't have to face Ned, but the bigger part could barely contain her disappointment. Was his absence from the office intentional? Had she misread his true nature all along?

Mr. Simonton led her into his posh inner office. "I trust Mr. Yates has taken good care of you."

"Yes, sir. Very...good." She cleared her throat. "Did you have a nice visit to Meridian?"

"Yes, yes. It was nice to get away. The missus hasn't seen her family in years. We had only planned to stay a few weeks, but it turned into a few months. It worked out well having Ned here to fill in for me. I see you and Belinda have kept him busy with this patent business. Your sister certainly isn't letting any grass grow under her while she recovers."

"No, sir."

Mr. Simonton picked up a sheaf of papers from his desk. "I have your application right here. Everything is ready for your signatures."

He indicated the correct spots, though Felicity could've found them herself now that she knew what was going on within the company.

"I always knew you ladies could carry the torch lit by your father. He would be proud of you for what you've done with this patent."

"It's Belinda's invention," she said.

He looked startled. "Not according to Mr. Yates."

Felicity was surprised Ned had even mentioned her to his boss. "I helped with some of the details and specifications, but this has been simmering in Belinda's head for years."

"I'm not surprised, really. Belinda is a businesswoman through and through. You've gained your own reputation around town since I've been gone. Your papa would be proud of how you managed the factory in Belinda's stead."

She started to minimize her role, then stopped. She had worked hard over the last two months and learned a lot. She made her own innovations in the advertising department. A lot more was going to change after Belinda returned to work.

"Thank you, sir."

Mr. Simonton slid the document into a linen envelope and handed it to her. "I hope Ned has been of assistance throughout this complicated process. Uncle Sam doesn't make things easy."

"No, sir. I mean, yes, sir. Ned has been very—helpful."

Mr. Simonton's chair groaned as he sank into the leather cushions. "He's a fine young man. I trust you've gotten to know him."

Felicity wasn't sure what he was getting at. "Yes, sir."

"I figured you would." He motioned her into the chair across from his desk.

Felicity preferred to leave. Especially now that the conversation had veered to someone she'd rather not discuss. Decorum dictated she accept his invitation. She perched on the edge of the chair and waited.

Mr. Simonton clasped his hands on top of his polished desk. "Your papa had great faith in you and Belinda. He told me so many times. He knew you would do right by the company. If he could see it now... Well, you girls—er, I'm sorry, you ladies, have outdone anything he ever dreamed of. His only regret, I'm sure, it that neither of you have married."

Felicity froze. "Excuse me."

Mr. Simonton chuckled. "He told me many times how he looked forward to grandchildren. He was disappointed when Belinda turned down her young man's proposal. I suppose she was more interested in learning the business than romance."

"Wait a minute. What?" Felicity interrupted, forgetting her manners. "Someone proposed to Belinda?"

Mr. Simonton didn't seem to notice her confusion. "We fathers always hope to see our daughters happily married. And we all want grandchildren." He chuckled. "As many as possible. But you young people have your own ideas, even if we think we know best."

Felicity still wasn't sure her ears were working properly. "Papa was disappointed that Belinda didn't accept her young man's proposal?"

Mr. Simonton finally noticed her confusion. "Naturally. He hoped you both would eventually marry."

"He might've wanted that before he got sick," she said.

He frowned. "I don't know about that. I'll never forget one of our last conversations. He made me promise I would encourage both of you to marry and live your own lives. You were still a child at the time, but he didn't want either of you to waste your youth in that factory."

He sighed. "I didn't think it was my place. You both seemed content, and I didn't feel it was my business to tell you how to live."

Content? She wasn't content. She was miserable.

He smiled and cocked a bushy, gray eyebrow at her. "I must admit when I met Mr. Yates, I thought to myself, 'Now isn't that a fine young man for Felicity Trego'. I'm not much for playing matchmaker. I believe the best way for young people to find love is to let nature take its course."

Felicity shook her head. "Love? But...what about the will? What about his fear that a son-in-law would try to take over the company?"

He narrowed his eyes and studied her as if looking at a stranger. "I don't remember your papa ever worrying about something like that. He trusted you both to choose men who would honor you and honor what you had built."

Felicity stared. That wasn't right. It couldn't be.

Mr. Simonton stared back. "I'm sorry if I offended you by mentioning Ned. I suppose I stuck my nose into your business after all."

"No, sir, it...it isn't that. It's just..." She stood and smoothed the front of her dress. "I...uh...really must go. Thank you for your help with the patent."

She stepped into the hallway and closed the door behind her. She leaned against the wall and struggled to draw a complete breath.

What had happened? She was tempted to go back into the office and ask Mr. Simonton to repeat everything he just said. Surely, she had misunderstood.

If Papa wanted her and Belinda to marry, he wouldn't have put the stipulation in his will. Mr. Simonton must know every detail and every declaration. Why wasn't he aware of the most important one? Had he forgotten? Or was there another explanation?

She had to see the will for herself. She couldn't go back and ask Mr. Simonton. He would think her a fool for not knowing Papa's wishes for her and Belinda. But there was a place to read the will without bothering Mr. Simonton.

Without a word to Catherine, she practically ran out to the street and climbed into her carriage. She drove as fast as she dared back to the factory.

She didn't bother driving around the building to the livery. She tied the horse to the railing that led to the offices and ran up the staircase.

Most of the offices were empty. The few open doors revealed staff preparing to leave for the day. She ignored them all.

She arrived at Belinda's office breathless and shaking. It took several attempts to locate the correct key on her ring and insert it into the lock. Finally, the lock clicked free and she pushed the door open.

It took another ten frustrating minutes to find the filing cabinet keys in Belinda's desk. Her hands shook as she tried to grasp the idea that no marrying stipulation existed in Papa's will. It wasn't possible.

She had nearly decided to bust her way into the filing cabinets with her bare hands when her fingers closed around the correct key. She went straight to the cabinet that held Belinda's personal papers. As she sifted through files, some slid out of the folders and fell to the floor. She didn't bother to pick them up.

Finally, she found what she was looking for. She sank into Belinda's chair and began to read. The lump in her stomach grew with each line. The legal jargon made for slow reading, but she understood enough to know what she was looking for wasn't there. As she turned over the last page, the words blurred in front of her.

It wasn't there.

No stipulation from a distrusting father forbidding her or Belinda from marrying existed.

Belinda had lied. Her entire life had been a lie.

Chapter Twenty-Six

Felicity stopped the carriage and stared at her house. She had never known a life outside these walls.

At nineteen, she left home for two years to attend the university in Boise. Belinda had tried to get her to go farther east, like New York or Boston where she had studied, but Felicity couldn't think of a reason to go so far.

At the university, she met women from other well-off families all over the west, some of whom she still wrote to today. The experience had been exciting, but more than anything, it was something to put behind her.

She had loved her courses in Literature and Philosophy, though she knew she would use neither once she got home. She studied homemaking and basic medicine and other classes women were required to take in order to someday become wives and homemakers.

The whole time she felt like a fraud. She loved learning to cook and entertain, but again, she knew she wouldn't use her new skills in Willow Wood.

Johanna did all their cooking, and if she or Belinda threw a party, the staff saw to the details. The other young women had been sent to school to prepare for marriage. Felicity went because Belinda strong-armed her into it.

Now she realized Belinda had strong-armed her into nearly every decision she ever made.

Though she knew Papa hadn't put the stifling requirements into his will, she didn't feel free. If anything, her burden was heavier than before. Her mind reeled. She wanted to run inside and confront Belinda.

How had she lied all these years? Why?

Clyde, her chestnut horse, wagged his head impatiently. He smelled home and knew a warm stable and hardy meal awaited him.

Felicity snapped out of her reverie and allowed him to pull the carriage into the drive. Shane came out of the barn to unharness the horse, but Felicity waved him away. She would take care of the gelding herself. She wasn't ready to face Belinda. She needed more time to herself.

She wasn't sure what she would say to her sister. She didn't want to react emotionally or irrationally. She wanted to think and pray about how to handle the situation.

Any time she jumped headlong into a situation, especially one with her sister, it ended badly.

She imagined what Belinda would say. The excuses she would make. She would rationalize her lies and only make Felicity angrier. She didn't want to hear excuses today.

"Mama left an hour ago," Shane told her as he closed the stable windows and made sure the trough was full of fresh water for Clyde and the other horses before he left for the night. "She said we could get more snow. Dinner's on the stove for you."

Johanna always left dinner on the stove. Felicity knew the boy was talking to give her time to tell him what was bothering her if she chose. She looked up at him. She couldn't call him a boy anymore. He was eighteen. Or maybe nineteen. She couldn't remember his last birthday. She couldn't remember a lot of things tonight.

"Thank you, Shane. You can go home now. I'm sorry I've been getting in later and later every evening and forcing you to wait on me."

"It's no problem, Miss Felicity. I use the time to read." He blushed pink at her surprised look.

"Miss Belinda loaned me some books. She's been reading with me some during the day when neither of us have much else to do."

Felicity was shocked. As far as she knew, Belinda was barely aware Shane existed. She must've been very bored stuck in the house day after day to bother helping him with anything. "What are you studying?"

He looked uncomfortable to talk about himself. "As you know, I've always been interested in horses. Other livestock, too. I've begun to notice similar health issues with your stock and the neighbors' horses I tend. Not that any of them are sick. I just pay attention to potential problems with their feet and knees and eyes. I figure the more I learn, the better I can care for them."

Felicity stopped brushing Clyde. "I'm impressed. I must confess I don't usually notice any of those things."

He stepped closer, his eyes bright with excitement.

"That's because you have me to do it for you. I know I have a lot to learn. I don't want to be a stable boy forever. Not that I mind working here for you and your sister. I appreciate the opportunity and all I've learned."

She hid a small smile as she went back to brushing the horse. "Of course."

Emboldened, he went on. "I'd like to manage one of the big farms someday. Or start a ranch. But I don't have any experience. I don't even have a horse. I want to learn, though. I'm not afraid to study hard. Mama can't afford to send me to school, but Miss Belinda has been very encouraging the last few weeks."

Felicity finished her job and rested one hand on Clyde's hip. "That's very admirable, Shane. Don't let your lack of education stop you from going after what you want. Equine care is a noble pursuit, as is using your free time here to study the subject."

"I haven't shirked my duties," he assured her.

"I never thought you did." She saw the young man as she never had before. He had started working at the stables when he was only six or seven with simple jobs. Slowly his responsibilities grew.

"Anything I can do to help you as you pursue your education, please let me know. Belinda too," she added.

She could tell from the look on his face, talking about it had encouraged him. "I will, Miss Felicity. Thank you."

"You go home, Shane. I'll see you in the morning. I'll close up the stable."

She watched him leave, then turned back to her work. She felt a little better after talking with him about his dreams and goals instead of fixating on her own problems. Now everything came rushing back.

The copy of Papa's will she had taken from Belinda's office was still in her satchel. Since seeing the words for herself, she had imagined a hundred ways to confront her sister.

No matter what she said, Belinda would have a perfectly logical reason to legitimize it. She would say she only wanted to protect Felicity. In reality, she was protecting the company. Always the factory.

Belinda may love Felicity, but her pride and Trego Leatherworks mattered more.

Ned obviously didn't believe she would be penniless if she married. Something had happened to scare him away. She remembered the trapped look in his face when she saw him outside Mr. Levenson's watch and jewelry shop. He couldn't get away from her quickly enough.

Why?

If her financial situation had nothing to do with his sudden loss of interest, there had to be another reason he no longer loved her.

Did anyone? Had anyone ever loved her?

She thought of some of the girls at school who only came to visit so they could see inside her fancy house and try on her fancy dresses. No one loved her for her. Not even Papa. She had idolized him. Had he loved her only for the way she looked up to him and for the unconditional love she bestowed on him?

She didn't want to give into self-pity. She didn't want to go inside and look at her sister's face either.

A worn Stetson hat sat on the tack box. She unpinned the hat she had worn to work and set it carefully on the tack box. She plopped the Stetson on her head.

She hefted a saddle off the rail and saddled her favorite riding mare. She looped the satchel with the patent and Papa's will over her shoulder and let it hang down her back. She rode out of the stable. She didn't bother to close the door behind her.

Chapter Twenty-Seven

Mrs. McClanahan set a cup of tea on the table in front of Felicity and sat down opposite her.

Felicity had been sitting in the kitchen for twenty minutes. The children showed her papers they'd done in school. Lucy told her about winning the school spelling bee and invited her to the awards ceremony next week.

Finally, Mrs. McClanahan shooed them out of the kitchen and freshened Felicity's tea. She rested her chin in her hand.

"All right. It's dark outside. You've worked all day. You look like you're about to shatter into a thousand pieces. Tell me why you're here."

Felicity took a tentative sip from her cup "I don't know where to begin. I guess I'm feeling sorry for myself and want someone to join me."

Mrs. McClanahan tilted her head. "I don't believe that. You're not the type. But something's on your mind. Spill it."

Felicity laughed. "Because you have other things to do?"

Mrs. McClanahan looked around the cluttered kitchen. The dinner dishes had been washed and put away, but school books littered the counter, and skillets for tomorrow's breakfast were waiting on the stove.

"I do have nine children to get ready for bed and another day. I want to spend some time with my Lord before I retire. But I'm not too busy to listen to a friend."

Felicity dug at a broken fingernail. She never had unkept nails before Belinda's accident. Now she was too busy to keep them trimmed and filed, and they were a mess.

"I wonder if anyone will ever love me for me. Just plain old Felicity without the Trego tacked on the end."

Mrs. McClanahan's face softened. "Honey, why would you say that? You have plenty of people in your life who love you."

Felicity shook her head. "I thought so, too, but now I'm not so sure. I found out today my sister has lied to me my entire life. It isn't just the lie I can't grasp but the reason behind it."

"Which is?"

"She wants to control me. She wants me to live the life she wants." She exhaled.

She was suddenly very weary. If Mrs. McClanahan had a spare couch or corner, she was tempted to ask to spend the night.

"Last week Ned told me he loved me."

Mrs. McClanahan reached across the table and patted her arm. "I knew it. It was written all over his face."

Felicity shook her head as tears threatened. "I'm not sure what Belinda told him, or what he assumed, but he hasn't spoken to me since. If he heard something terrible about me, no matter how terrible, shouldn't he seek me out and ask for my side of the story? That's what I would do if I heard a rumor or if I got a thought in my head all on my own. Especially if I loved the person. Why didn't he do that?"

"I don't know, honey. It could all be a big misunderstanding."

"Or it could be he doesn't really love me. Not a true, selfless love that lasts forever."

She inserted her finger in the handle of the teacup but changed her mind and didn't drink.

"That's why I think no one loves me the way I need them to. Belinda loves me because she can keep me under her thumb. I've been her obedient little lap dog all my life. I do whatever she tells me to do. I sit at home with her every night and we read together or do needlepoint.

That might be enough of a life for her, but it isn't enough for me. I want a family. A husband."

"It's only natural," Mrs. McClanahan said.

"It isn't what Belinda wants. She's greedy. She doesn't want to share me with anyone, and she doesn't want to share our money. I think she cares more about the money than she does me.

"She always said we couldn't marry because our husbands would try to take the company from us. I believe it's more than that. If we married, we would eventually have children. Her wealth would fracture. She would have to share what she has with nieces and nephews and in-laws and whoever else might worm their way into our lives."

She ran her finger around the rim of the teacup. "The fewer people in Belinda's life, the less likely someone will ask something of her. Challenge her position. All she had to do was continue her lie to me. I'm so gullible, I made it easy for her.

"As for Ned, I don't know what happened to him. He's avoided me like the plague. Maybe he thinks I'm too rich. Or too poor. All I know is nobody loves me for me. Even the children here love me because I bring barrels of pickles and sugar for pies. Will anyone ever love me for what I am right now? Not for what I can do for them or what role I can fill?"

She couldn't go on. Mrs. McClanahan's eyes filled with tears. The sight of them was her undoing. She burst into tears. Mrs. McClanahan circled the table and gathered her into her arms.

"Honey, honey," she crooned in Felicity's ear. "Even if all that were true, which I'll never believe, you are not alone. There is one who loves you just as you are right this minute. God will never leave you or love you any less, whether you're rich or poor."

Felicity sniffed and tried to pull herself together. "I know. I'm sorry. I don't want to feel sorry for myself, but that's exactly what I'm doing."

Mrs. McClanahan found a faded handkerchief in a stack of freshly washed laundry and pressed it into Felicity's hand. "I've never met your sister, but I'm sure she loves you more than she loves her own self.

"As far as Ned, well, I just don't believe he only cares about what you can do for him. That young man has a heart of gold. After how he's shown my boys what a real man is like..."

She shook her head. "No, I refuse to believe he's been using you. I know love when I see it, and, girl, that boy has it bad for you."

Felicity smiled under the handkerchief. "I want to believe you. I want to remember the look on his face when he told me—"

Pounding sounded at the front door. Both women gasped in surprise. Hope rose in

Felicity's chest. Was it possible? Had Ned gone to the house to talk to her, and when Belinda told him she hadn't come home, he guessed she was here?

One of the children opened the front door. "Mum!" Frannie cried.

They leaped out of their chairs. Heavy footsteps stomped in their direction. Before either could react, the sheriff's frame filled the doorway. Over his shoulder, Felicity saw Wes Harrison. He pushed past the sheriff.

"You!" he shouted, pointing at Felicity. "I should've known you'd be here. See, Sheriff. That proves it. Arrest her and then find that little thief."

Mrs. McClanahan recovered first. "Who are you calling a thief? What's the meaning of this, Sheriff? I demand an explanation."

The sheriff looked as irate as Mr. Harrison. "We're looking for Tim. Where is he? He's under arrest."

Chapter Twenty-Eight

Wes looked around the kitchen. "Where is he? I know you're hiding him. Tim! Come out, boy, and face the music."

Mrs. McClanahan pushed past Felicity and stood directly in front of the sheriff. "You better get him out of here, Sheriff. No one comes into my house shouting and carrying on. His big mouth is scaring the children. This isn't right and you know it."

Felicity looked at her in disbelief and then at the sheriff. He looked grim. She knew it was serious. She needed Ned.

"What is it you're accusing Tim of stealing?"

Wes sneered. "I knew he was trouble the first time something disappeared out of my shed. I tried to tell you the day you came to my house the boy was no good. All you wanted to do was mollycoddle him. Now look what's happened." He jabbed a finger near her nose.

Mrs. McClanahan turned her anger on him. "You better not be saying my boy's no good. Sheriff, get him out of here or I won't be responsible for his safety."

Wes crowded closer. "He's not your boy. He's nobody's boy. Worthless piece of trash blowing through the streets, dirtying up our town. Ain't a one of 'em any good."

Felicity gasped. Over his shoulder, she saw several scared faces framed in the living room doorway.

Sheriff Deavers looked at Mrs. McClanahan. "Where is he? Hopefully we can get this all cleared up, but I need to see the boy."

For the first time, Mrs. McClanahan looked uncertain. "Well, I...I'm not sure where he is. He didn't come home today. I thought he was working."

"See there, Sheriff," Wes crowed. "What'd I tell ya?"

Sheriff Deavers barely acknowledged him. "Why would he take off unless he had something to hide?" he asked, almost gently.

"Probably because he knew he'd be railroaded without proof," Felicity answered for her.

Wes set his hands on his narrow hips and leaned toward her. "Oh, I got all the proof I need. Stuff was always coming up missing when he worked for me. Once a thief, always a thief. Well, I tell you what, I'm going to get my pound of flesh for every last thing he stole."

Felicity opened her mouth to reply. The sheriff put a placating hand on the man's arm. "Now, Wes, let's not get too carried away just yet. As soon as we find the boy and recover your things, we'll make sure justice is served."

"It sounds to me like you've already tried and convicted him," Felicity nearly shouted.

"We've not made any judgments yet," the sheriff said. "If the boy would show himself, it'd be a lot easier getting to the bottom of things."

"Do you have an arrest warrant?" Felicity asked. "If not, I suggest both of you get out of here now."

Sheriff Deavers swung his head around to look at her. He looked like he wanted to say something, but he knew he was in the wrong, as was Mr. Harrison.

He took a deep breath. "Is he here, Beulah? I just want to ask him some questions."

Mrs. McClanahan squared her shoulders. "You're not asking him anything as long as that..." She jerked her thumb at Wes. "...man is in my house."

The sheriff looked at Wes. "Go wait outside."

"I'm not going anywhere. That delinquent stole valuable tools outta my shed. I'm not leaving without 'em."

Malachi leaped out of the doorway. "Tim didn't steal nothing."

Sheriff Deavers clamped his hand on Malachi's arm.

Wes wheeled on the sheriff. "What'd I tell you, Stan? They're all in on it. Ain't there a law against covering for a thief?"

Felicity grabbed the sheriff's wrist. "Let go of that child. He hasn't done anything wrong."

The sheriff sheepishly dropped his hand. Even if he thought Malachi needed brought under control, he didn't want to face a Trego in court for harming a child.

"If you don't have a warrant, then go wake up Judge Greer and have him write you one." She glared at Mr. Harrison. "I hope you have a lot of evidence because if you disturb the judge with nothing more than ridiculous suspicion, you'll never sell another thing in this town."

Wes looked like he wanted to say more but thought better of it.

The sheriff raked his fingers through the shaggy growth on his chin. "We might as well go, Wes. I'll talk to the judge in the morning."

Wes's eyes flashed. "That little thief will bury all my stuff by then."

Mrs. McClanahan put her finger within an inch of the man's face. "If you call that boy a thief one more time, the sheriff'll have to arrest me for assault."

Sheriff Deavers wagged his head. "Let's go. We'll be back tomorrow, ladies, with an arrest warrant."

"Fine," Felicity spat. "Just don't plan on talking to Tim without an attorney there to represent him."

The sheriff shook his head at Wes as if second-guessing his decision to come out here tonight.

"Wait a minute," Wes blustered. "We ain't leaving, are we? She knows where that boy is. You need to search her house." He leaned around the sheriff and directed his voice into the house. "I know he's in there," he shouted.

"Come on, Wes. Ladies, we are coming back so don't get no fool notions in your head."

"You can rest assured I would never stand in the way of you carrying out the duties the county hired you to do."

As soon as the door closed behind the sheriff and Mr. Harrison, the smaller children ran forward into Mrs. McClanahan's arms.

"Is Tim in trouble?"

"Is he going to jail?"

Hazel and Jane buried their faces in her apron and cried.

While Mrs. McClanahan settled the children, Felicity turned her attention to Mary and Malachi, the only two who remained separated from the group.

"Where's Tim?"

They looked at each other.

She stepped closer and lowered her voice. "I can help him, but I have to know where he is."

They looked at each other again.

"Malachi," she said sharply. "Where is he?"

Mary nudged him and nodded. "He knew they were coming. Mr. Harrison has had it out for him for months."

"But why? Tim wouldn't have..."

"No, ma'am. He didn't steal nothing. It's Mr. Harrison. He's been looking for an excuse... Especially after you talked to the sheriff about what he did to Tim's arm."

Felicity groaned. This was all her fault. But how could she not have gotten involved when she found out about the beatings?

She squeezed both their arms. "Don't worry. I'm going to get help for Tim. If he comes back, tell him to wait here."

"We can help, Miss Trego," Mary said.

"No. You'll be more help to Mrs. McClanahan with the children." She gave their arms another squeeze, and then told Mrs. McClanahan she was going for Ned.

"If we don't find Tim first, we'll be back in the morning and go with you to the jail."

Mrs. McClanahan nodded tearfully. "Keep him safe, Felicity. Don't let Wes Harrison get his hands on him again."

Felicity hurried out to her horse. She wasn't sorry she had confronted Mr. Harrison about flogging Tim. But she was sorry the man wasn't going to let the matter drop.

Chapter Twenty-Nine

At the end of the lane Felicity turned off the road and cut across open fields to reach the boardinghouse while avoiding the congested streets where the sheriff might see her.

She kept the old Stetson pulled low on her head, confident no one would recognize her if spotted. The sheriff would figure she was going after Ned, but she didn't want him to know she was also searching for Tim.

At the opposite side of town, she picked her way back onto the road and rode to the boardinghouse. She hated to think of what the residents and Mrs. Crothers would say when she rode into the yard this time of night, but it was a business call. Her heart beat faster at the thought of seeing Ned. It didn't matter now that he might not be as eager to see her. She was here for Tim, not herself.

Nearly every window on the bottom level of the boardinghouse was aglow. There was no point in trying to keep her arrival a secret. Though she'd never stayed at a boardinghouse, she knew how they worked. She rode straight into the yard and dismounted.

"Felicity Trego, is that you?"

"Yes, Mrs. Crothers. I apologize for the late hour. I need to see Mr. Yates."

The woman stepped onto the porch and squinted. "Are you all right, Felicity? What's wrong with you head?"

Felicity touched her head and then chuckled. She removed the Stetson. "I wanted to spare my good hat. Is Mr. Yates available?"

"Well, Felicity, I never thought I'd see you wearing a grimy old Stetson. I almost didn't recognize you."

"It's me all right. Is Mr. Yates—"

"Felicity?"

She looked past the proprietress and saw Ned in the doorway. She nearly collapsed in relief. "Ned, I...is there someplace we could talk?"

He edged out the door past Mrs. Crothers. She looked from him to Felicity. Her eyes lit up. "You young people don't stay out too late," she said, chuckling. "We're due for snow." She looked accusingly at the dark sky. "Never know when it'll get here."

Ned waited until she closed the door behind her and then turned to Felicity. "What's the matter?"

A lot of things, she wanted to say.

Instead, she pushed her selfish thoughts aside. "It's Tim. The sheriff came to Mrs. McClanahan's tonight. He threatened to arrest him."

Ned grabbed her arm and pulled her farther away from the door to a darkened corner of the porch. "Arrest him? He's a kid."

Her heart surged at the compassion in his voice. He truly cared for Tim, for all the children. He just didn't love her.

"They say he's a thief. Mr. Harrison accused him of stealing tools from his shed."

"He wouldn't steal anything."

"I agree, but he's not at the house. Have you seen him? I thought he might come to you."

"He isn't here. Not that I know of anyway."

Frustration filled Felicity. "I don't know where else he would go. We need to find him before the sheriff does. Or worse, Mr. Harrison. He's on a tear. I don't think he's interested in letting the law find justice."

"Does Malachi know anything?"

"I think he and Mary might know where he's gone, but they wouldn't say. Can you come with me? We can get another horse and search."

"Of course." He looked into the darkness. "Are you in the carriage?"

"No, I'm on horseback, but we can ride double back to the house."

"Good. Let me get a heavy coat, and then we'll go around back and look through the barns before we leave. You might be right. Tim could've come here and he's hiding somewhere."

Ned ducked inside to grab a coat and hat. He shrugged into it and took her hand to lead her around the house and through the yard.

Felicity tried to ignore the heat of his hand on hers. She knew he only wanted to protect her from tripping and falling in the darkness, but she couldn't help enjoying the contact while it lasted.

It only took a few minutes to deduce Tim was not hiding in the barns or sheds. They went back to where Felicity's horse was tethered. She mounted first and slid forward in the saddle to make room for Ned. He gently wrapped his arms around her.

The ride through Willow Wood's side streets only took a few minutes. Felicity looked up and down the dark, quiet streets, hoping to catch a glimpse of Tim. She could barely focus with Ned's arms around her.

"If only I hadn't sent him to the Harrisons to work," she said, when they reached the Trego mansion.

They both dismounted and walked toward the stable. "Their son died from blood poisoning a few years ago. They've been in a bad way ever since. Mrs. Harrison is like a shell of who she used to be. I hoped Tim could bring some life to their home."

Ned brushed his hand down her arm. "You're not responsible for Mr. Harrison's behavior."

She nearly crumbled at the tenderness in his voice. "Maybe not, but if something happens to that boy..."

Ned put his hand in the center of her back. "It won't."

Without thinking. Felicity leaned into him. His arms went around her and drew her close. She breathed in the scent of leather and soap that was so completely male. She felt so secure and safe in his arms as if everything would work out as long as he was near.

Ned removed the Stetson from her head and ran a hand over her hair. He pulled back suddenly, throwing her off balance. She saw a surprised look on his face in the moonlight, as if he hadn't realized what he was doing.

She didn't have time to decipher what the look meant. He said he loved her, and now he obviously realized he was wrong. She didn't know what had changed his mind, but she didn't want a man who could fall in and out of love so easily. Life was difficult enough.

She pulled open the stable door on the metal track and went inside. She took the satchel off her shoulder and stowed it in an empty tack box. Belinda was probably anxiously waiting to see the patent agreement. Felicity didn't really care right now what Belinda wanted. She had more important things on her mind.

Just as she lowered the lid of the tack box over the satchel, she whirled around. "I left the stable door open when I went to Mrs. McClanahan's."

She looked around the darkened barn. Ned had lit a kerosene lantern, but it did little to light the interior. She lifted her eyes to the loft. "Who's here? Shane? Tim?"

Movement sounded at the back of the stable. A boy stepped out of the shadows. "It's me, Miss Trego."

"Malachi?" She and Ned rushed to him. "What are you doing here? How did you get here ahead of me?"

She realized the answer since she and Ned had spent time looking for Tim at the boardinghouse.

Mary stepped out beside him. "We want to help."

"You shouldn't have come. You heard Mr. Harrison. He's in a dangerous mood."

The young people looked at each other and then studied the stable floor.

Felicity opened her mouth to repeat her admonition. Ned stepped up beside her. "Where's Tim?"

They exchanged glances again. "If we don't find Tim, the sheriff and Mr. Harrison will."

Ned watched them a moment, and then directed his voice toward the rafters. "Tim, come out. We know you're here."

Mary began to cry. "He didn't do it. He didn't steal anything."

"It's all right, Tim," Ned said to the rafters. "We're here to help, but you have to talk to the sheriff."

After a moment of silence, they heard feet shuffling down the ladder from the loft. Felicity ran to him. "How long have you been here?"

"Since this morning."

"I brought him, Miss Trego, when I came to work," Mary said. "I knew no one uses the loft very often."

"It's all right, Mary, but he can't stay here."

"I just wanted to hide until things settled down," Tim said. "I heard Mr. Harrison had accused me of stealing his tools. I knew he'd convince the sheriff I was guilty. They're friends."

Ned put his hand on Tim's shoulder. "Just because they're friends doesn't mean they can convict you of a crime if you didn't do anything."

"I didn't," he insisted.

"You're probably going to need more than just your word."

"That isn't fair," Felicity cried. "What about innocent until proven guilty."

Ned didn't look so certain. "Mr. Harrison's respected in this town. Tim's a kid. And an orphan."

Felicity gritted her teeth. "I can't believe this. Do you think anyone will believe him?"

"It'll be hard to convince the sheriff. Tim had opportunity, and motive, too. He's a poor kid with no money and no legal means of getting any."

"What are we going to do?"

"The only things we can. I'm going to defend him, and he's going to tell the truth."

Felicity wanted to put on a brave face for the children's sake, but she felt like bursting into tears.

"I know what happened to Mr. Harrison's tools," Tim said.

Felicity gasped. "You know who stole his tools? Oh, thank goodness. All you have to do is tell the sheriff and this whole matter will be over."

"I can't. It'll be easier for everyone if I take the blame myself."

Felicity grabbed his arm. "You could be in real trouble here, Tim. If you don't tell the truth, the sheriff will put you in jail."

"It doesn't matter. I can't let him hurt Mrs. Harrison."

"Mrs. Harrison? What does she have to do with it?"

"She's the one who stole the tools."

Chapter Thirty

Felicity and Ned rode quietly down the alley behind the jailhouse. They had convinced the children to go home to the orphanage to set Mrs. McClanahan's mind to rest, and they would take care of everything else.

It was after ten o'clock and Willow Wood was quiet. It was a weeknight so most of the miners and railway workers were already abed, preparing for another workday tomorrow. Tinny piano music flowed out the batwing doors of The Pick and Shovel saloon, but only a few voices could be heard within.

Lights shone inside the jailhouse. They left the horses at the end of the alley and crept on foot along the side of the building. Halfway down the wooden structure, they recognized two voices. Raucous laughter and bawdy talk erupted with regularity.

"It sounds like their moods have improved," Felicity whispered.

"Until one of them reminds the other why they started drinking in the first place. But let's take advantage of their camaraderie while we have the chance."

They went back to the horses and headed out of town. They stuck to the roads this time since it was too dark to risk going cross country. Most lights were out in the houses they passed so they didn't worry about being spotted or questioned. Their biggest concern was the impending snow.

The Harrisons' property was nearly the first they came to outside of town. Ned reached out and caught Felicity's arm at the edge of the yard.

"You don't go riding up to someone's house this time of night. People shoot first and ask questions later."

Her eyes widened in the moonlight.

"Hullo, the house," Ned called in a voice just loud enough to carry across the yard.

A cat darted under the edge of the porch. Livestock shuffled inside the barn. A lantern moved inside the house. The door opened, and they saw a woman silhouetted in the doorway, the lantern in one hand, a rifle in the other.

The woman raised the arm holding the lantern. "Who's there?"

"It's me, Flo. Felicity Trego. And Ned Yates, the lawyer from town."

A moment passed and the lantern slowly lowered. "Well, come in, then."

Felicity smiled in relief at Ned, though she wasn't sure he could see her face.

"Why are you out at this hour in this cold?" Flo asked when they dismounted and walked onto the porch. "Wes isn't here." She was still dressed, but her hair was down and there were no shoes on her feet.

Felicity ignored the first question. "We know. We just saw him at the jail. He's tying one on with the sheriff."

Flo sighed in weariness. "That means he'll be mean and surly all day tomorrow." She propped the rifle in the corner and headed through the small front room to the kitchen.

"Can I fix you some coffee?" She looked at Ned and gathered her hair into her fist, obviously remembering she wasn't properly dressed to have a man in the house.

"No, Mrs. Harrison," he said quickly. "We won't stay but a minute. We apologize for the inconvenience and the late hour, but we have an important matter to discuss before your husband comes home. It's about Tim."

The woman looked even more tired. Felicity jumped forward, pulled out a chair, and guided her into it. "Can I fix you some coffee, Flo? Tea?"

The woman's faded brown eyes gazed into Felicity's. Her chin quivered. Felicity squeezed her hand, hoping she wouldn't cry, but she would comfort her if she did.

"Tea would be nice. Everything's on the stove."

Felicity quickly set the kettle over the heat.

"Ed wasn't always this way," Flo said. "Oh, he was always hard like his pappy. Liked things done a certain way. I 'spect most men are that way." She looked at Ned.

He gave her a small smile and sat down across from her while Felicity found a cup in the sideboard.

"After Tyrus died—he was our boy—" she explained for Ned. "Wes just got...unreasonable. I know losing Tyrus hurt him. But it hurt me too. He couldn't see past his own grief. It didn't help that he lost a lot of business in his shop. Who'd want to come out here and deal with a man who never had a charitable word for anyone?"

Her question didn't require an answer, and they didn't give her one.

Felicity set a saucer over the tea to let it steep and set the cup in front of her.

Flo gazed intently at Felicity. "I never thought he'd hurt that boy. He said he was just trying to teach him something."

Felicity sank into the chair next to her. "How long has it been going on?"

Flo took the saucer off the teacup and stared into it. "Almost since the beginning, I reckon. I tried to make things easier on the boy. Wes, he's so pig-headed. Nobody can talk to him when he gets that way."

"What happened to the tools?" Ned asked.

She looked up sharply, as if prepared to defend herself. Her shoulders slumped. "Money was tight. Wes wouldn't give me any for things I needed here in the house. Mrs. Endicott could only look the other way for so long. I had to pay my bills. I sold something he didn't use anymore to settle my account at the store. He didn't seem to notice so I did it again. Then I realized..."

She poured a dollop of cream into the tea but didn't drink any.

"Wes just kept getting worse. It's the grief, Felicity. He's a good man. Or at least he was. He can't reconcile losing our boy. Neither can I. I can't take it anymore."

She took a sip of tea with a shaky hand. When she set it back in the saucer, some sloshed over the edge.

"I'm leaving. I'm going home to Wisconsin. I already wrote my ma and told her I was coming. I needed money for the train so I sold whatever I could get my hands on."

Felicity and Ned exchanged looks over her bent head. "Your husband thinks Tim stole his tools," Ned said. "He brought the sheriff to the orphans' home tonight to arrest Tim."

Flo drew her lips into a thin line. It was obvious she already knew.

Felicity laid her hand on her arm. "I'm sorry for all you've lost. But you have to tell the sheriff what you told us. He believes Mr. Harrison. You can't let Tim take the blame for something he didn't do."

Flo sat back in the chair, pulling her arm free. "I'm sorry for that. But you don't know what it's like. He isn't just mean to Tim." Her voice shook. "I can't keep living like this."

Felicity looked helplessly across the table to Ned.

Ned clasped his hands on the table and leaned forward. "After you're gone, they'll still blame Tim. He doesn't have anywhere to go. You'll be gone, but they'll hunt him down and make him pay for your husband's missing property."

She seemed to falter but looked away. "I'm sorry about that. Tim's a good boy. When they don't find the tools on him, they'll know he's innocent."

Felicity's patience snapped. "No, they won't. They'll accuse him of selling it already or hiding it somewhere. You said yourself how hard Wes is. He'll never let it go."

Flo pushed out her chair and stood. "It's late. You should go. I need to finish what I have to do before Wes gets home. I'm leaving on tomorrow's train." She moved toward the door. Felicity and Ned had no choice but to follow.

She opened the door and waited for them to go through. After they went out, she said, "Felicity, you're a good Christian lady. I hope you believe me when I say I care for Tim. He's blessed to have you in his life. I know this seems unfair of me, but if you care anything for my safety you won't tell Wes where I'm going."

Felicity swung into her saddle, and she and Ned turned toward town.

"I don't feel like a blessing to Tim," she said after they left the yard. "I'm the one who set this whole situation in motion."

Ned caught hold of her sleeve and brought her to a stop. "Stop blaming yourself." His voice was firm. "All you did was show those children the benefits of an honest day's work. There's no sin in that. You can't hold yourself responsible for the actions of every person they meet in their lives."

"I know, but—"

"No." He tugged on her sleeve. "There are no but's. God never put the responsibility of each person on our shoulders. All we can control is ourselves. The only one responsible for Mr. Harrison's temper is himself. God doesn't blame you, and it's vanity for you to blame you."

Felicity started to rebuff him but realized he was right. She would always hate what had happened to Tim and the situation in which he found himself, but to blame herself was giving herself too much power.

"Everyone knows I'm vain. Belinda always says..." She brushed aside the thought. She didn't want to think about Belinda right now.

The clouds shifted and she could see Ned's expression. She wondered if he was thinking of kissing her. It wasn't far from here where he'd pulled the buggy over and kissed her and told her he loved her.

The look on his face now didn't hint at a kiss. His gaze was searching and quizzical, as if trying to solve a riddle when he didn't like the obvious solution.

His face cleared. They started forward again, moving quickly to put distance between themselves and the farmhouse in case Mr. Harrison came home sooner than expected and caught them there. They rode in silence until they came to a secluded parallel road that would take them to the boardinghouse while passing fewer houses.

"Do you think we said anything that might get through to her," Felicity said over the creaking of leather.

"I don't know. She was pretty scared."

In the moonlight, Felicity could barely see his profile. He looked distracted. "If she doesn't tell the truth, Tim may never have a chance for a good life in Willow Wood. He'll always be marked a thief."

A few moments passed before he responded. "Hopelessness is a heavy burden, especially for a young person. So is being at the mercy of people who don't care if you have a future or not."

Felicity wondered if he was thinking of his real parents. He hadn't told her the whole story of why he ran away when he was a boy. Maybe he never would. Only unthinkable circumstances would make a child decide he was better off on his own than with the people who gave him life.

"A man has to have hope. Without it, life isn't worth living," he said. "I don't want Tim to forget that."

"What about you, Ned? What do you hope for?"

He stared at her, his gaze again searching. She wished she could muster the nerve to ask him what he thought he would find.

"My hopes are irrelevant."

"That's not true. God placed the capacity for hope in all our hearts."

"Then I hope Tim gets out of this mess."

Disappointment settled over Felicity like a shroud. She was glad he cared more so much for

Tim. At the same time, it broke her heart to think he no longer cared for her.

Chapter Thirty-One

"Where have you been?" Belinda shouted from the parlor.

Felicity's shoulders drooped wearily. Before she had entered the house, she took Papa's will out of the satchel and slipped it in the front of her dress. A confrontation was imminent once she told Belinda she knew there was no stipulation about marrying.

Tonight, she didn't have the strength for it. She took the satchel off her shoulder and smacked it down on the desk where Belinda sat in her nightdress.

"There's the patent. I know it's all you care about."

Belinda stared at her. Felicity noticed her eyes were red-rimmed from fatigue and perhaps fear.

"I don't care about the patent." Belinda's voice softened. "I was worried about you."

The tenderness surprised Felicity, but she was tired and frustrated, and most of it was due to Belinda.

"I'm sorry I worried you. I was actually here a few times, but I had to go back out." Some of the irritation slid out of her bones as exhaustion took over. She sank into the chair across from her sister.

"The sheriff and Wes Harrison went out to the orphans' home to arrest Tim. Wes says he stole some of his tools."

Belinda's face went white. "Oh, Felicity, how terrible for you to find out one of those children is a thief."

Felicity growled in her throat. "He isn't a thief," she said through clenched teeth. "None of them are. Mr. Harrison is wrong. I rode to the boardinghouse to let Ned know what's going on. Then the two of us went to the Harrisons to talk with Flo."

"Why did you do that?"

"Because she sold the tools without telling her husband. I'm afraid I can't provide more information than that right now."

Belinda pursed her lips in thought. "Why did you and Ned Yates get involved in the matter?"

Felicity bristled at Ned's name on Belinda's lips. Their relationship was none of Belinda's concern, especially since they no longer seemed to have one.

"Wes needed someone to blame, and Tim was the easiest target. In the same way he switched the boy for not working quickly enough. He's a mean, bitter man who wants others to hurt the way he does."

Belinda flinched. "Felicity, I'm so sorry."

Felicity knew Belinda's sympathy was real. "Neither of us could stand by and watch Tim be punished for something he didn't do. Even if he did it, he deserves a fair trial, and he won't get one unless we got involved."

Belinda snagged her bottom lip. "I'm sorry I was suspicious. I've been stuck in this house for too long. I fear I'm becoming a nosy old lady."

"Becoming?"

Belinda laughed. "I'm glad Tim has you on his side. And Ned."

•••

What do you hope for, Ned?

Ned stared at his face in the mirror. He was no closer to an answer to Felicity's question than he had been last night when she asked him.

After she said the words, he very nearly wrapped his arms around her and kissed her sweet lips. He had thought of doing exactly that all evening.

At the same time, he couldn't stop seeing the look on Father's face every time Mother came home with another stack of hat boxes or bills from the dressmaker's with no regard to the worry lines etched into his face. He couldn't convince her he no longer made the same money as in years past. Either Mother couldn't understand or she chose not to.

"Felicity isn't your mother," he said aloud as he dragged the razor along his jaw.

He hadn't slept well since the day he saw Felicity in the jewelry store admiring the necklace. Last night had been the hardest. He could no longer tell himself he didn't love her. That he could forget her and move on with his life. He had no one in Willow Wood. He had no one back in Omaha. His sisters blamed him for the demise of the family fortune. His parents were gone, and now it looked like he had lost Felicity as well.

What do you hope for, Ned?

He wanted to tell her his greatest hope was that she could love a man with no money. A man in debt who might never amount to more than he was right now.

Several times during the evening he got the impression she wished he would. But then he would remember Father's anguish when Mother told him he wasn't the man he used to be.

Ned couldn't risk hearing those words from the woman he loved. He dried his face and dumped out the soapy water.

Even if Felicity was a carbon copy of his mother, his parents had loved each other. Despite their troubles and disagreements over money, they had a good life together and loved each other to the end. If either of them were here to ask, he was sure they would say their love had been worth the effort, and they wouldn't trade a day they shared together.

Ned wasn't so sure. He didn't want to marry a woman he would grow to resent. Or worse, would come to resent him.

He barely noticed when he heard pounding on the door downstairs. He was used to residents coming and going at all hours and impatient delivery drivers sometimes kicking the door when their arms were too full to knock properly.

"Mr. Yates," Vesta the maid called up the stairs. "Mr. Yates, come quickly."

Straightening his tie as he went, Ned hurried down the stairs. Felicity stood framed in the open doorway. Mary was just over her shoulder. Both wore weary and worried expressions.

"What happened?"

Felicity stepped inside. "The sheriff went to Mrs. McClanahan's while the children were having breakfast. Can you believe it? He waltzed right in and carted Tim off to the jail."

Ned grabbed his hat off the hat rack at the front door. "I still have your horse from last night. Do you want to wait, or go ahead and I'll saddle him and catch up with you?"

"That'll take too long. I have the carriage. Can you come now?"

Instead of answering, he grabbed his coat and held the door open for them to go out first. It only took a few minutes to reach the jail. Ned hadn't set the carriage's brake before Felicity jumped down on the other side with Mary right behind her.

By the time he entered the jail, Felicity had already toed off with the deputy Ron Dawkins. "I'm here to see Tim," she was saying. "He better not be in one of those cells if you know what's good for you."

The sheriff unfolded himself from his rickety desk chair. "He isn't, Miss Trego. I put him in the back room so he won't have to interact with the two drunks I brought in last night from The Pick and Shovel."

Felicity folded her arms across her chest. "He should be out here where everyone can see him. You surely don't think he's a dangerous criminal."

"The charges are theft, Miss Trego. It's a serious matter."

Felicity opened her mouth to respond. Ned stepped in before she found herself charged with disturbing the peace, or just plain annoying the sheriff.

"Isn't Mr. Harrison's presence here a conflict of interest? Or has he been deputized?"

Wes rose, a little unsteady on his feet. His eyes were bloodshot and it looked like he hadn't slept a wink last night. If he had a brain in his head, he would've been at home begging his wife not to leave him instead of boozing with the sheriff.

"Consider him an interested party."

"Well, so are we," Ned said firmly. "I want to see my client."

"Your client?" Wes slurred. "That kid ain't got no money for a fancy pants city lawyer."

"I'll pay whatever it costs," Felicity exclaimed.

Ned couldn't help smiling at the indignation in her voice.

The sheriff continued to look at Ned. "Ain't no need for all that. This isn't an official questioning. We're just trying to get to the bottom of what happened to Mr. Harrison's belongings."

"Since we already know what happened, there's no point in wasting everyone's time," Wes put in. "You and Miss Trego might as well get on out of here. This will only take a few minutes."

"Shut up, Wes," the sheriff said.

"I want to see Tim," Felicity said loud enough to wake the drunks in the back.

"And I'm not going anywhere," Ned said, just as loudly. "You're not asking that boy one question without me."

The sheriff's head swiveled from Felicity to Ned. He looked a little dizzy. Perhaps the liquor from last night had an effect on him, too.

Wes straightened further. "This isn't a trial. We don't need lawyers and nosy women and all this nonsense. As soon as that boy gives me back my tools, we can forget the whole thing."

All eyes turned to the sheriff. He looked confused and a little uncomfortable.

"No, no, Mr. Yates is right. Let's not give him an excuse to ride over to the circuit court and overturn whatever we find out today."

Mr. Harrison was losing what was left of his patience. "We can't keep wasting time. I done told you, Stanley, I just want that boy to admit what he done. He can give back what he has and work off the rest."

"He's not working one day for you!" Felicity's cheeks were angry red spots.

Mr. Harrison held out his hands plaintively. "I just want to solve this."

She ignored him and turned to the sheriff. "If you continue to carry on with this farce, you have to do it right. Take him to the county seat. I'll ride with Mr. Yates. Mary, you go back to my house and tell Belinda what's happening. Then saddle a horse and go to the orphanage."

"She can't start barking orders, can she?" Wes blustered. "Her money don't mean nothing in here."

Sheriff Deavers looked properly offended. "Nobody's money, or lack of it, means anything to the rule of law in this town. But I've known the Tregos my whole life. Her name carries a lot of credibility. If Felicity says the boy's innocent, I'll listen hard to his defense. I'm beginning to wonder if your tools even disappeared, Wes, since you're working so hard to hurry this along. You wouldn't be the first man to fall on hard times and claim his property was stolen."

"Now, Stan..."

"This has gone on long enough," Felicity snapped. "Where's Tim? Tim?" she called out, making all the men jump and Ned hide another smile. "He better not have one mark on him, Sheriff."

"You know me better than that."

"I thought I did, *Stanley*."

Deputy Dawkins appeared in the doorway, holding Tim's arm.

"I'm here, Miss Trego," Tim said. "I'm all right."

Felicity, Ned, and Mary hurried across the room to him. Felicity reached him first. She pulled him into her arms and glared like an angry she-bear at Wes Harrison.

The sheriff sighed heavily and hitched up his pants. "Clear my desk, Ron," he said to the deputy, "and pull up some chairs. Let's see if we can clear this whole thing up right here, right now."

Mary hugged Tim and Felicity and prepared to leave. Felicity led Tim to the first chair at the table and sat in the one next to him.

Ned joined the deputy in arranging the rest of the chairs. They quickly ran out so the men used an upturned barrel and a dilapidated milk crate. Just as the last one was placed, the door opened and Flo Harrison stepped inside.

Chapter Thirty-Two

Wes leaped to his feet, amazingly sober. "Flo? What are you doing here?"

She looked across the room, and her gaze locked with Felicity's. Felicity smiled encouragingly. She could read the fear in the woman's face. She wondered if Flo would tell her husband she was leaving. Maybe that's why she'd come; to do it in the safety of a room full of witnesses.

Flo's gaze slid to the sheriff. "You can let that boy go, Sheriff. He didn't take anything."

Wes lifted his chin. "You stay outta this, Flo. You always tried to mollycoddle the boy when all I wanted to do was teach him something. Let me and the sheriff handle it."

She barely glanced at him. She reached into her reticule and pulled out a wood-handled file about ten inches long. She laid it on the desk.

"Hey, that's my pappy's wood rasp." Wes scooped it up and examined the handle, worn smooth with age and use. "I've been looking everywhere for that."

"I know you have. That's why I brought it back."

"What'd'ya mean? Brought it back from where?"

Flo directed her words at Tim. "I'm sorry, boy. I never took anything he still used. I thought I'd be gone by the time he noticed things were missing."

Wes squinted at her. "Gone where?"

The sheriff scooted back his chair and stood. "Why don't you have a seat, ma'am, and tell us exactly what happened?"

She looked around the table. Her eyes stopped at Felicity. "I never meant to hurt nobody. I just wanted to...I had to get home."

"Flo, what are you saying?" Wes asked again.

"Have a seat, ma'am," the sheriff repeated.

She finally sat and twisted the cloth top of her reticule. She stared at her hands. "I'm leaving you, Wes. I'm going home to Wisconsin. I wasn't going to tell you. I didn't want you to come looking for me."

"But...why are you leaving? I don't understand."

For the first time since she met the man, Felicity felt a little sorry for him.

"I know you don't understand," Flo said. "That's the problem."

"Mrs. Harrison, you need to explain what you're doing here," the sheriff said. "We're questioning this young man, and unless you have something to add..."

She dipped her head. "I do, Sheriff. I took the tools. I needed the money." She looked at her husband. "I'll pay you back for what I already sold. It may take a while, but I'll make sure to send you every penny from Wisconsin."

"What? No. I don't want the money. I want...why are you leaving me?"

She looked at him like he was dense. "I can't live with you anymore, Wes. Especially after what you did to that boy."

The sheriff rocked back on his heels. "What did he do?"

"I already told you, Sheriff," Felicity cried. "You dismissed me when I told you about the stripes he laid on Tim's arms."

The sheriff pretended he didn't hear. "Go ahead, ma'am."

Flo picked at a broken thumbnail. After a few moments she looked at her husband. "You blamed me when Tyrus died. It wasn't my fault he was messing with that ax. You could barely look at me. You still can't. I lost him, too, and now I lost you. I can't stand seeing that look in your eyes anymore. As if I've done something wrong. As if you're disgusted that I'm still alive and Tyrus is gone."

"Flo, no. That's not how I look at you. I need you."

"You don't need anyone. You prove that every day."

Tears sparkled in his gray eyes. "I never blamed you for what happened. I was just so hurt. I thought if I had been home that day, he wouldn't have been chopping wood and he wouldn't have cut his foot. I didn't blame you. I blame myself."

"Doesn't really matter anymore who you blame. Yourself. Me. God. Maybe we were only meant to have Tyrus a short time. I don't understand it either. But Tyrus is gone and I can't keep taking your anger at God and anger at the world."

He lunged across the table and grabbed her hands, making her drop her bag. "Please, Flo, don't go. I didn't realize what I was doing to you. I didn't mean..."

Tears ran down his whiskered cheeks. "You're right. I took it out on you and everyone around me."

Flo removed her hands from his and got out of the chair. "Don't bother apologizing, Wes. It's too late. My pa done sent me the rest of the money for my train ticket. I packed my trunk. All I need to do is hire a wagon to haul it to the station for me. Like I said, I'll send you what I owe as soon as I can."

He shook his head. "I don't care about the money. I only care about you. Don't go. I'll be alone."

"You've been alone for four years, Wes. You just didn't know it."

•••

No one spoke on the way back to Mrs. McClanahan's. Tim sat wedged in the back of the carriage. Felicity couldn't get the image of Mr. Harrison's tears out of her head. She hadn't believed the man was capable of such emotion. But she understood Flo's resolve not to listen. He had hurt her deeply.

She thought of the lie Belinda had told her. The lie she started the day Papa died to keep Felicity bound to her.

Her anger toward Belinda had dissipated some, but mostly because she hadn't had time to think about it. Maybe it wasn't a malicious lie, but one Belinda fashioned in order to protect herself and control Felicity. Wes had hurt Flo and Tim in order to protect himself. It was unacceptable, but she understood it now. A little.

"I don't know if it's in Flo's best interests to stay, but I hope somehow they can work it out."

Ned nodded thoughtfully. "Marriage is for better or for worse. I guess they've had their share of worse."

"I need to repent for judging Mr. Harrison so harshly without knowing what he's been through. It goes to show you never know another person's heart."

"Not until you ask," Ned muttered under his breath.

Felicity frowned and looked at him. He leveled a look back. She wanted to ask if he had something to say. She didn't want to be like Mr. and Mrs. Harrison; for the person she loved to think he knew how she felt but be a mile off.

"I never knew they had a son," Tim spoke up from the back of the wagon.

Felicity and Ned jerked around to look at him. Felicity had nearly forgotten he was in the carriage. From the look on Ned's face, he had, too.

"I didn't know they had anybody," the boy continued. "Mrs. Harrison is a nice lady. She always tried to make things easier on me. I hope she doesn't have to leave town."

"Sometimes people can't stay in a bad situation," Felicity said gently.

"And sometimes they have to know when to stay and fight."

Felicity and Ned looked at him in surprise. It didn't sound like he was talking about the Harrisons anymore. He slumped back behind the buggy seat and didn't speak again until they reached the orphans' yard.

The children spilled out of the house as Ned brought the carriage to a stop near the back door. Mrs. McClanahan elbowed her way through the crowd and enveloped Tim in her arms.

"It's over," Felicity said. "Tim is going to be all right."

The children cheered.

"Don't ever think you can't talk to me about whatever's going on with you," Mrs. McClanahan scolded as she held him close.

"I won't, Mum," he said, his voice muffled against her breast.

After thanks and more hugs, Ned and Felicity climbed back into the carriage and headed back to the boardinghouse. "We've been taking this route a lot lately," Ned observed.

"I think I could take it in my sleep."

They rode in silence a few minutes. As they neared the spot in the road where Ned had kissed her, the horse seemed to slow. Felicity wasn't sure if it was wishful thinking, Ned's intentional slowing, or a tired horse. The carriage came to a stop. She snagged her bottom lip and looked at Ned.

He shook his head, and a smile lit up his stormy-sea green eyes. "When you yelled back at the jail for them to bring Tim out, I thought I was going to have to pry you off of Wes Harrison."

Now that it was over, Felicity could smile at herself. "You almost had to. Treating that boy like a criminal. He never should've been put inside that jail—"

Ned leaned across the seat and kissed her.

"Oh. I..."

"You had nothing to gain by helping that boy. If he had stolen those tools, it would've destroyed your credibility in this town. No one would give you another nickel to help support the orphanage. You would've become a laughingstock."

"I don't care if anyone laughs at me. I know Tim..."

He raised his hand to stop her rant. "That's my point. You believed in him, and you were willing to risk everything to help him, even if it meant whipping Wes, the sheriff, the deputy, and me, too."

She tilted her head and smiled playfully. "I would never whip you, Ned."

"I appreciate that. I was a little nervous for a while."

She laughed, relief flooding through her. This was the old Ned. Playful. Honest. Gentle. The Ned she had fallen in love with.

As soon as the sensation came over her, it disappeared and was replaced by sadness. He told her he loved her but then decided he didn't, and he hadn't spoken to her for nearly two weeks. Her heart couldn't take the pushing and pulling. She was better off in the house with Belinda where every day was exactly like the one before.

Ned sighed and stared at the floor of the carriage between his feet. "I've been a fool, Felicity."

"What? When?"

"The day I saw you buying the necklace. I was a fool. I know you like beautiful things, and I can't get them for you. I didn't want to grow to resent you for spending money on things I can't afford. I know you want a man who's wealthy in his own right. That will probably never be me. The last thing I want to do is disappoint you. I never want to see the look on your face that I'm not the man you thought I was."

This time, she held up her hand to stop him. "Wait a minute. What necklace?"

"The one at Mr. Levenson's shop. The one that made your face light up. The one I couldn't afford to buy for you if I live to be a hundred."

"What are you..."

Then she remembered. The humiliation of that day came flooding back. Mrs. List and Mrs. Milstead laughing and squealing and suggesting she wear the diamond necklace to her wedding. A wedding that would never happen.

"How did you know about that?"

He looked away again. "I saw you through the window. I wanted to talk to you, but then I saw you with them, and I saw how happy the necklace made you."

"You thought I would love a necklace more than you?"

He winced. "I told you I'm a fool. I thought you wouldn't respect a poor man. It was completely unfair of me. I let my own fears and experiences with money and the problems it causes a happy marriage dictate my actions. Can you ever forgive me?"

"I can forgive you, Ned, but I don't understand where you got the idea I would only love a wealthy man."

"That's what... Never mind. It was my mistake."

"Did Belinda tell you that?"

His lack of an answer told her what she suspected was true.

He grabbed her hands. "Don't blame Belinda. I shouldn't have listened to her. I know you, Felicity. I've been reminded of that during the last twelve hours when I saw how you were willing to fight the world to protect Tim.

"You would fight a mountain lion to protect the ones you love or what you believe in. I told you the other night I love you. Since then, I've only grown to love you more."

Felicity's heart swelled. "Oh, Ned."

"I can't buy you diamonds. Not right now. But I want you in my life. I want you to marry me. But there's one thing."

Her bones felt like melted wax. *What now?*

"I want to give Tim a home. I want to adopt him. I'm not sure how to do that since I live in a boardinghouse. But it's been on my heart since the day we went there to work on the roof."

"Oh, Ned, do you mean it?"

He squeezed her hands. "The woman I marry would have to be willing to become the mother of a teenage son the first day. Do you think you can do that?"

"Live in a boardinghouse with you and a teenage boy? I think we'll have to work on that plan."

He kissed her again. "Is that a yes? Will you marry me?"

"Oh, Ned, I've been waiting for this my whole life."

He put his hands on either side of her face and drew her close. Just before their lips touched, she stiffened.

"Wait. There's still the issue of the diamond necklace." She nearly laughed out loud at the panic in his eyes.

"What issue?"

"You said you know I'm a fighter. Well, there's something else you need to know. I do like beautiful things. I like dresses and hats, and dare I say it, diamonds."

"Okay." His panic was visibly mounting.

"This shouldn't come as a surprise to you, Mr. Yates, but I have a lot of money. I can pretty much buy whatever I want, and many times I do. As long as I have the money, and as long as my purchases don't displease the Lord or threaten my family's health or livelihood, I'll buy a diamond necklace for every woman in this town if I choose to."

He laughed and rested his forehead against hers. "I would never expect anything less."

Chapter Thirty-Three

Belinda met Felicity at the door. "What happened? Is everything all right with Tim? Mary never came to work this morning. I've been worried out of my mind."

Felicity felt sorry for her until she remembered much of her grief was of her own making.

"Everyone's fine. Flo Harrison came to the jail and confessed she sold her husband's tools because she needed the money. Mary was at Mrs. McClanahan's when Ned and I dropped Tim off. She'll probably be here later today."

She watched Belinda leaning heavily against her cane. "You shouldn't be on your feet."

"I'm getting stronger. Dr. Dutton said it's good for my circulation to move around as long as I don't put much weight on my foot."

"Let me help you back to your chair. You look flushed."

Belinda didn't resist. "I'm fine. I was just worried about Tim and Mary. And you."

Felicity positioned herself under Belinda's arm and helped her back to the desk in the center of the parlor.

When Belinda was seated, Felicity lifted her foot and placed it on the stool. She straightened. "You don't need to worry about me, Belinda. I'm going to ask Mary to come here and stay with you until you're back on your feet."

"What do you mean? Where will you be?"

Felicity took a fortifying breath. She had never stood up to Belinda. As far as she knew, no one had. Not even Papa.

"I'm going to stay at the hotel for a while."

"The ho—"

Felicity went on as if she hadn't spoken. "I may as well tell you. Ned and I are getting married. I'm going to live at the hotel until after the wedding. And after, well, I'm not sure. I suppose I'll buy a house. Something small until Ned and I can build—"

"Wait a minute!" Belinda shouted. "Stop! What are you talking about? You can't get married. You know what Papa wanted."

"Stop, Belinda. Don't say another word. Don't bring Papa into your lies. You've blamed him for your deceit long enough."

Doubt crept into Belinda's bottomless blue eyes. Felicity could see she was measuring how much Felicity may or may not know.

"You're talking nonsense, Sister. Moving to the hotel where everyone will know our business. I never heard anything so absurd. What will people say?"

"Didn't you hear what I said? I'm getting married."

"I heard you. And didn't you hear what I said? You can't. What will you tell Mrs. McClanahan? That place needs you."

The last of Felicity's patience snapped. "Enough, Belinda! I read Papa's will."

Belinda's eyes widened, but she was wise enough to keep her mouth shut.

"It's upstairs in my suite," Felicity said. "I know Papa did not forbid us to marry. He wanted *you* to marry."

The color drained from Belinda's face. Felicity felt a stir of sympathy for her sister but not enough to quell her anger.

She put her hands to her own cheeks. They were flaming hot. She took a deep breath to bring her emotions under control. She wiped her palms on her skirt and sat across the desk from Belinda.

"Who was he?"

"Who was who?"

"The man Papa thought you loved enough to marry."

Belinda glanced away. "Nobody."

"I don't believe you. Did he leave town? Is that why you hate men?"

"I never said I hate men. I just..." Belinda exhaled. "I don't believe a person should get credit for something he didn't do just because he's a man."

"I don't either, but don't change the subject. I'm not getting out of this chair until you tell me his name."

Belinda wouldn't look at her. "You know him. Carl Rayburn."

Felicity scrunched her forehead. Why did that name sound familiar? She gasped. "Carl Rayburn? The handsome older gentleman at church who owns the tailor's shop?"

"He's not older. He's my age."

Felicity chuckled in spite of her anger. "Yes, that's what I meant. But what happened? Why didn't you..."

She stopped. If Carl had jilted Belinda or broke her heart, it might be difficult to discuss.

Belinda stared at her hands. "I wanted to make Papa proud. He loved you. You make it easy for everyone to love you. Not like me. I have to work to make people notice me. To make them respect me."

Her expression hardened. "But I did it. Everyone in this town knows who I am. I wanted Papa to know too. I wanted to improve the factory—make it a success—so he would love me the way he loved you."

"Belinda, no—"

Belinda went on. "I couldn't do that and be a wife. A woman has to make choices, Felicity. I chose the factory and Papa over Carl. I made my choice, and I'd do it again."

Felicity sympathy evaporated into the night air. She slammed her hand on the desk, making Belinda jump.

"You didn't make only your choice. You made mine too. You made up a story and kept it alive my whole life. Because you didn't want to marry out of some warped sense of duty or greed, you convinced me I couldn't either. You wanted to keep me here in your misery with you. You decided what you wanted and you made sure I had the same thing."

Belinda shook her head. "It wasn't that. I wanted to protect you. I wanted to protect the company."

Felicity licked her lips to control the rising flood of anger. She needed to remain calm. She wouldn't let Belinda add insult to injury by legitimizing her actions.

"No, you wanted to protect yourself. You talk all the time about how a woman should have the right to decide how to live her life the same as a man. You took that right away from me. The only woman whose rights you truly care about is you. You're selfish."

Belinda flinched as if slapped. "Oh, Felicity, I don't know what to say. I am selfish. By the time you were ten years old, I knew every man in this town would come calling on you. Even then, you were beautiful and witty and charming. I was afraid, Felicity. I didn't want a man to come in here and take over what we built. Even if it wasn't intentional, I know how the world works. Women do the work and men get the credit."

Felicity trembled with rage. "Huh uh. Don't play the martyr here. 'Poor Belinda. Nobody loves me so I'll destroy my sister's life.'"

"That's not what I'm doing."

Felicity was tempted to slap the table again. Or Belinda. She let out a slow breath to keep her voice from quaking.

"You're still blaming this on me. You made up this whole lie so I wouldn't allow a man to come in here and take what you built. Don't deny it, and don't you dare tell me you were only trying to protect me. You don't care about me. The only thing you care about is how people think of you. If they don't love you, then you'll make them fear you."

Belinda opened her mouth as though to defend herself but closed it again.

"How did you see this ending, Belinda? The two of us living out our lives in this house, building up the company, and then what? What would happen after we were gone with no heirs to take over? Leave it to the town to manage until they ran it into bankruptcy?"

Belinda snagged a handkerchief from her sleeve and dabbed the end of her nose. "I don't know. I guess I thought after we were dead, I didn't care what happened. But...oh, I'm so sorry. I was wrong. Please, tell me you weren't serious about moving to the hotel. I can't lose you."

"I can't live with someone who lies to control me. You lied to me from the day Papa died. You perpetrated that lie in every action we took. And then you had the nerve to blame it on Papa. I can't forget what an evil thing you did to keep me under your thumb. I won't."

"No, I..." Belinda heaved a shuddering sigh. "I told myself all these years I did what I did to protect you, but I...I guess you're right. I knew I would lose you someday. I guess I thought I had to lie and manipulate to keep your love, just like I thought I had to earn Papa's. I didn't want to lose you, Sister, and God forgive me, I didn't want to lose the factory."

Felicity slumped back in the chair, exhausted. "I'm glad you finally admitted the truth."

"So am I. Everything I did was a lie. I even lied to Ned. Can you believe he's the first man I ever feared? Except for maybe Carl Rayburn. I knew that first day you came home after meeting him at the office, he was the man who would steal you away from me. I'm sorry, I shouldn't have said that. He couldn't steal you because you don't belong to me."

Felicity stared unseeing at the pattern on the wallpaper. "You had no right."

Belinda lunged forward and grabbed her hand. Felicity didn't pull away.

"I know. I'm so sorry. I put my selfishness and pride for the factory over everything else. Even you. I didn't want to lose you. I was afraid of being alone."

"I never would've left you alone, Belinda. Not if you had told the truth. But now, well, I don't know."

Tears streamed down Belinda's face. "Please don't say that. You have every right to hate me. If I were you, I would hate me."

Felicity wasn't sure what was left to say. She was tired of the whole mess. "I don't hate you. You're my sister. But I don't know if I can trust you again."

"I don't blame you. But can you give me a chance to earn it back? I don't deserve it, but I want to make it up to you. And to Ned. I'm sure he thinks I'm a monster."

"He's not like that."

"You're both so much better than I deserve. I'll do whatever you ask to make it up to you."

Felicity wasn't ready to let go of her anger. She wanted to hurt Belinda as much as she had been hurt. But she was her sister. They were all the family each other had. And she did love her.

"There is one thing you can do."

"Anything. Whatever you want. I'll pay off Ned's creditors. I'll build you the biggest house in Willow Wood."

Felicity shook her head. "Nothing like that. I know I need to pray about trusting you again. I'll also pray about moving to the hotel. I don't want to leave here out of anger or spite. In the meantime, I want you to forgive yourself."

Belinda's eyes darkened. "I don't understand."

"I know. You don't know how forgiveness works. I want you to go to church with Ned and me on Sunday. I want you to know."

"Anything you ask."

"Don't do it for me. Do it for yourself."

Chapter Thirty-Four

Mary slid the ornate ivory comb into the back of Felicity's hair. "Miss Trego, look. What do you think? Isn't she pretty?"

Belinda tilted her head from side to side to critically examine Felicity's upswept hair. "Mary, my sister is always beautiful, but yes, it's lovely. You do excellent work."

Felicity turned from the mirror to face Belinda. Her smile widened. She hadn't stopped smiling all morning. She still couldn't believe she was getting ready for a wedding.

Her wedding.

Mary blushed under the praise. "At Mrs. McClanahan's I was in charge of getting the girls ready for school and church. I learned how to make any sort of hair shine."

"You only made one error."

Felicity swiveled back to the mirror in alarm while Mary searched to wrangle a wayward curl.

"No, not there." Belinda touched Mary's hand. "You called me Miss Trego again. You're living under our roof now. You're part of this family. No one in my family calls me Miss Trego."

"Yes, ma'am."

"Not ma'am either. It's Belinda."

Mary bit down on her bottom lip. Felicity grabbed her hand and squeezed. "We're both so happy you're here."

"I'm happy, too." Mary's voice quavered. "I never thought I'd have my very own family. I was twelve when I went to live with Mrs. McClanahan. I figured I'd never leave. Nobody wants the older girls, unless it's to work in a kitchen or for diapering babies."

"Not in this house," Belinda said sternly. She immediately softened. "Unless you want to. I'd rather send you to college. I tried to convince Felicity to go to Boston where I studied, but she wouldn't leave Idaho."

The color drained from Mary's face. "Boston? Oh, no, please don't make me go there. I want to stay right here in Willow Wood and work with you at the factory, if it's all right,

Miss...Belinda. I just got a family. I don't want to leave it."

Tears welled in Felicity's eyes. She resolutely blinked them away. She didn't want to walk downstairs to greet her groom with red eyes and a puffy nose.

She looked at Belinda in the mirror's reflection. Belinda seemed to have the same problem.

Belinda blinked away her tears. "Whatever you want, Mary. I'd never try to bend a young woman to my will."

Felicity snorted.

"Anymore," Belinda amended.

Mary looked from one sister to the other, clearly lost.

"Could you go downstairs and see if Johanna needs anything," Belinda asked. "I'd like to speak to my sister for a moment before her wedding."

After Mary ducked out of the room, Felicity stood and went to Belinda. "This house is about to become a lot more crowded with you adopting Mary, and Ned and Tim moving in with us."

Belinda laughed. "I never dreamed I'd adopt a grown woman."

"She isn't a grown woman. Even if she was, she needs you."

Belinda sniffed. "I guess I need her too. I certainly couldn't let you move into that boardinghouse. Mrs. Crothers would keep you up all night chatting, and you'd miss your shift at the factory."

Felicity laughed. "Is that the only reason? Are you sure you wouldn't miss me?"

"I'll miss you terribly, Felicity, even with all of you here. You'll have your own home soon enough, and then I suppose, babies."

Color rushed to Felicity's cheeks. "That's usually how it works."

Belinda straightened the collar of Felicity's dress. "I wanted to ask you something before we go downstairs."

She went to the bureau drawer and took out a black velvet box. She opened the lid and turned it to Felicity.

"Papa's pocket watch?"

She nodded. "I would like to give it to Ned as a wedding gift. But I wanted to ask you first. It's half yours."

"Oh, Belinda, that would mean so much to him."

"He's family now. Willow Wood is down to one spinster Trego sister."

"Not necessarily."

Belinda's eyes narrowed. "What does that mean?"

Felicity arched her pale brows. "I invited Carl Rayburn to the ceremony."

Belinda gasped. "You didn't."

"He's in the drawing room right now with the rest of our guests."

"Oh, dear." Belinda patted her hair and straightened her bodice.

"He never married, Sister. He's been living in that big house on Union Street all these years. Maybe he's been waiting for you."

"Well, now, I don't know about that."

"We'll never know until you go downstairs and offer him a piece of wedding cake."

•••

Ned stood next to the parson in the square of sunshine in front of the huge bay window.

Felicity wanted to marry at the mansion to make things easier for Belinda, who still couldn't walk without her cane. Always thoughtful, even on her wedding day. One of the many reasons Ned loved her so much.

He tugged at his tie and resisted the urge to look at his watch again. All eyes in the room were fixed on him and would remain so until Felicity and Belinda made their entrance. He wished they'd hurry up. He'd been waiting for this moment since the end of November when Felicity agreed to marry him. Six hectic, exhilarating weeks ago.

Tim waited beside him in the hushed room. Ned had always dreamed of having children, but he never expected to be the father of a teenage son before he turned thirty. He smiled at the thought of it.

Tim saw him staring and smiled back, though it was obvious he had no idea why.

Tim had moved into the Trego mansion two weeks ago. Last night, Ned spent his final night at the boardinghouse. After a honeymoon train trip touring Utah, Colorado and the Grand Canyon in Arizona, he would move into Felicity's suite at the top of the stairs.

He had teased her about making room for him among the armoires and hat boxes. In the spring they would begin construction on their own house on the north edge of town.

The drawing room was filled to capacity with about fifty guests. Mrs. McClanahan sat in the front row with most of the children from the orphans' home. Lisette Dutton sat in the next row. Her husband Grayson, the former federal marshal turned rancher, sat beside her, cradling their baby girl Jo against his broad chest.

Across the aisle, Ellie Lundy, the Tregos' neighbor, sat with her cousin Harper Kinski and Harper's husband Logan.

Ned remembered Hugh Lundy, half of the Lundy List Corporation, but he had never met Ellie until today. She was reed-thin and dressed in black mourning clothes, reminding all in the room of the tragic and shocking events that culminated in her father's death last August.

Jessa Hammersmith was Felicity's only friend who had to decline the invitation to her wedding. Felicity had understood. Jessa's baby was only a few weeks old, and with more snow expected, she wasn't comfortable taking the little man out into the weather.

In the back row, Flo Harrison sat next to Mrs. Sanders, the parson's wife. Ned had heard Flo moved into the parsonage while she and Mr. Harrison worked to reconcile. He closed his eyes and sent a prayer of blessing heavenward for the success of their marriage. They had already lost their son. They shouldn't lose each other too.

At a signal missed by Ned, Johanna began playing Wagner's Wedding March on the piano. His stomach tightened as the room's collective gaze turned toward the arched doorway.

Hazel and Jane, dressed in matching cream velvet dresses, proceeded Felicity and Belinda into the room, dropping paper flower petals they had cut from newspapers onto the floor.

Belinda sat down in the empty chair next to Mr. Hughes and the ceremony began.

Ned couldn't take his eyes off his beautiful bride. He still couldn't believe the Lord had blessed him with such a kind, warm, genuine wife. As Reverend Sanders began to speak, Ned vowed to the Lord to honor and cherish her and never give her a reason to regret accepting a poor country lawyer's wedding proposal.

He snapped back into focus when he realized Felicity, Tim, and the reverend were staring at him. Behind him, a few people snickered.

He wondered how much of the ceremony he had missed during his ruminations.

"Do you, Norbert..." Reverend Sanders intoned.

Jane and Hazel exchanged horrified glances. "Norbert?" they hissed to each other.

Felicity barked out an unladylike laugh.

Ned leaned toward the parson. "Please, Reverend, I prefer Ned."

He hadn't spoken as low as he thought since everyone in the room joined in the laughter, Felicity loudest of all.

He would remind her of this moment in years to come if she ever tried to talk him into naming a son after him.

The End

Coming Soon

If you have enjoyed Felicity's story, or any of the books in the Willow Wood series, please take a moment to leave a review on Amazon, Goodreads, or any other marketplace or blog that allows reviews. Honest reviews are the best way for new readers to discover my books.

Then, download a copy of the next book in the series, the much anticipated:

Chapter One

March, 1892

The ground shifted under the horse's feet. Ellie Lundy stiffened in the saddle as if the grip of her legs around the horse's body would keep it upright. The only thought roaring through her head was that she shouldn't have chosen this trail. The last few weeks had been unseasonably wet. That, coupled with winter thaw from a heavy snow accumulation, had made a trip into the mountains this morning reckless at best. At worst, she may have just gravely injured herself or the horse.

Last night at the hotel as she prepared for her outing, she had questioned her decision to go into the mountains this early. The winter had been long and cruel.

The last few days had teased Willow Wood's citizens with the promise of spring, which sometimes didn't show its glorious face until May. She was tired of winter. Tired of staring out the window and waiting for temperate work conditions.

Two paintings were commissioned for a hotel in Billings. Another was expected at a courthouse in western Colorado. It wouldn't be long before the leaves on the trees began to open. The painting of a sunrise through leafless trees for a Denver businessowner couldn't wait another day. Ellie had work to do, regardless of winter thaw and half frozen mud that seeped through her boots.

She had left the hotel in Scottstown at four a.m. to reach the spot she discovered last month during a scouting mission.

It had been a productive morning. Her easel was in place just as the sun's first rays broke over the horizon.

As the morning came alive, Ellie captured every splash of color, forgetting her earlier doubt about venturing so far into the mountains. Even the scant clouds had contributed to what she envisioned for the painting.

Now the canvas and her supplies were secured in the saddlebags. She was confident she had created the perfect start for an Ellie Lundy original the businessman and his heirs would admire for generations to come.

As long as she got herself and the canvas back to the hotel in one piece.

Saturn whinnied and reared his head less than a heartbeat before the mountain's vibration traveled through the horse's legs and into Ellie's saddle.

She was halfway to the ridge that would provide the easiest route back to the hotel where a livery hand would see to the mount while she went over her work. She was tired from the long morning but too excited to think about rest and sleep.

Her plans flew out of her head as the strange vibration turned to a rumble. A rushing, crashing, ground-shaking rumble that seemed to echo through every sinew in her limbs.

The rumble roared over her like a tidal wave. Dust rose into the air, stinging her nostrils and lungs and obscuring her view.

Panic and fear rose inside her. Her first act was to get the terrified horse out of the way of the heaving mountain hurtling itself at them. She leaned over the pommel until she was nearly flat against the Saturn's neck and buried her fists in its mane. She urged it off the trail to her left and away from the brunt of the avalanche.

The horse leaped off the trail just as the ground seemed to disappear under its hooves. A rock about the size of a melon glanced off Saturn's right shoulder and barely missed Ellie's chest.

The heart-pounding roar continued as the horse leaped farther away from the trail. Through the dirt and debris, Ellie saw the vegetation beneath the horse's hooves had been laid flat from the winter's thaw.

Fresh panic rose inside her as the horse fought for traction on the slick slope. Saturn whinnied in fear and alarm as his hooves lost purchase. Ellie ripped her feet free from the stirrups and pushed her body away from the direction of the horse's fall as hard as she could. Her teeth clacked together and she tasted blood as she landed hard on her right side. Ignoring the pain shooting through her shoulder, she forced herself into a roll to avoid the falling horse. Its massive body hit the ground not four feet from her. Its hooves were a blur as they rushed at her face.

She flinched, but the blow never came. Her eyes were still clenched shut when she heard the horse leap to its feet and charge into the brush.

Ragged breath pounded in her ears as she hugged the mountain beneath her. Blood ran over her lips and dripped off her chin. Gingerly, she ran her tongue around the inside of her mouth. No broken teeth, thank goodness. She poked her tongue between her lips and winced as she found the source of the blood. Her upper lip was already swelling under her probing tongue.

She started to lift her hand to find the wound. Pain exploded from her right shoulder. She warily opened her eyes to survey the damage. From the degree of pain, she half expected to see a tree limb impaled through her shoulder or her arm hanging by a tendon.

Both shoulder and arm were perfectly intact and whole. "Thank you, God," she said.

The quickly breathed prayer reminded her of her cousin Harper, who had come to Willow Wood last year to help Ellie through her depression. Harper had married Logan Kinski, and the couple lived with Ellie in her mansion in Willow Wood. Logan was building a cabin on their ranch north of town. He and Harper hoped to move into it before their baby was born later in the summer. Harper was hesitant to leave Ellie. Ellie was just as hesitant for Harper to move out. She loved her cousin and wanted to keep her close. But it wasn't fair to Harper. She and Logan deserved their own life. And Ellie needed to learn to stand on her own two feet, even during an avalanche.

The avalanche.

It was only then Ellie realized the earth was silent and still, save the erratic pounding in her chest.

No crashing rocks. No falling trees. No panicked panting from the horse. All was completely still.

She remained flat against the earth as she caught her breath. Not far away, a bird landed in the brush. A breeze whispered through the thin branches over her head. Somewhere below, a deer or other cautious animal moved into the open. The world was already restoring order upon itself.

Ellie needed to do the same. She rolled onto her left side—which thankfully did not scream out in pain—and began the careful inventory of her injuries.

Her right shoulder and wrist had taken the brunt of her fall. She wiggled her toes inside her boots and shifted her legs. Her right hip hurt nearly as much as her wrist and shoulder, but she was able to pull her legs toward her chest and maneuver into a seated position. She lifted her left hand to her face. Her eyes were still in their sockets, and her ears were still where they had been her whole life. Her nose smarted, but she could inhale without difficulty. She found the source of blood on her top lip. She reached under her skirt and tore off a length of her shift and held it against her lip.

As she waited for the blood to clot, she looked around. Saturn was nowhere in sight. The sorrel had either run over the ridge or back down the hill toward the stream. She wondered if he would come if she whistled. Whether he would or not didn't matter since she couldn't do much whistling with a split lip.

She couldn't see the top of the ridge from where she sat, but she thought she had been nearly there when the earth began to move under Saturn's hooves. She was at least three miles from Scottstown. In all her trips through the area, she had never seen a farm or cabin between the ridge and the tiny settlement. If Saturn wasn't waiting for her on the ridge, it would be a long hike back to the hotel, especially with her hip and shoulder complaining with every step.

She struggled to her feet and straightened as best she could on the steep incline. She groaned in dismay at the damage around her. Most of the trail had been obliterated by the rockslide. Huge boulders balanced precariously against each other. Navigating the mountainside would be dangerous and nearly impossible. Unless she could find the trail the horse had taken.

Shaking aside images of irritated hibernating snakes the rockslide may have exposed, she reached for a tree root to hoist herself past the first rock.

Something called out. Loud. In pain. And close.

Ellie froze in her tracks. On the hillside it was impossible to tell from where the sound had come. She trained her ears and listened. Silence. Had it been her imagination? Or from farther away, and her pain and fear had amplified the sound?

Before she could take another step, the sound came again, like a horse or other animal in pain or distress. Saturn may have gotten spooked and run into the avalanche. If so, there wasn't a thing she could do for him. She couldn't leave her faithful mount hurting and alone either.

She picked her way through the rocks and debris until she came to a spot that provided a clear view to the top of the ridge and the open sky beyond. She was tempted to forget the horse and begin the climb. Her body ached from head to toe. Once she arrived in Scottstown, she would send someone to see to the injured animal. Immediately, she dismissed the temptation. It would take at least three hours for her to reach help and another three for rescuers to find this spot. By then, it would be too late for whatever lay broken among the rocks.

She turned in the direction of the sound and continued her trek around the face of the mountain. She had only made about fifty feet of progress when she heard the sound again. Louder and more distinct.

It wasn't Saturn. Whatever was out there had been caught in the epicenter of the avalanche. Whether a horse or mountain cat or bear, something was dying on the other side of the hill.

She pulled herself along, grasping at footholds and hand holds and refusing to think of snakes hiding among the trees.

When she was a girl a father of one of the boys at school had killed a rattlesnake in the mountains. The boy brought the decapitated snake to school to show off to his friends and terrify the girls. Ellie had bad dreams for a month after.

After ten minutes of carefully stepping from one rock to the next, she realized she hadn't heard the sound again. Perhaps whatever it was had succumbed to its injuries, and she was wasting precious daylight and energy searching for it. She climbed onto a large boulder to see if she could catch sight of the source of the noise.

Not six feet in front of her, she saw it. If she had continued around the boulder in her original path she would've nearly stepped on the magnificent creature's head.

The horse's broken body was angled up the hill toward her. Huge, terrified eyes stared at her. Its sides heaved in pain and exertion.

"Oh, no," Ellie cried out in alarm and dismay at its suffering.

She knew horses and recognized the large red bay was as big and powerful as any of the horses Papa used to keep in the stables at home.

"You poor thing," she said in a soothing voice. The horse looked nearly delirious, but she didn't want to scare it further. Forgetting her own pain, she crouched on the rock to crawl closer. There wasn't a thing she could do but keep the proud animal company as it died.

Then she saw the saddle cinched around the horse's heaving side. An empty saddle.

She stood and looked over the horse. "Hello?" she called softly. She didn't want to panic the horse anymore than it already was. She was also aware loud noise could trigger another avalanche. "Anyone there?"

She listened but didn't hear anything over the horse's labored breathing. "Hello?" she called out louder, though she didn't expect a reply. If the horse was this bad off, she could only imagine the state of the rider.

The least she could do was find the body and take note of the location to make it easier for men from Scottstown to recover the remains.

She picked her way down the mountainside to circle the horse. The bay either heard her or sensed her presence. It gathered what was left of its strength and struggled against the pile of rocks that pinned it.

Ellie's heart sank at the horse's distress, but she kept going. The animal was beyond help. As she scanned the hillside, she nearly wished she wouldn't find whoever had occupied the saddle. Last summer her papa had been thrown from a horse and killed. She had been the first to reach his body that night. She would never forget the sight of his broken body or the way his blood had mingled with the rain and ran like a river toward the gutter.

Bile rose in her throat at the memory.

"Where are you?" she cried out, forgetting the threat of another rockslide. "Answer me. You're not dead. I'm here. I'm coming."

Twenty feet past the horse, she spotted the man nearly concealed under the rocks. He wasn't moving.

Enjoy the rest of Ellie, the next book in the Willow Wood Brides Series.

I hope you enjoyed this excerpt. To get to know me and my other titles better, I'd like to gift you with a free download of *A Promise for Josie: A Willow Wood Prequel*. Simply follow the link and sign up for my newsletter to get the free download of the story that started the *Willow Wood Series*.

After a broken promise and a broken heart, is love worth the risk?

About the Author

Teresa Slack loves reading, writing, and falling in love. Creating clean and wholesome western romances where rugged cowboys still sweep independent women off their feet was an easy choice for her.

She writes from her home in the beautiful southern Ohio hills, which she shares with her husband and rescue dog and rescue cat. Any errors and typos she blames on the cat randomly running across her keyboard.

www.ingramcontent.com/pod-product-compliance
Lightning Source LLC
Chambersburg PA
CBHW070754280626
47162CB00016B/286